THE HEALER'S LOVE

THE HEALER'S LOVE

Kierra L. Rose

First paperback edition July 2020

Book cover by Creative Ankh
Proofreader Pittershawn Palmer

ISBN 978-1-732-4767-1-4 (paperback)
ISBN 978-1-732-4767-0-7 (ebook)
ISBN 978-1-732-4767-2-1 (hardcover)

https://thenakedfirefly.wixsite.com/thenakedfirefly

In Memory of

Brandon Lewis,

Adell Hall,

my grandmother Catherine Davis,

& grandfather Henry Cutler

Dedicated to
my children,
who were so patient with me during the editing process,
and to my husband,
who is the inspiration for this love story

ACKNOWLEDGEMENTS

First and foremost, I would like to say, this book was definitely a learning experience when it came editing. I want to thank KaShay for Alpha reading for me as well as catching developments issues that should have been caught.

I want to thank Becca and Krista for Beta reading for me and believing in this story to finish it all the way to the end.

Thank you to my writing/sistahood circle, Black Girls Who Write for being the support system I needed in my life. Through the hiccups of getting this project baby out in the world, you women came through for me without me asking. What you have done for me, I pray I can pay forward plus more to you all. I love yall.

Thank you, Alesia, for being a sister to me from our childhood to now. I know we'll get to where we need to be.

Thank you, Ashley D. for not only being my doula during my pregnancy but also a friend to push me to finish the book.

I want to thank my sister-in-law Ashley L for not only volunteering to read my writings when they were in need of help but for also being my first patron, believing in the stories I was meant to tell.

Of course, I want to thank my parents for having me and being supportive of my love to tell stories from the very beginning and introducing me to the written word before I started school. And most of all, for loving me and all my writer girl weirdness.

I want to thank in my writing community for being supportive during this process and especially during the grueling days of editing. You will never realize how much it means to me.

There are so many people I want to thank but that's another book within itself. I want to thank all my friends and supporters: past, present and those in the future.

And I want to thank those that have come into my life and taught me both the positive and negative of life, you don't realize how much your actions have given me inspiration for the next projects and stages in my life.

CHAPTER 1

Foul body odor and the faint scent of peppered food riddled the air of the Igbalaian miniature bus. Iyanda clutched her Adire print messenger bag close to her midsection, sipping in small breaths through her wrinkled nose. Omodunni, her onisegun teacher, slept undisturbed in the seat next to her, the older woman's head resting against the sun-warmed window.

Not only was it the hottest time of the year for the island of Igbala but also a heavy time for tourists. People would come from around the globe to the Jewel of the Pacific to lounge on the black sanded beaches, visit the hidden waterfalls, tour the Portuguese historical landmarks, and soak in the warm sun until their skin burned. Some, loving the easy surface of the Igbalaian life, stayed, oblivious to the discomforts of the natives.

Many of the Igbalaian homes wore the bright colors of the jungle parrots, hoping the visitors would keep returning to the tropical paradise. And they would, especially for the annual Bones Festival. A celebration and remembrance for the locals and also a time when the stingrays would come closer to shore, ready to deliver their messages to the spirit world. But for vacationers, the festival was a time of drunkenness and promiscuity.

The bus bounced over a deep pothole, lurching the unseated passengers forward. A man slammed into Iyanda, knocking her into the seat ahead of her. Grabbing her right shoulder, she stifled a scream through clenched teeth. Sucking in air, she gingerly examined the injured area.

Thankfully, it was still in its socket.

She cradled the arm closer to her side. With narrowed eyes, she scrutinized the fallen man.

Either ignoring or not noticing her, he stumbled to his feet and went back to balancing himself within the traffic weaving vehicle.

Iyanda didn't expect remorse or apologies during the summer; it was too hot for the typical Igbalaian courtesies. She turned back around.

"Don't let it get to you," Dunni said, her eyes now open. "He had a long day as well. Most of them have. You had it easier."

"Easy?" Iyanda signed. *"We were up before the sun."*

Dunni reached inside her large Adire print healing bag and pulled out a small hand towel. She wiped the sweat trickling down her neck, only to have more replace it.

"Yes," Dunni said, placing the towel back in her bag, "but you have eaten. How many meals do you think these people have received today? Do you think any of their employers fed them for a job well done?"

Iyanda lowered her chin at her selfish thinking. She ate breakfast before training and a midday lunch prepared by the grateful family of a patient.

"We always have to remember, Iyanda. Orisha Osanyin gives us the gift to heal the body as well as the soul and mind. As we cleanse ourselves each morning before we present our offering to Him, we must do so with an untroubled heart."

Iyanda shifted in the uncomfortable bench chair, the springs of guilt digging into her skin.

"What troubles you?" Dunni asked.

"Nothing," Iyanda signed.

"Today you confused the mango leaf with that of the jackfruit."

Iyanda's hand flexed around her bag's handle, remembering the customer in the marketplace. Dunni's bell-shaped earrings rushed her thoughts with their tinkling. Taking a breath, she signed, *"It was the heat."*

Dunni made a low humming noise as if pondering over what Iyanda told her. "I see. Then maybe it's a good thing I come with you."

Iyanda knew the real reason for Dunni wanting to come with her. Despite her destination being in the opposite direction, the older woman insisted on riding with Iyanda to Stingray Cove. Because of the whispers of young women being attacked by foreign men, this time of the year was not suitable for Igbalaian daughters to travel alone. Unfortunately, for the women, the Council swept the incidents under the rug to avoid negative publicity.

Iyanda needed time with her troubling thoughts. But they were interrupted by the bus's jolting halt.

The sudden stop propelled forward those exhausted standing commuters, who had forgotten to brace, to the floor. Iyanda sucked in air as her shoulder was struck again. As passengers righted themselves, they claimed the now vacant seats.

Talaka Village. Home to Yoruba and indigenous descendants.

The door swung open, inviting the odor of burnt garbage and decay to join the cocktail of offensive stenches.

"It's strange to look at one's home, and not wonder if the deities saved you," Dunni said, the melody in the voice ebbing.

Iyanda stared out the window at the security shuttered businesses and trash-filled streets. An elderly man dragging a dolly full of groceries shuffled by three women and a flashy-dressed male. The women tried to entice the older gentlemen with their bodies and words. When he ignored them, the younger man taunted his manhood.

Iyanda turned her head from the disgusting display of disrespect.

"Can you believe it was once the most beautiful village on Igbala?" Dunni asked. "The freshest fish ever caught."

"I grew up not too far from the fish market," Dunni said, her voice breaking. "Everyone came from miles to taste my parents' cooking. They really knew how to make others feel good with their food. Then the first American restaurant opened. Talaka Village was never the same."

"My people, my home, were seduced by the extra money. We sacrificed tradition and morals for what we believed would give us wealth."

Iyanda touched Dunni's shoulder, wanting to share her mentor's pain.

Dunni sniffled. "It didn't. First, it was prostitution, and then children robbed their elders. Poverty soon took up residence. I left with my big sister, but my parents stayed. They were willing to work among the garbage, wanting to help restore what once was."

Dunni sighed. She looked at Iyanda. "Do you know why I heal people in Talaka?"

Iyanda shook her head.

"It's because no one else will. Other oniseguns fear being polluted by the people who lived here, my people."

Iyanda's hand slowly dropped to her lap. What Dunni said was true. The majority of Stingray Cove residents refused service to anyone from Talaka Village, much less step over the village border. Those who came from the spurned community tried to hide their accent, a distinct blend of broken Igbalaian Creole and bastardized English.

People left the bus, insulting and cursing the driver as they descended the narrow steps.

"You can walk," he retorted, his lips curled in a surly snarl. He closed the door after new passengers climbed aboard. The rusted vehicle lurched forward before merging back into traffic.

"I swear they give this job to anyone now." Dunni leaned her head back and closed her eyes.

Iyanda rubbed her sweaty hands across her knees, wanting them to stop bouncing. She peeked at Dunni. How could she tell her mentor the news?

The older woman peeked at her from under lowered lids. Iyanda snapped her attention to the bobbing heads in front of her.

Dunni used a crooked finger to turn the younger woman's face toward her. "The person who has nothing to hide should not do anything in secret."

"I wasn't hiding," Iyanda signed.

"Oh no?" A small smile revealed dimples in Dunni's cheeks. "Then why stare at me with sad eyes?"

Iyanda turned her attention to the back of the driver's head. He was too young to be balding. Her mind calculated the herbs needed to form the perfect ointment for the man's condition.

Sweat rolled between her breasts, tempting her to wipe away the irritation. Biting the inside of her lip, she ignored the elder's eyes boring into her.

Dunni gently touched her hand.

Tears blurred Iyanda's vision. A rolling storm formed in her chest as she swallowed the lump in her throat.

She took a breath. It was now or never. She looked at Dunni. *"I can't come to any more classes."* Iyanda dropped her hands into her lap, wishing they would disappear.

Dunni frowned. "What are you talking about?"

Iyanda paused before signing, *"I-I have to stop my training."*

"You have six months left, Iyanda. Why do you give up?"

Iyanda shook her head, the storm within her growing. *"I don't give up. My family-."*

The bus came to their stop. Iyanda and Dunni stood, brushing past the shoving oncoming crowd. Thankfully they managed to exit the bus without being trampled or tumbling down the loose steps.

Iyanda inhaled the fresh, salty air of Stingray Cove, a slight breeze cooling her sweat covered body. The streets bustled with tourists shopping, eating, and sightseeing. One brazen couple, beet red from the blazing sun, paused to take a picture of her and Dunni. They smiled at the women as one would viewing a finely carved sculpture and then walked off without a word. Iyanda frowned. They were becoming bolder each year.

She glanced at Dunni, wondering if her mentor was just as annoyed as she was with the tourists. The older woman studied her, causing a sheepish Iyanda to look at her feet.

Using her toe, she played with a small rock on the paved dirt. They had to go in separate directions. Iyanda took a step forward only to have Dunni stand in her way. Iyanda attempted to go around, but no matter which way she went, the other woman blocked her departure.

She lifted her head.

"You are one of my best and brightest students," Dunni said. "You can be the most successful onisegun on the island and you throw it away, for what?"

Dunni's pained eyes tore into Iyanda's soul.

"My family needs the money to finish paying off the building," Iyanda signed.

"We have always had an arrangement." Worry lined Dunni's brow. "Do you need more time?"

Iyanda shook her head.

A shadow came over Dunni's face, her disappointment pinching at Iyanda's heart.

Dunni was more than her teacher and mentor; she was family. When Iyanda stopped speaking, it was Dunni who found a way for everyone to communicate with her.

Bowing her head with a heavy heart, Iyanda walked away.

She dragged her feet toward her family's boutique. Waving to the familiar storekeepers, she feigned a smile for all to see. Some waved back, while others frowned at her existence.

Her with no father.

Her with no words.

Her mother abandoned by her husband.

A disease, the shame Iyanda bore, many avoided at all costs.

Iyanda resisted rushing back and telling Dunni she would continue. Not now. Her family needed every penny to finish paying the building off. Nana B would disagree. She would argue Iyanda could finish the last six months for there was plenty of money to spare and if not, Nana B would find a way.

Iyanda stood in front of the adjoining stores and focused on the pastel pink establishment called WAISTED. Since her girlhood, loud talking and laughter filled the bright boutique.

Today was no different.

The women of her family and a few regular customers move around, their mouths wide in laughter, their faces beaming with joy. The store belonged to her grandmother Nana B. Among the native clothing and carvings, the waist beads took center stage. Her grandmother would say each bead told a story about the wearer, who they were and who they had been. A tradition passed down from mother to daughter since before the Yoruba captives were brought to the island.

Unfortunately, many young women who left the island neglected the tradition, which hurt Nana B's and many of the other elders' businesses.

Nana B.

Her grandmother would know something was wrong before Iyanda stepped into the store. The shame the older woman would feel knowing her granddaughter was giving up.

Iyanda shook her head.

No, she needed more time before going inside WAISTED or even her own store.

Iyanda walked across the street and took a seat on a wooden bench facing the two stores. Shutting her eyes against the merriment, she allowed the tears to flow down her cheeks.

* * * * *

It had been four years since Emiliano laid eyes on the mansion he once called home. School had called him abroad while the death of his father drove him to stay away.

For two weeks since his return, Emiliano avoided the Petty estate by picking up his sister from school or having her dropped off at his apartment.

He didn't recall the mansion being so small. The brick-red exterior was still in good condition, primarily because of the groundskeeper's staff and not by any order of his mother. The chalk-white shutters shone in the mid-morning sun as the freshly washed steps both beckoned and repelled him.

Getting out of the car, Emiliano inhaled the fresh scent of watered hibiscus, canna lilies, and mature citrus trees in the courtyard. Paved bricks formed a sun shape in front of the house; the courtyard's threshold to visitors and his childhood imagination.

His brows knitted at the sight of an Audi parked in front of the garage. He couldn't recall anyone in the area with that make and his mother hated to drive.

Rushing up the smooth white stone steps, he entered the house, scanning for any signs of his mother and sister.

He called out to them, his voice bouncing off the high walls.

Nothing.

Emiliano made his way to the sitting room, where his sister would entertain her best friends or be nose-deep in a book.

Empty. Still. Cold as the gray furniture and white walls. A simple room Emiliano's mother loathed and his father had loved.

He strode to the winding staircase, trying to ignore the jittery feeling in the depth of his belly.

He shouldn't have left that day. When she begged him to stay, all he did was promise he would return. Promised she would be fine.

His throat tightened. He should have taken her with him. It would be his fault if anything happened to Yesenia.

"Yesenia!" he hollered.

His jaw clenched when he didn't receive an answer.

He called for her again, taking two steps at a time up the winding staircase. Bursting into his little sister's room, he strode into the vast yellow space and looked up at the white loft bed.

"Nia," he said, as he tried to steady the worry in his voice.

He scanned for any sign she was hiding.

No movement.

Going back into the hallway, he searched the other bedrooms. Finding no trace of his mother either, he rushed downstairs, hoping to find one of the house staff members.

Just as he reached the bottom step, the sound of laughter echoed from the kitchen. He followed the sound to the pool patio. His heart rate slowed on seeing his sister and mother safe.

He frowned at the white man in a business suit hovering over his mother as his sister stood nearby. Yesenia glimpsed over her shoulder when he stepped out into the sun.

Yesenia beamed. "You're here!"

Emiliano looked between the man and his mother.

"My son," his mother, Quilla Petty, said in a singsong voice. "I wondered if you were going to visit me."

"You say it as if you missed me," Emiliano said dryly. He glanced at Yesenia. "Ready to go?"

"I have to get my bag." Yesenia scooted passed him into the house.

"Four years is too long for any child to be away from their mother." Quilla took a sip from her champagne flute. "Of course, being on the island for two weeks without sending word is rude." She eyed him. "She must be something, whoever she is, to make you forget your manners."

Emiliano's jaw clenched. He had taken a woman back to his apartment for a few drinks, but she quickly lost her appeal when she revealed she only dated wealthy men. He allowed her to sleep it off in his bed while he took up residence on the couch. The next morning, he had a taxi take her to wherever she needed to go.

He narrowed his eyes at his mother. "Still stalking me?"

"You're my son. With you being heir to Petty Trading Company, your safety is my first obligation. I know everything. What you do, who you meet. And reliable sources have informed me you've been picking up Yesenia from school or paying her driver to bring her to you."

"You should be used to men disappearing," Emiliano said with a disgusted snort.

Quilla's lips tightened. The years had not been kind to his mother, and she was sensitive to it. Her once slender figure was now an ancient mystery hidden within the short, rotund woman reclining before him while her now plump cheeks made her look almost angelical, for once.

Emiliano glanced at the man, his eyes drifting to the older guy's hair. *Who told him gelled spikes at his age was a good look?*

Following her son's gaze, Quilla's face brightened. She reached for the man's hand. "This is Edward."

The man bent to kiss Quilla before nuzzling her nose.

Emiliano looked away, clenching his jaw. Her behavior wasn't a surprise to him, but he wished his mother would be more discreet around his sister.

"May I speak with you a moment, Mother?"

Quilla glanced at her son then back at Edward. "I must see what my child wants."

"Of course, my dear."

British. Emiliano scoffed. Of course.

Emiliano led his mother a few paces away before asking in a low voice, "Who is this man?"

"I told you his name is Edward," she said, fluttering her ridiculously long eyelash extensions.

Emiliano pressed his lips together. "Don't play games. Who is he to you?"

Quilla smiled up at him, the apples of her cheeks becoming rounder, making her fat face almost innocent looking. "He's my lover."

"You would bring a strange man around your daughter?"

"She's a big girl. What I do and with whom is my business."

"Coming from the woman who can't mind her own," Emiliano muttered.

"Emiliano, I'm ready." Yesenia waited at the door.

"Anything else, son?" Quilla's brow raised, her eyes daring him to continue.

Emiliano smirked. "Yeah, remind your boyfriend he can't stay the night unless you get my permission."

"Make sure you two are here when I return," Quilla said, a strained smile evident on her face.

Pleased at knowing his mother wouldn't try him, he turned on his heels and made his way to his waiting sister.

CHAPTER 2

Emiliano Petty eyed the pink boutique WAISTED. Like most of its neighbors, it was a hole in the wall disguised as an upscale trinket shop for tourists. It didn't impress him, but Yesenia insisted on coming to the store since he received her wakeup call.

After treating her to a birthday lunch and shopping in Pleasant Heights, he made the twenty-minute drive to the boutique.

Approaching the store, sonorous laughter and talking echoed into the streets. Igbalaian women. Their laughter remained full and rich even through struggle.

One of the few stores in the area with an AC unit, cold air welcomed them in from the sweltering afternoon heat. Emiliano shivered as the sweat on the back of his neck turned cold under his locs.

Eyes settled on them as the women greeted them in unison with a song of warm reception. His nostrils detected a faint scent of licorice beneath the smells of freshly churned Shea butter, lavender oil and pure black soap.

"Emiliano?"

Emiliano smiled at the familiar face. Meeting her halfway, the scent of jasmine blossoms tickled his nose as he hugged her tightly. It comforted him to once again see the woman he considered to be more of a sister than a friend. On more than one occasion, she came to Emiliano's rescue from playground bullies or false rumors in middle school. Giving a final squeeze he released her.

"Lily Poe, how long has it been?" Emiliano asked.

"High school graduation," she said.

"What are you doing here?"

"Buying some waist beads and getting a new outfit. Adeyemi always knows how to get my clothes to fit just right." She glanced at a dark brown woman straightening shelves.

"Still looking good."

It wasn't a lie. Lily Poe Tuboson had always been a bit on the chunky side, but time had distributed the curves into the right areas, and, as always, she loved every ounce of her size. She smiled at the compliment and with a couple of pivots, giving him a full view of her assets, which were covered by the brand new green Adire skirt and yellow blouse.

"What are you doing back?" Lily Poe asked. "For the Bones Festival?"

"No. For this charming young woman," Emiliano said, putting his arm around Yesenia.

Yesenia playfully pushed Emiliano away.

"She demanded I be back for her fifteenth birthday," Emiliano said.

Lily Poe smiled at Yesenia, shaking her head. "You've always had your brother wrapped around your fingers."

"Toes too, if I allowed it," Emiliano said, chuckling.

Lily Poe and Yesenia smiled, rolling their eyes at his teasing.

"What brings you to our side of town?" Adeyemi asked in Yoruba.

Emiliano focused on the deep, clay brown woman before him. She wore the classic make-up common among the women of Stingray Cove. With her youthful appearance, he wasn't sure how to address her, but he felt she was of his mother's age group. Her full, glossy red lips curved into a brilliant white smile as her dark brown eyes focused on him.

"My sister," he responded back in Yoruba, "heard about this place and had to come here. Since my mother won't be back until later today, I wanted to grant her request."

"Did you want to buy waist beads or something else?" Adeyemi asked.

"I'm not sure what she's interested in buying."

Yesenia disappeared among the racks of colorful clothing.

"I will help her, Sir." The woman trailed after his sister.

Emiliano leaned against one of the counters. Out of the corner of his eye, he spied an older dark-skinned woman. With her round frame sitting erect on a stool, she was a lioness overseeing the movement of her offspring. Her dark, steely gaze followed, Yesenia and the other woman.

Sitting in a corner not that far from her was a freckled-face young woman with a cream complexion. She batted her lashes in his direction, making him shift against the counter. An older woman with similar skin tone and French features nudged the younger one and scolded her for not working.

"How long have you been back?" Lily asked.

"About two weeks," he said, turning his attention to her.

"Plan on going back?"

Emiliano shook his head. "If I do, it'll be when she graduates."

"It's time you came home. The island needs you. Not enough progressive members on the Council."

"What makes you think I want the position?"

Lily Poe leaned on the counter next to him. "Because if I know you, and I do, you won't let your father's work go unfinished."

The corners of Emiliano's mouth turned up. She was right. His father, Jack Petty had once been one of the many men who made decisions for the island. With each being able to trace their lineage back to the original generals of the Rebellion, their position on the Council was their duty as well as their birthright. He had once dreamed of sitting in the chair before his father's death, now the time was here, and he shook with the thought of claiming it. Would he be able to complete what Senior Petty had started?

He paused upon hearing Yesenia's broken Yoruba, praying it was the word perfume he heard. Her American accent revealed her lack of study of their father's native tongue.

The freckled-face woman, Tambara's eyes bulged out of her mousy face. She grabbed the attention of the other creme-colored woman, who approached him with somewhat of a regal air.

"We don't sell things like that. If you want it, go to one of those American stores," the older woman said in broken English.

Emiliano's jaw tensed at the harsh tone directed at his sister.

"Ola, don't be rude," the dark-skinned matriarch scolded in Yoruba.

"We don't sell it," Ola repeated in the same unkind tone.

Yesenia's head tilted to the side, averting her eyes from everyone which was her way of internalizing the words said to her. Watching her blink fast made him want to shake the perfume out of the woman. Did she talk to all of their customers like this, knowing the penalty if one of the tourists were to report them?

He felt sixteen again. Barely able to defend himself, he had been completely helpless to protect his baby sister against their mother. She had ignored the hungry cries of the toddler, angered at the little girl for earning a shade of brown skin. When he had tried to feed the young Yesenia, Quilla threatened to throw him out. He couldn't risk leaving his sister with the woman.

"We don't sell popular perfumes," the red-lipped woman from earlier said. "We make them from herbs."

She took his sister's hand and led her to a door at the back of the store which had a sign hanging on the top jamb: IYANDA'S EWE.

"She hasn't come in yet, ma'am," another woman said, coming from a backroom behind the counters.

Emiliano took a double take of the woman behind the glass counter. Even with a pixie cut, she had a familiar smile and round face. He knew her. He just couldn't remember where from.

Adeyemi let out an exasperated sigh. "Thank you, Gaiana." She smiled at him and Yesenia. "I'm sorry, our herbalist is not in. Come back another time."

Emiliano nodded. After saying goodbye, he led his sister out of the store.

"Will you bring me tomorrow?" Yesenia asked.

Emiliano walked to the driver's side of his car. "Even if I have to gag Mother to get you out of the house."

A movement across the street caught his eye. Three men crowded a woman sitting on a bench. She wore the traditional garb and headwrap of an Igbalaian woman. She avoided eye contact with the men. Emiliano wanted to believe she was playing hard to get, as some of the women in Stingray Cove tended to do, but then she pulled away from the touch of one of the men.

"Emiliano?" Yesenia asked.

"Stay here," he commanded, making his way in the direction of the group.

The man who was rejected, grabbed her arm and pulled her close.

"You think you better than any of these whores around here?" the man hollered at her in American.

Emiliano shoved the man away from the woman, making sure to use his body as a shield between her and her attackers. The three men, almost as tall as him but bigger in body, threatened his personal space with flaring nostrils and hard eyes.

Emiliano locked gazes with the tough guy. The man's red face expressed the possible explosion if Emiliano didn't vacate the premises.

Emiliano smirked. "You gentlemen seem to be lost."

"We were having a friendly conversation with our friend," Tough Guy said, his eyes darting to the seated woman.

Emiliano followed his gaze. The woman kept her head down and was visibly shaken. He glared at the head punk.

"I think the lady wants to be left alone," he said.

The men laughed.

"Who does this dude think he is?" one of the other men jeered.

"I think he wants her for himself," the other said.

"Well," the tough guy stepped closer to Emiliano, their noses almost touching "We saw her first. Get missing or we'll do it for you."

Emiliano squared his shoulders. "Get back on the ship that brought you or I'll have you banned from the island." His eyes narrowed when he saw Yesenia heading in their direction. He didn't want to have to kill anyone if something happened to his little sister.

"Let's just kick his ass and finish with her," one of the men said.

Tough Guy's eyes couldn't hold their hardness. His once defiant gaze was wavering.

The crime for any tourist causing trouble and being involved in anything illegal was to be banned entry into the island. But that only happened if someone in the higher social class reported the offender.

Emiliano wasn't sure at first if they were tourists but the ringleader's change in attitude verified it.

"Let's go," Tough Guy commanded.

"Dude," the other men objected.

Tough Guy walked away, not looking back at his companions. "I'm not missing out on some fun before the ship leaves."

The other men glared at Emiliano and the seated woman then followed after their friend.

"What the hell, Brother?" Yesenia exclaimed at his elbow.

Emiliano gave her a stern look. He would address her language later. "I told you to stay at the car."

He looked down at the woman. "Are you okay?" he asked in Yoruba.

She gazed up at him. Her eyes, unnaturally innocent for a woman her age, were large obsidian stones threatening to envelope her face. Sweat glistened on the tip of her flat, Nubian nose. He had seen a face similar to hers in WAISTED. She gave him a small smile, her eyes moist with tears.

Before he could say a word, Yesenia collapsed to the ground. His heart dropped to the pit of his stomach. "Nia!" He knelt at her side.

The woman, getting up from the bench, rushed to his sister as well. Unsure of what her intentions were, Emiliano pushed her hand away from Yesenia's unconscious body. As he did so, their gazes met and her unnatural dark eyes pleaded with him.

Emiliano frowned. Certainly this woman didn't mean any harm, but could she help? Panic gripped his stomach as people passed, oblivious to his unconscious sister's body. Were they so wrapped within their enjoyment they didn't notice when others needed aid? Sizing up the woman, his heart told him to trust her.

He let out a slow breath of resignation. He was willing to take the chance.

"Help her, please."

* * * * *

Iyanda handed the young teen a small teacup.

The girl raised a brow at the appearance of the dark reddish-brown liquid inside the cup.

Iyanda smiled. Placing her hands under the girl's cupped hands, Iyanda urged her to drink.

The girl downed the concoction then pushed away the empty cup, her sweet face twisting in disgust. The floral scent of hibiscus and chamomile flowers always threw off customers from the surprisingly bitter taste.

"I hope I don't throw it back up," she said.

Iyanda placed the teacup down and picked up a nearby miniature chalkboard and piece of chalk, she scribbled on it.

The girl frowned at the writing.

"She can't read Yoruba very well."

The man's voice sent vibrations through her. Iyanda took a cursory glance his way, lingering on his face longer than she should. His eyes reminded her of the sun setting behind the ocean's horizon, warm and magnetic. A couple of stray dark brown locs framed his handsome angular face. He and the girl carried the same Igbalaian Yoruba features except where the teen's complexion was of a rich reddish brown, his was of a warm yellow brown.

Lowering her gaze, she handed him the board.

He scanned it before handing it back to her. Her heart skipped a beat as his penetrating gaze threatened to hold her hostage.

"What did she say?" the girl asked.

His eyes bore into Iyanda. "You need to drink the tea for three days. It'll help with dehydration."

The girl groaned.

"Does it also help with cheating girlfriends?" the man asked in a humorless manner.

Iyanda grimaced at the flippant joke.

The girl used her hand to hide her face and groaned. "You are so embarrassing."

Iyanda scribbled some more on the chalkboard.

"Can you not talk?" the girl asked.

"Nia," the man said in a chiding tone.

Yesenia waved a hand in Iyanda's direction. "She keeps writing. Can she talk?"

Iyanda shook her head. Her knees weakened under his scrutinizing gaze. Even though he said nothing, Iyanda knew the man was thinking the same thing, judging her and coming to a decision about something he knew nothing about. Dropping her chin to her chest, she inhaled, needing to control the internal trembling.

"You must get all the guys' attention," the girl muttered, smacking her lips.

Iyanda internally laughed. To be so young again and believe a boy was the beginning and end.

The man made a tsk-ing noise. "Excuse my sister. She forgets her manners."

The girl waved him off. "It's true. Guys always want a quiet girl. That's what mama says."

"You think I'm like that?" Emiliano asked.

"You're different, Emiliano. You're, like, cool. Minus what you said earlier."

The girl focused back on Iyanda. "You have a lot of plants. Can you make me a perfume? I want one to catch my crush's attention. It has to be different, once you make it, you can't make it for anyone else."

Iyanda nodded then scribbled on the board.

Emiliano leaned over and read it. "I will ask the Earth for what you request. It will be ready in three days."

The girl held out her hand. "I'm Yesenia Petty and this is my awkward, big runaway brother, Emiliano Petty."

Iyanda smiled, took Yesenia's hand and gave it a light shake. She gave a slight head nod to Emiliano.

Carrying the bag of loose herbs for her tea, Yesenia took the lead and together they walked to the door.

Iyanda's heart quickened as Emiliano cast a final glance her way. When the door closed behind them, a sense of quietness settled over the room. She sighed and placed the board on the counter.

"You're here, Iyanda?" Gaiana said, sticking her head into the store.

Iyanda gave a wispy smile and signed, *"Were you late again?"*

Gaiana giggled. "I promise I won't be late tomorrow, boss lady. Did you need anything?"

Iyanda shook her head. Gaiana's head slid back into WAISTED, shutting Iyanda back into the quiet of her store.

Going to the back room, she stopped in front of a small mirror. She unwrapped her brown headwrap, each fold of the cloth falling at her feet. She trembled at the memory of the tourist men who mistook her for a promiscuous woman. They had touched her.

No one came to her aid, except him.

Her mass of thick, black coils spilled over her shoulders. She raised her hand, running her hand through the tangled softness.

Soon it wouldn't be her property to touch anymore. Sure, now she could fashion it in the traditional halo braid, but the moment the vows were spoken, her husband could decide whether she would have a head full of black coils or shaven to his delight, even down to what color headdress she wore could be his decision. All she knew, it was a traditional law that she was okay with not following if possible.

She began to braid one side of her hair. Tears burned the back of her eyes as she locked each strand in its prison, forming them into the halo of her promise.

CHAPTER 3

Emiliano joined his sister and mother for dinner later in the evening, claiming his father's chair as his own.

Quilla stared him down. "What makes you think you can sit there?"

"I'm sure he wouldn't mind me keeping his chair warm until you find some other man to do it for me."

Quilla pursed her lips. "Where were you two today?"

"Birthday shopping," he said in Yoruba.

He smirked as his mother's eye twitched. She hated the language. It wasn't her native tongue and while married to an Igbalaian man years ago, she never bothered to learn the native or Creole tongue, thinking it beneath her.

"Emiliano, you know I hate when you do that."

"Shopping," he responded in Spanish.

"And where did you take her?" she asked.

"Does it really matter?" he answered in a short tone. Did she not realize he was a man and didn't have to answer to her anymore? His mother did have a right to know where he took Yesenia. If anything, his sister was safer with him, but he held his tongue. Not wanting to fight with anyone else for the day, Emiliano wished to recharge instead of having to deal with his mother's adolescent attitude.

"She came home with grass!"

The brown-skinned herbal woman came to his mind. What was her name? They had not even bothered to ask. An average beauty with large, dark innocent eyes. Her brown skirt hugging her round, shapely hips and her narrow waist...

He shifted in his chair and faced forward. "Take your seat, mother."

Quilla scowled at him before sitting in her chair at the other end of the polished dining table. Seconds later a butler and two maids placed before the three diners a bowl of chowder.

Emiliano peeked over at Yesenia. She gave him a small shrug before placing her cloth napkin on her lap. He stared at the thick soup, chunks of potatoes poking out of the white milky substance.

"When did we start eating chowder?" he asked.

"Mother's new boyfriend likes it," Yesenia said, her lip curled in disgust.

Quilla shot Yesenia a warning look which caused the young girl to avert her eyes back to her bowl.

Emiliano leaned back into the chair, wanting to keep his distance from the bowl. His mouth watered at the memory of his late grandmother's soft beans, garri and baked chicken.

"Now another man can make decisions in this house?" he asked.

"What are you implying?" Quilla asked.

The sound of approaching footsteps brought a smile to her lips.

Seconds later, the tall, gray-haired, lightly tanned man from earlier walked in wearing a dark blue suit and brown winged tipped shoes.

A little overdressed in Emiliano's opinion. He viewed the others at the table. His mother wore a low cut, form fitting gown while his sister wore a pastel pink ruffled dress.

Emiliano frowned.

They never ate dinner dressed up unless there were guests. And his sister certainly didn't wear ruffles.

Edward walked over to Quilla, kissed her forehead then made his way to the other end of the table, mumbling his excuses for why he was running late. He stopped short upon noticing Emiliano sitting at the head of the table.

He raised a brow.

"Young Master Petty. We weren't formally introduced." His accent was thick and heavy with sarcasm. "Home on holiday. You are welcomed here."

"I know." Emiliano placed his elbows on the table, leaning forward with crossed arms, he cocked his head to the side. "This is my house," he said, raising his brows. He wanted the man to challenge him about this fact.

The man's smile became strained. "Yes, of course."

The two men stayed frozen in their spots, Emiliano in his father's chair, the strange man standing and waiting for Emiliano to move.

Emiliano studied the man. He had to be older than Quilla. The lines etched deep in his skin reminded Emiliano of the ugly pugs his mother used to keep as pets. Too incompetent-looking to be a lawyer and definitely not straight-laced enough to be an accountant. Whatever the position, Emiliano guessed the man had some experience in acquiring other people's assets.

Emiliano smirked. Too bad for the man Quilla had no money to give.

The man rocked on his toes before clearing his throat.

Emiliano gestured to one of the waiting staff members to give the gentleman a drink of water. Yesenia coughed into one of the cloth napkins bringing everyone's attention to her. Emiliano's breath steadied when he saw a small smile appear behind the napkin.

His sister glanced at her mother who shot her a disapproving look. Yesenia quickly straightened her face and placed her napkin back on her lap. Quilla frowned at her son.

A young woman wearing a white maid's uniform brought a glass of water on a tray to the dignified standing man. The man glared at Emiliano.

"Won't you join us for dinner?" Emiliano asked.

Emiliano indicated with an outstretched hand to the chair beside Quilla at the other end of the table. The man glanced at the chair then looked back at Emiliano in disbelief.

"Problem?" Emiliano asked, eyeing the man.

Edward shook his head and murmured it wasn't a problem at all. He turned and headed to the chair offered to him.

"Don't forget to get your water," Emiliano said. "Don't want that cough to get worse."

The man snatched the glass off the tray and stormed to the other end of the table. Quilla moved to the chair designated for the man and offered her own. His blue eyes spoke volumes of how he was going to make Emiliano pay.

"What do you do, Edward, is it?" Emiliano asked.

"I-."

"He's a banker," Quilla interrupted.

"How long have you been on Igbala?"

"Only a few months," Quilla answered.

Emiliano eyed his mother. "Is he a man or a boy needing his mother to speak for him?"

"Don't you dare take that tone with me," she rasped.

"Or what? You're going to make me wear ruffles too?"

Quilla glared at Emiliano. "It's a sign of good breeding to dress for dinner."

Emiliano's eyes fixed on Edward. "The British are known for being the definition of good breeding."

"Emiliano!" Quilla's dagger filled eyes dared for him to continue.

And he was willing to cross the line.

Yesenia's distressed expression begged him to stop.

Emiliano gritted his teeth. He needed his mother to know of his disapproval of this man, her past, her ways. With a final glance at his sister, he blew through his nostrils the breath of temporary surrender. He focused back on the bowl of chowder. Opening his cloth napkin, he placed it on his lap and picked up his spoon.

"Yummy," he said before taking a taste.

After dinner the man left and Yesenia went to bed early. Emiliano relaxed in his father's study, a book opened in his lap. He read the words, but he listened as his mother's angry steps made their way to his father's study. He didn't bother to lift his eyes from the book when she stood before him.

"What was the meaning of you being rude to Edward?" Quilla demanded.

"What was the meaning of you allowing him to think he's head of this house?"

"Who I allow into this house is my business."

"No, who you allow in your bed is your business. This house," Emiliano said, sweeping his hand in the air, "is my business."

Quilla stuck her chest out, her hands on her wide hips.

"American schooling has made you forget the rules of my house," she said.

He locked eyes with her. "This was Father's house and he made it quite clear in his will that the estate and everything else was to be in my hands. They are your rules. I'm not obligated to follow them. However, this house, until further notice, is my house. If you don't like it, the door is always open."

"What have I done for you to treat me like this?"

"Besides being a crusher of the souls of everyone who loved you."

"I loved your father," she said in a low, firm voice.

He looked back at the pages, dismissing her. With a huff, Quilla stormed out of the room.

Putting the novel down on his lap, Emiliano stared at the shelves lined with his father's collection. When he was a boy he would sneak into the sun-lit room to run his fingers over the smooth, burgundy spines of the books he could reach on his tiptoes.

How many had his mother allowed her boyfriend to touch and claim?

* * * * *

Iyanda slid past her mother within the narrow passage provided by the stove and kitchen counters. Careful not to get her brown skirt caught on the hanging cabinet door under the sink, she moved to put dried dishes into their assigned spots. She turned off the whistling tea kettle and moved it to a cool eye on the stove.

Going back to the sink she slid her hands into the hot water and began washing the dishes. She stared out the kitchen window, rubbing the soapy sponge in a circular movement over the same plate. The ending of her training haunted her thoughts.

The touch of Adeyemi's gentle hand startled her.

"What bothers you, my child?" Adeyemi asked.

Iyanda shook her head. She knew she could tell her mother anything, except her conversation with Dunni. Her mind raced for an excuse for her emotional state.

She removed her hands from the warm water and wiped them on her skirt. She signed, *"Do you believe it's possible to achieve anything without money?"*

Adeyemi's face softened. She caressed Iyanda's face, smoothing the wrinkles above her brow.

"Nana B is not concerned about the business and neither am I." Adeyemi said in a soothing tone.

"I know, I just want to know how you feel about me not finishing my training?"

"You don't need that training. All that money we spent and for what, herbs and tools you won't need. Pretty soon, you'll be getting married. This marriage will be good for you. It'll give you a name, something your father took away from both of us. Picture the doors this could open. Playing doctor with people is not a position you want, there is no good standing for that. I want the best for you, and I know Nana B would agree with me."

Iyanda's lips turned up in a strained smile. Her hands couldn't communicate what her heart wanted to say to her mother. Adeyemi always thought it was foolish for her to pursue such a career. The door her mother believed would be opened through her marriage to Mason was the very door Iyanda wanted to slam shut and barricade. Adeyemi wanted her daughter's social status to rise in hopes that it would take away the stigma placed upon her.

Iyanda had loved Mason, once. They had known each other since childhood, and he had been a constant in her life after her father abandoned them and her brother left. He was her first boyfriend. When he became her first lover, he changed. He started flirting with other girls, sometimes when she was present and his hands, once so gentle, left her upper arms sore and bruised. He had even voiced to her mother that all she needed was to be under the right man to correct her and her choices.

To show she was in agreement with him, Adeyemi accepted the bride price, placing Iyanda in an unofficial marriage. Thankfully for Iyanda, she didn't have to live with him until the marriage papers were signed.

"Now take Nana B her tea." Adeyemi handed Iyanda a heated teacup and saucer then shooed the younger woman out of the kitchen.

Iyanda walked through the living room, careful to steady the cup on the small plate. Setting foot out onto the closed-in porch, she found her grandmother on the black wicker loveseat, her eyes closed, too peaceful for her own comfort. Placing the cup down on the small table, she leaned close to Nana B, listening for the elder woman's breathing.

"I'm fine, ọkàn mi."

Iyanda stood straight, relief washing over at hearing her grandmother call her by the pet name she had given her, "my heart".

Nana B opened her eyes. Through squinted eyes she looked up at Iyanda. "More of that medicine?"

"Nana B, it'll help your stomach pains," Iyanda signed.

"My stomach is fine." Nana B fanned herself with the small palm leaf.

Iyanda knelt beside the older woman and batted her lashes. *"For me, ọkàn mi."*

Iyanda pressed fingers to her lips and giggled when Nana B sighed and looked away, the corners of her mouth curling into a light smile.

Nana B sucked her teeth then reached for the cup. Iyanda readily gave it to her then took the empty spot on the loveseat beside her.

Nana B sniffed. Taking a small sip, she wrinkled her nose. "It will kill me."

"Nana B."

Nana B lightly chuckled then drank some more of the bitter herb.

"Feel better?" Iyanda signed.

Nana B made a small hmm sound before placing the cup back on the table.

"Your mother is talking about your marriage again?" Nana B asked.

"She's excited about the wedding."

"Are you?"

Iyanda averted her gaze from Nana B's scrutinizing stare. Of course she wasn't excited about the wedding or marriage. But to express otherwise would break her mother's heart, and Iyanda had already decided it had been broken long enough.

Iyanda fidgeted on the loveseat, wanting to disappear into the house or even in the darkness of the backyard, anywhere but under Nana B's gaze.

"A shift is coming," Nana B said.

Iyanda's grandmother stared out into the pitch blackness. Since Iyanda could remember, Nana B had a special connection to the Ancestors of Igbala. Through her dreams, they sent the seasoned woman messages. Warnings, Nana B would call them, for the people to take heed to.

Iyanda wanted to ask what type of shift.

"Not sure yet," Nana B said, as if reading her mind. "But when it happens-." the older woman looked at her. "You be ready, ọkàn mi."

CHAPTER 4

The mid-morning sun warmed Emiliano's back as he approached the grand government building. The blue bricks, faded by the sun's enduring brightness, retained their strength to keep the structure through time's damage. The council building was one of the many remnants of Portuguese rule.

He surveyed the sixty-seven windows, each dark and barred from the threats of old, his eyes resting on the thirtieth window on the top floor. A small smile crept on his lips. While his father had been in the council meetings, young Emiliano would run outside in the courtyard. After imagining the man on the horse statue was an enemy Portuguese soldier, he would count the windows then run inside to his father's designated office, staring out at the design he had created with the white stones on the manicured grass.

Emiliano walked inside, passing through the tall, metal doors into an airy hallway. Sitting at the guard's desk was a salt and pepper, slender man. Emiliano stopped at the counter and requested to sign in.

The guard's eyes drifted from a magazine he was perusing up to Emiliano's face. His eyebrows raised, his face lighting up. "Mister Junior Petty!"

Emiliano studied the man's face. There had only been one man who called him that. Was it possible the gentleman still worked there?

"Mr. Ope?"

The man crossed his arms across his chest, a small smile in the corner of his lips. "What have I always told you?"

Emiliano smiled at the childhood memories of the bright eyed, gruff speaking man allowing him to patrol the halls of the building. "Uncle Ope."

Uncle Ope came from around the counter and gave Emiliano an unusually strong hug for someone his age. The older man released him, marveling at how much the younger man had grown and looked so much like his father.

"It's been quiet around here, since your Baba's death," Uncle Ope said, his face sagging.

Emiliano's heart stuttered at the mention of his father. Uncle Ope was right, the building felt different, as if his dad's presence had been the much needed coolant to keep the engine running smoothly.

He leaned close to Uncle Ope. "As his son, it's only fitting I make a bit of noise," he said in a voice above a whisper.

Uncle Ope smiled then let out a noise of excitement. Emiliano motioned for the older man to quiet down then flashed him a smile.

"You make your father proud," Uncle Ope said. "I'll sign you in." He motioned for Emiliano to go.

Assistants hustled by, oblivious to his presence, burdened by the tasks bestowed upon them. Managing to stop one, he asked them where the council members were meeting. They pointed him in the right direction then hastened away.

Emiliano tensed as he strolled down the long hall. It had been almost eight years since he had walked past the large portraits of council members past and present. He paused at his father's image. Jack R. O. Petty was inscribed in gold beneath his image. The dark, reddish-brown man sat erect with a look of sternness on his face and a gleam in his eyes. Emiliano stood tall, poking his chest out a bit, mirroring his father. He smiled at seeing the corners of the man's mouth curled up in a knowing grin, one that Emiliano believed held all the secrets of the world. The older man was never one to stay sour-face for long, unlike the other members.

"I'm here, Baba," Emiliano said to the image. "I'll finish your work. I promise."

Emiliano continued to the tall, curved doors at the end of the hall. Entering the doorway, he was greeted by a newly refurbished waiting area. An older man, with his nose in a newspaper, was seated on one of the red brocaded chairs lined along one of the walls. A dark cherrywood secretary desk sat adjacent to the forest green door. Vibrant paintings of Igbala covered the walls, like small windows, ones the Council would never care to look out. Stepping inside, he was greeted by the receptionist.

"I'm here for the council meeting," Emiliano informed her.

"I'm sorry but only members can be here," she said.

"Are you Jack's boy?" the older man asked.

Emiliano eyed the man. Was this man another one who had graced his childhood? Minus the lack of black hair, the skinny, square head and pointed nose were familiar to him. "Elder Seye?"

The older man smiled bringing Emiliano to bow, mindful that his hand touched the ground.

Elder Seye righted Emiliano. "Don't be silly, boy. I hate that bowing thing. I'm no king." He waved at the receptionist and began walking toward another door.

"You are an elder." Emiliano walked beside Seye. "You have earned that respect."

Seye lightly chuckled. "Your father used to say the same thing." He stopped and gave Emiliano a small smile. "He was a good man."

Emiliano stood tall, his heart swelling with pride. It was good to hear Jack Petty had left a positive legacy with others and as his son, Emiliano intended to achieve the same. He squinted to hold back the tears.

Seye touched Emiliano's shoulder. "'He who leaves a good legacy behind will be fondly remembered for his generosity'. You have his heart. You were his pride and I know he raised you right."

Emiliano glanced at the closed door. "I want to finish my father's work, Elder Seye."

"Times have changed. People change. What the people wanted Jack wanted. Since his death, their voices have gone unheard. Don't be discouraged when you walk in here. Hide your feelings in front of these sharks. If they suspect that you are even a little bit nervous, they will destroy any hope you have of accomplishing your father's dream."

If Emiliano hadn't been anxious before, Seye's words quickly changed everything. Jack Petty had wanted to give those in the lower-class power against the abuse of the higher status and tourists. He believed they shouldn't have to endure such mistreatment; those days had died during General Boaventura's rebellion. There were many other issues the man had on his list, each ranked in importance, Emiliano wasn't sure if he would be able to fight with the same passion as his predecessor.

Seye opened the door and walked inside, Emiliano trailing behind him. Five older men dressed in traditional garb talked among themselves inside the small room.

"Brothers!" Seye said in Yoruba drawing the men's attention. "Eight years ago we lost one of the greatest among us. Chairman Jack Ropo Ògúndáre Petty. Now God has looked upon us and given us Jack's son."

He placed his hand on Emiliano's shoulder. Emiliano looked at the apathetic expressions of the other members, his stomach turning. Had he made the right decision?

"He has come to claim his father's chair, once again making this high council whole." Seye smiled at Emiliano and indicated at the chair located on the right side of the head.

"We have not agreed to this," said one of the members.

Emiliano recognized the rotund man as Honorable Mobolaji. As a boy, Emiliano thought the man sweating profusely had nothing to do with the hot summers of Igbala but with the lies and deceit he spewed at the council table. Emiliano had never been brave enough to tell his father, in fear of being reprimanded for disrespecting an elder.

Mobolaji dabbed at his face and neck with a soiled handkerchief. His hard eyes avoided contact with Emiliano, instead focusing on Seye.

"What is there to agree to?" Seye asked. "The chair is rightfully his by blood."

"Chairman Petty chose a woman of foreign birth, tainting the bloodline of the council," Mobolaji said.

"Have you lost your senses, Brother? How many of us have a pure bloodline? You yourself have Portuguese blood in your family."

Mobolaji sucked his teeth. "I am not trying to claim the Chairman's chair. I know my place, but this boy does not. He left and has been in America for the past four years. Our schools were not good enough for him. He doesn't respect his own culture or traditions. He is as foreign as his mother."

"I agree with Brother Mobolaji," another member, Honorable Iles said. The short man stood behind Mobolaji, as if using the bigger man's frame as a shield. "We have decided on another, someone whose blood is pure and is of the island."

Seye's mouth fell open. "Has this been brought to the Head?"

"It has and the seat is to be given to the young man of our choice," Mobolaji said with his head high.

"You cannot give a seat to one whose family line was not one of the Generals," Seye argued.

"We can and have," Iles said.

Emiliano's fingers clenched and unclenched. He wanted to wrap his hands around the haughty Mobolaji's thick neck. Who was this other man who was vying for his father's chair, a spot he had earned by birthright? For a moment a tinge of guilt settled in his mind concerning his absence. Maybe if he had stayed and claimed the seat three years ago, there would be no talk of another. Maybe if he had been more involved in the politics of the island while away, this wouldn't be an issue. When he left physically, he chose to leave mentally, for fear of dwelling on the absence of Jack.

"You have forgotten the Council's custom, Honorable Mobolaji." A man wearing a cream-colored suit stood. Remaining tufts of black hair clung to the scalp, lining the bald spot on the man's head, giving him an older appearance.

"I have not forgotten anything, Barrister Tolu," Mobolaji said. "Times have changed and so should we."

"If the man you have chosen wants the seat," Tolu said, "he will have to be chosen by the Head. And I feel you and your followers have not been completely honest."

"Are you calling me a liar?" Mobolaji's eyes narrowed at Tolu.

"One does not hide something in one's hand and yet swear that one knows nothing about it," Tolu responded.

Mobolaji's glistening face reddened at the proverb. "The decision has been made by the Head."

"Not the final decision," Tolu said. "We are to vote and in two months, the Head shall choose who will sit in the Chairman's seat."

Emiliano studied the faces of the men in the room. Narrowed eyes shooting daggers at one another, each pondering what the other's decision would be. Adrenaline rushed through his body as he waited. Why the hell was this even a choice?

"Fine," Mobolaji finally said. "Two months we will vote and allow the Head to give their final judgment."

Leaving the room, Seye escorted Emiliano to the main door.

"Do not worry. The Head has always cared about tradition. This will not stand."

"This is my father's legacy," Emiliano said. "How can they just give it away as if it were used goods?"

"There are many who want to change the way things are done to line their pockets."

"And they are allowed to keep their positions?"

He remembered his father saying the same thing at the dinner table every night. He thought of placing more women on the council, making the gender ratio even, that all voices would be heard. His mother had waved it off, believing it was foolish to challenge powerful men and had told him he should be happy that they could live like royalty because of his heritage.

"These men, like you," Seye said, "have the original Council's bloodline. Only one can change it and I do not believe they are aware of what is happening. Your father tried to bring it up and even had a few suggestions before," Seye trailed off, his expression dropping.

Then it was time to inform them, Emiliano thought.

"Who is this person they want in my father's seat?" Emiliano asked.

"I'm not sure. Probably someone under Mobolaji's guidance. Don't worry, I will find out for you."

Emiliano left, shielding his eyes from the bright sun. His blood boiled, urging him to storm back inside and take what was his. But he couldn't. It was not what Jack would do. He stared at his shaking hands. He exhaled, willing himself to calm down. What could he do?

His mother's bloodline had been called into question and yet he discerned she was not the issue. Those men wanted to erase what Jack had started, even if that meant hindering his son from finishing the work.

He stormed across the government building's courtyard, not caring to call for a car to pick him up. Outside the gate, his vision was clouded to the cars honking in traffic and the people hustling by, their gaze glued to the ground. He paused his thoughts upon seeing out of the corner of his eye a woman, selling pots of herbs, leaning against the large stone wall protecting the government building.

Emiliano felt his pulse slow as he thought of the innocent-eyed woman at the herbal shop. He hadn't thanked her for what she had done for his sister. Spotting a flower peddler across the street, he rushed over and bought a small bouquet. He smiled at the bright yellow irises before hailing a taxi to the other side of Stingray Cove.

* * * * *

Iyanda threw some rosemary sprigs and lavender flowers into a stone mortar, crushing them with the matching pestle. The soft scent of lavender relaxed her mind, her version of morning coffee.

Last night when she had left Nana B to her beading, Iyanda had headed back to the kitchen. Before she could step a foot inside, her mother Adeyemi had bolted from the room into the bathroom. Uncle Onuoha, her aunt's husband, had strolled out of the kitchen with menacing green eyes and a smirk on his lips. Adeyemi had locked herself in the small bathroom and wouldn't emerge until the next morning with dark circles under wide nervous eyes and disheveled hair, her movements skittish.

For as long as Iyanda could remember, Nana B didn't care for Uncle Onuoha. She had claimed that Ola only married him because he was a Yoruba man with wicked green eyes. Each night he made her scream and plead for him to stop as the sound of hands striking flesh reverberated through the house. He always made sure Iyanda's grandmother was in a deep sleep before he started, recalling a time when the older woman put her bamboo knife to his throat as he slept on the couch. She promised that if she ever saw signs of the abuse again, she would make sure his body wouldn't be recognizable by his ancestors. The six-foot giant of a man became craftier about the location of his abuse.

But Iyanda believed Nana B knew and was just waiting for Aunt Ola to confess. Iyanda questioned why Aunt Ola didn't report him, Adeyemi told her it would be no good without another man to confirm it to the authorities. It was hard on Igbala for women to prove abuse. There were successful cases but only because someone would take pity and come into agreement with the woman.

The chime of the store door guided her from her thoughts. Wiping her hands on a nearby hand towel, she rushed out to the front of the store.

Yesenia Petty stood at the door with her hands clasped in front of her. "Do you speak Portuguese?"

Iyanda nodded, giving the girl a questioning look. It was a bit early for a girl like Yesenia to be out. Was she not feeling well again?

Yesenia held her hands up with palms out. "I feel fine. I've been taking the tea," she said in Portuguese.

Iyanda raised a brow.

"I want to learn about plants, like you," Yesenia said.

Iyanda scanned the store, thankful no one else was nearby to hear the girl say that. She gestured for the young woman to come inside. Iyanda picked up the small chalk board from the counter and a piece of chalk. She began to scribble something down then pause. The girl had asked if she could speak in Portuguese. Was there a chance she wouldn't be able to read Yoruba? Erasing what she had written, she wrote in the language that Iyanda never thought she would have to use again when she graduated high school, then handed it to Yesenia.

The girl read, *Why would you want to do that?*

"Because I want to be smart like you," Yesenia said. "I've lived on Igbala most of my life and I'm embarrassed to speak Yoruba. Either my accent is not Igbalaian enough or I get a word wrong. I can't even speak creole. I know English, Spanish and Portuguese well but this is my home too, I should know everything about it. I want to learn the names of the plants beside tree and flower."

Iyanda smiled. She sympathized with the young girl. Many of the upper-class Igbalaians had forgotten the knowledge and ways of their Yoruba ancestors and chose not to learn it. The art of natural healing classified one as belonging to the lower class and Yesenia definitely didn't fit the category.

Even if they could get past the young girl's economic status, there was the matter of Iyanda training her. An onisegun had to get special permission from authorities to instruct someone from Pleasant Heights.

She wasn't an onisegun.

Iyanda chewed on the inside of her bottom lip as she stared at the eager teen. To take such a risk could cost Iyanda not only the chance to finish her own training but could land her in jail, causing her family undo stress.

She shook her head.

"Oh please, Miss." Yesenia clasped her hands together under her chin.

Iyanda walked behind the counter, the girl stopping at the invisible barrier.

"I know the risk you would be taking but I would be taking a risk too."

Iyanda scoffed. Yesenia would never know risk. The worst that would happen to her would be the disapproving glances of elders in Pleasant Heights and travel restrictions to Stingray Cove.

Iyanda walked to the back room, hoping the distance would muffle the sound of Yesenia's voice.

"Haven't you ever wanted something so bad you would do anything for it?" Yesenia asked.

Iyanda stopped mid-step. Of course she had.

"I would sacrifice everything if I could have one piece of what my Baba loved."

Iyanda looked down at her hands.

She had tried to gain her father's love. Daily she showed filial respect and obedience toward him. She had tried loving and doting on her father only to be turned away by his scorn. Whenever she uttered a word to him or in his presence, he would ignore her or lash out at her mother in anger.

Eventually, she stopped speaking when he was around to protect her mother as well as herself. Her brother encouraged her to talk when he was present, their father not daring to come for her as long as her big brother was around. When her father left, she felt she could finally have her voice back but by then it was too late, she had forgotten the words.

Her brother who had been helping her to gain her voice back, left for Nigeria never to return.

She had lost her voice to gain her family back and yet they still were not within arm's reach. Now the opportunity to be her island's healer was slipping through her fingers day by day.

She lost her voice. What right did she have to take someone else's?

Iyanda walked back to the counter to find Yesenia staring at her feet. She touched the young woman's slumped shoulders.

Yesenia looked up.

Iyanda gave a slight nod, bringing the brightness back to the girl's face and eyes. Yesenia flung her arms around Iyanda's waist.

"Thank you! Thank you!"

Iyanda pried the tight grip loose then held Yesenia back. Grabbing the chalkboard and chalk, she scribbled something then handed it to Yesenia.

Yesenia read out loud, "Be here early every day. Don't tell anyone. The first time you're late or tell, I can no longer teach you."

Yesenia nodded. "Don't worry, I can keep secrets." Hurrying to the door, she paused. She looked back at Iyanda. "What's your name?"

Iyanda thought back to that day. They hadn't made the proper introductions. At the time, it was business as usual for her. Most of the privileged didn't bother to ask her for her name, and she didn't willingly give it to them. But this time was different. She wrote her name on the board.

"E-yan-da," Yesenia read. "I like that. I have to find out what it means." She left the store.

Iyanda stared at her name. A name given to her by her grandmother. One that many couldn't pronounce if they weren't Igbalaian. A name her father had despised.

A special name, her brother had once said. Her lips curved in a small smile.

She liked it too.

CHAPTER 5

The warm afternoon sun glinted off the glass counters, making Iyanda squint against the glare. The warm, minty smell of her tea filled her nostrils, giving her a sense of peace and wellbeing. Just as she exhaled, Gaiana popped her head in.

She motioned for Iyanda to follow. The excited woman guided Iyanda into WAISTED. When her gaze fell on her fiancé, Mason King, her stomach clenched, despite the smile she forced to her face.

He had been gone for almost a year, traveling Europe and the Middle East, becoming cultured. He hadn't changed in appearance much. Clothed in black pants and matching buttoned shirt, a bright red jacket finished the look. He still wore garments that not only underscored his domineering presence, but in Iyanda's opinion, seemed too formal for most occasions.

Mason reaped from the benefits of his successful hairdressing mother. After his father was robbed and killed, Ms. King was forced to raise her son by herself while achieving her dream of owning her own shop. Sacrificing and saving for twenty-two years, Ms. King now owned three salons, two spas and a hair care product line, upping their status to middle class.

His dark, smooth skin reminded Iyanda of the dark purple Odessa Calla Lilies she saw grow in garden hotels. The light bounced off his cheeks, causing a silver glow, mesmerizing many a lady he encountered. The low fade on the sides of his head shaped the black hair on top into a sleek box. He licked his thick, dark brown lips then smiled his charming, perfect white smile. He held out a blue wrapped gift to her.

Adeyemi had approved of him and he paid the full bride price. Soon Iyanda would have to ignore the tightening feeling in her ribs whenever he was around.

Iyanda glanced at the others in the store.

Gaiana's wide eyes spoke of the excitement brewing inside of her, threatening to explode over into the room. Iyanda couldn't be sure if Mason's presence or his gift were the cause of Gaiana's excitement. Gaiana had made it clear in the past she thought it was wonderful Iyanda and Mason were getting married, always loving a love story between couples who had known each other since childhood. If only her friend knew, would she feel the same way?

Mason's eyes narrowed as he held the box.

She looked over at Adeyemi. A white-toothed smile spread across her mother's beautiful face, her eyes expressing her approval. Iyanda looked back at the gift. She nodded in appreciation then accepted the box.

She undid the shiny paper, handing the discarded wrapping to Gaiana, revealing a cotton candy pink show box. Lifting the lid, her eyes widened at the contents.

"Well, let the rest of us catch a glimpse of this great gift," Aunt Ola said.

Iyanda reached inside and pulled out a black, eight-inch stiletto. The toe portion of the shoe was elevated by a hollowed-out platform that threatened to make the wearer topple forward with each step they took. A beautiful intricate pattern made out of lace shielded the foot except the toes and the side of the heel.

Iyanda's eyebrows knitted together as she stared at the shoes. She glanced at Gaiana, searching for a clue as to how to accept such a gift. It wasn't her style, but she didn't want to be rude.

"All the women in the Middle East are wearing them," Mason said, beaming with pride.

"How do you know what they are wearing under all those robes?" Nana B asked.

Mason chuckled, his slanted eyes void of warmth toward Nana B. He locked eyes with the older woman.

"I only associate with fashionable women. And they helped me with my gifts for my two favorite women," Mason said.

Tambara sneered. "There is nothing fashionable about Iyanda."

Nana B, Gaiana and Adeyemi cast a warning look at the envious woman. Tambara stood unfazed.

Mason's booming laugh echoed in the small space. "So, true!" he exclaimed as he tried to catch his breath.

Iyanda shifted, her eyes darting between the varied expressions on the women's faces. Her cheeks warmed at the comment. It wasn't the first time Mason agreed with someone's embarrassing remarks against her.

He wiped at the corner of his eye and said, "She just needs the means to be that woman." He winked at Iyanda.

Iyanda feigned a smile. Mason never missed a moment to remind her family of their lack. The smile disappeared when Nana B joined the group.

"Insulting my family was not why you came to visit, Mason." Nana B's cold, hard eyes focused on him. "What is it you need?"

"I'm taking Iyanda to lunch."

"That is up to her," Nana B said.

Adeyemi nodded to Iyanda to go.

"Do I have to?" Iyanda signed.

She preferred to finish her work. Going out with Mason meant she would have to find some way to communicate since he never bothered to learn sign language. And usually the date began and ended with her words going unnoticed and him controlling everything.

"He's a good man. Be thankful he wants you," Adeyemi signed.

Iyanda sighed. Looking back at Mason, she caught him checking out Tambara. She turned away, silent anger creeping through her veins. She had tried to ignore his wandering eye during their relationship, wanting to believe it would get better the closer it got to the wedding day. She suspected he had talked to her cousin on a more intimate level at one time, but she hoped she was wrong. Handing the box to Gaiana, she made her way to the store door.

Mason grabbed her arm. Snatching the box from Gaiana, he held it out to Iyanda.

She frowned.

"Change into these," Mason ordered, releasing her.

"It's lunch," Nana B defended. "Why does she need to wear those?"

"Because my woman needs to wear what I buy her." Mason glowered at Iyanda.

She grabbed her grandmother's arm when the older woman took a step forward. Iyanda looked into the dark eyes, shaking her head. She mouthed it would be okay, wanting the tension between Nana B and Mason to ebb.

Finding a stool, she changed her flat sandals to the stilettos, her feet tight and compressed like the canned anchovies Aunt Ola bought.

"May the heavens be with me," she thought.

CHAPTER 6

Iyanda slid into the booth, her pulsating toes breathing a sigh of relief. She couldn't understand why she had to wear the circulation cutting shoes off to come to Caetano's. They had only eaten at the casual Portuguese restaurant one time before. It happened while they were in high school. Mason had scrimped and saved every penny to buy her a slice of birthday cake from here and made sure to have just enough to buy drinks so they could have a seat in the building. A thickness formed in her throat at the memory. It was a sweet gesture, a last genuine one before she gave herself fully to him. A night she wished she could take back.

"I don't know what that hostess's problem was," Mason said. "All she had to do was look and she would have seen this table. It's not the best but I guess it will do."

What he didn't know was the bartender went and spoke to the manager for her. After the argument and bribe attempt with the maître d', the owner of the restaurant interfered. She offered them a seat at the bar until a table was cleared but when Mason made it worse, security was called and they were given a choice to leave. While he stewed in his embarrassment, the barkeep signed to her, promising to help them get a table.

"And that bartender better keep his eyes off of you, if he wants to keep his low-paying job."

Iyanda glanced at the copper-skinned man behind the bar. He gave her a small smile before going back to work. He walked over to the owner, Ms. Riviera as they waited. The beautiful, light brown woman smiled up at him, batting her lashes. For a second she narrowed her eyes at them before focusing back on the bartender. She came into his personal space, too close in Iyanda's opinion, and whispered in the man's ear. Flicking her long black hair back, she strutted away, the blue dress accentuating her slim curves.

Mason stared at her, his eyes gentle. "I'm glad you're not like other women, you know not to talk over a man."

Is he serious? When was the last time he heard me speak? Iyanda thought, giving him a quick smile.

"When we get married, you can have your little garden, but you're done giving herbs to people. I don't need my wife passing out medicine to strange men."

Taking out her notepad she wrote, *"I treat women and children too."* Then slid it over to him.

Without looking down, he brushed it across the table back to her. "I feel like that plot was a waste of money, I mean why will you need to play with weeds after having children? You'll be too busy being pregnant and keeping my house to do anything else." He chuckled at his own joke.

Before he left, Mason had purchased her a small unit of land in a community garden, telling her it was something to keep her out of trouble while he was gone. Adeyemi told her it was a loving gift and Iyanda should appreciate it. She wanted to, but inside she knew this energy wouldn't last.

"I heard from my mother that I am being considered for Council Chairman. Who would've thought doing the hair of Honorable Mobolaji's wife would have its benefits?" Mason scoffed. "Imagine, pretty soon I'll be able to come in here and that uppity ajẹ will learn how to show a man some respect. And you'll have the honor of being seen with me."

A waitress came to the table before Mason could finish talking. "What can I get you good folks?" she asked in Igbalaian Creole.

Mason sneered. "Someone not from Talaka Village."

Iyanda's hands squeezed her knees. She wished the booth would swallow her into its red fabric.

"I'm sorry. I thought you were from Talaka Village," the woman stammered.

"What the hell does that mean?" Mason roared. He stood, towering over the now timid woman.

Iyanda clenched her teeth. Mason's father was born and raised in Talaka Village, a fact Mason wanted to remain hidden. Because of his features, those of the island automatically assumed he was of the repulsed community. She grabbed his hand and gave it a small tug.

He glared at her before snatching away. He focused back on the waitress. "Say it."

"Say what?"

"Show me the proper respect you would show a man."

Iyanda and the woman exchanged looks. Mason was fuming and Iyanda knew it could get worse. She cast a glance at the bodyguard from earlier. He was looking in their direction, ready to clear the room if necessary. She tried again to get Mason's attention.

"I'm sorry, Sir. It won't happen again," the waitress said.

Mason nodded and smirked. "Good." He reclaimed his seat. "I'm ready to order. I want the Chef's special and get her something."

Iyanda felt sorry for the now nervous server. She picked up her pen only to have the woman place her hand on hers. She frowned at the woman

"My brother told me you use sign language." The waitress looked in the bartender's direction.

Iyanda lowered her gaze, trying to control her smile. She looked back at the woman and gave a slight nod.

The waitress pointed at a device in her ear. *"My brother went out of his way to help me learn when I was a child. I'm glad to use it with someone other than him."*

Iyanda giggled. It reminded her of how her brother used to teach her English, wanting it to be a secret language for them, it was too bad she wasn't a quick student.

"What can I get for you, ma'am?" the waitress signed.

* * * * *

Emiliano wished he had chosen better footwear as he climbed the hill. The uneven cobblestones threatening to ruin the red outsole of his suede loafers made him rethink his sanity. Clasping the sweat-drenched flowers in his hand, he ignored the fluttering butterflies in the depth of his stomach. He reminded himself to deliver the bouquet as a thank you, nothing more. He took tentative steps toward the connected stores.

He was mulling over what other excuse he could give for being on that side of town so late in the day, when the young woman with the fawn complexion came walking from the other direction.

"Emiliano, you came back!" She rushed over and greeted him with a kiss on his cheek.

"How are you?" He tried to search his memory bank for the woman's name. He knew it started with a 'T'.

"Great, now that you're here." She batted her lashes at him.

Emiliano cleared his throat. "It was good to see you-."

"Tambara," she volunteered.

"Tambara. I have to take care of some business."

"Your sister has grown so pretty. She is always in the magazines with her school and your mother." Tambara complimented, either oblivious to him trying to leave or not caring. "I can't believe she's about to be fifteen."

"Thank you."

"I especially love the articles with you and her. She is growing into a fashionable woman and you are her big, strong brother." She caressed his bicep.

"So, when is the party?" Tambara's eyes glazed with lust.

"It starts tomorrow night. It's a bunch of my sister's friends and their parents. I was hoping to pick up her gift today. Is the lady here that is making it for her?"

"No." She eyed the flowers. "Is that who you brought the flowers for?"

Emiliano raised a brow. "A thank you gift for what she did for Yesenia."

The brightness in Tambara's eyes became cold. "When she gets back, I'll give her the message."

An obvious lie.

"So, who is keeping you company at the party?" Tambara asked.

Emiliano shifted away from her hands. "No one." He shrugged. "I probably won't stay long."

Tambara stepped closer, pressing her ample bosom against his chest. A whiff of floral body spray assaulted his nose. She lifted her face up to his.

"That sounds lonely," she said in a low voice. "A ride is better when you're with someone else."

Emiliano smiled. Slowly he backed away from Tambara and the stores.

"Have the lady give me a call when she returns," he said.

Emiliano walked down the hill, far enough until he was sure Tambara couldn't see him anymore. Darting down a side street, he followed the path around a few stores and brightly colored shacks and apartments until he reached the other side of the building. Peeking around the corner and seeing the coast was clear, he snuck inside the herbal shop. He winced at the bell chiming above the door.

Dried herbs and flowers hung from the ceiling, offering their fragrances of sweet and bitter. A tray of hot tea sat on the counter next to the door with a sign asking patrons to take one. He poured himself a cup and took a small taste. Sweet with a hint of mint.

He called out. No one answered.

Walking to the counter he called out again. "Anyone here?"

A light touch on his back made him turn around. There she stood. A warmth hummed in his chest as he devoured her figure, her beauty. He frowned. She was standing three feet away. He knew he had physically felt someone touch him. At least, he thought he did.

Time paused as they stared at each other. He appraised the way her dark green skirt hugged her round, shapely hips and the way her blouse tried to hide her narrow waist. Instead of a headwrap this time she wore her hair in a braided halo.

His shoulders slumped at seeing the symbol of engagement interwoven on her head.

Engaged.

Of course she was.

A small grin appeared on her full lips.

"Hi." He handed her the flowers, wanting to kick himself for not thinking of something else to say.

She gave a slight nod.

He cleared his throat. "I came to see if my sister's order was ready. And to give you these."

She softly gazed at the bouquet then sniffed, her thick lips curling into a smile. If only he were the flowers, he would bathe in the admiration.

He admired the sway of her hips as she hurried behind the counter to a backroom. She came back with a jar of water. Placing the flowers inside, she slid out a chalkboard and piece of chalk from underneath the register. She thanked him for the flowers then explained to him it wouldn't be ready for a while. Maybe one to two days.

"Then I'll see you at the party?" Emiliano asked.

She paused, blinking as if to register what he said. Relief washed over him when she nodded.

"With everything that happened the other day, I never caught your name." he said.

"Didn't give it," she wrote. She lowered her gaze, the coy smile on her lips making his stomach flutter.

He chuckled. "Ok, well, what's your name?"

"Iyanda," she wrote.

Emiliano reached for the chalkboard, his hand brushing across hers. His heart pounded as her gentle eyes caressed him, reaching deep to a place he had forgotten.

"Sorry," he said. He slowly moved his hand away from hers, the light charge from the touch still tingling in his arm.

"What's going on here?"

Emiliano turned.

Adeyemi. Her red lips pressed together as she eyed them. The woman's nostrils flared as she looked between him and Iyanda.

He stammered. "I-I was in the area and checking to see if my sister's order was ready."

The woman looked in Iyanda's direction.

Looking between both of the women, he now saw a small resemblance. He guessed from the way Iyanda averted her eyes the other woman had to be the mother.

Iyanda gathered the chalk and chalkboard, nodded in Emiliano's direction, then rushed to the back room.

"It will be delivered to you when it is ready, Mister Petty," Adeyemi said, her words coated with a final warning.

Emiliano wanted to kick himself.

He left the store, the tingle fading the moment he stepped over the threshold.

CHAPTER 7

Iyanda walked beside Adeyemi, careful to avoid eye contact with anyone of the male gender. After Emiliano's visit to the store two days earlier, Adeyemi scolded Iyanda for being so careless.

"What if Ms. King had walked in?" Adeyemi had asked. "What then? She wouldn't want you in her family and neither would anyone else." For the rest of the night Iyanda had kept to Nana B's side, helping the older woman make waist beads.

The odors of pepper-spiced goat meat and freshly baked bread mingling with the scent of ripe fruit and sweat richened the Igbalaian air. The vendors calling out to passing people and haggling with customers made Iyanda long for the serenity of her herbal shop. Mid-morning was the best time to attend the market however, each weekend attracted more and more merchants and not enough space.

"There are more àlejò each year," Tambara said, her nose wrinkling as a tourist couple passed.

"They're here for the Bones Festival, Tambara," Adeyemi said. "Their visit helps the island."

"It's not for them," Tambara shot back.

"Be nice," Nana B said in a warning tone.

Tambara was right. The festival wasn't for the outsiders. It was for Igbala.

The government closing the island off to tourism during the time of the festival, they decided, would not be in the best interest of their pockets. So, the residents had to suffer through as their most cherished of celebrations were tarnished by the tourists' lack of respect and understanding.

Iyanda wanted to agree with her older cousin, but to do so would put her in more hot water with her mother. As the older women argued with Tambara, Iyanda browsed the wares of the nearby stalls, inhaling the natural scents of the handmade soaps. They had come to the market hoping to find cloth for new dresses and also to catch up on any current news, things she didn't care for at the moment.

Her long, brown fingers, still charged by Emiliano's touch, danced over the soft materials at a merchant's stall. She paused.

"It's hand-woven, Miss," the merchant said.

Iyanda admired the fabric. Her fingers caressed the black, burgundy, and sea green pattern. She envisioned making it into an agbada for Emiliano and to be able to see him enter into a room and command the attention of all wearing the luxurious robe.

"Your husband would love you more if you wear this," the merchant said.

Iyanda blushed. With a small smile, she gave a slight nod then walked away.

Stroking her arm, she moved to the next stall. The rhythm of the marketplace no longer held her attention. The merchant's words buzzed in her head. *Her husband.*

Not Emiliano.

Mason. Mason would be her husband. He would burn the material, not wanting her to represent anything of their roots, her being.

Catching a glimpse of a young couple at a stall, Iyanda watched as the man paid a merchant then clasped a cowrie bracelet around his woman's wrist. The woman, not giving the token of love a moment to rest against her skin, threw her arms around the man's neck, showering his face and lips with kisses.

There was a time she and Mason were like them. She never received a cowrie love token, but he showed he cared in other ways. In middle school, he had been lovestruck with her, bringing her hibiscus flowers every day to place in her hair. He protected her from the teasing when her father had abandoned the family. At sixteen, he lost his patience. She stopped speaking. The flowers stopped. He became the one doing the teasing, claiming it was all in fun.

Peeling her eyes away from the amorous couple, she spied a familiar face.

She squeezed her eyes shut. Taking a breath, she calmed the fluttering in her belly before taking a peek.

Dunni. The older woman knelt behind her layout of various herbs.

She hadn't spotted Iyanda yet, but the moment she lifted her head…

Iyanda looked behind her. Her family was still browsing but the distance between them and her were shortening with each step. If they saw Dunni, they would want to catch up on news and Nana B would ask about the healer training. Then she would have to explain everything. She couldn't face her grandmother's disapproving face.

Panic set in. Looking between the two parties, Iyanda crept down a path leading further into the market. Her heart pounded. Each voice behind her sounded like her mother's. On nearing the market house, she quickened her steps. She knew the market house would be the last place the women would step into.

Outsiders wishing to operate their businesses in the marketplace had the abandoned warehouse gutted and remodeled to accommodate the numerous stalls and stores. Nana B refused to shop inside the market house, claiming the outsiders were taking away the money from the already struggling Igbalaians.

Slowing down, Iyanda turned, scanning the crowd for her family's faces.

She sighed. They hadn't followed her. Iyanda turned around.

The market house was just as crowded as the outside market. The delicious aroma of cooking meat reminded her she had not eaten yet.

She decided to eat first before going to look for her family. Walking in the direction of the food area, Iyanda took a quick glimpse behind her.

Her mind relaxed upon not seeing her mother.

Not paying attention, she walked into something hard. As she stumbled back, someone grabbed her wrist and pulled her up. She steadied herself against the person. Certain her legs wouldn't give out on her before she looked up.

Iyanda cast a glance up at the person holding her close.

* * * * *

Emiliano tried to ignore every cell in his body responding to Iyanda's lush feminine curves. His fingers ached to unravel the damned halo braid she wore and explore and tease every part of her until she…

She pulled away, averting her eyes. Rubbing her palms rapidly together, her full, dark brown sugar lips mouthed, what he assumed, was an apology.

He frowned. Before he could ask her what she was doing, a couple of uniformed men approached. They eyed Iyanda and Emiliano.

Emiliano's jaw tightened.

The Sem Mácula Law.

An archaic law of Igbala put in place by the Portuguese conquerors used to distinguish the class of master, slave, and native. Being put to rest after the rebellion, classes were demolished for a while. Until the residents of Pleasant Heights, his mother included, decided the law needed to be revived and enforced upon those of the working class while over-protecting the upper class and tourists. With one word he or anyone from his class could have Iyanda beaten in the streets.

"Everything okay, Mister?" one of the men asked in broken English.

The uniformed men rested their hands on the beating sticks secured to their hips.

Her eyes pleaded with him.

Emiliano eyed the officers. "We're fine."

Taking her hand, he led her away from the men. Once he felt comfortable, they were out of their sight, he turned and looked down at her.

"From now on, do not apologize to me in public," he said. "You never have to worry about me reporting you."

She gave a slight nod.

He gave her hand a gentle squeeze. "Come on."

She gripped the strap of her bag, her narrowed eyes studying him.

"Just want to buy you some coconut water." He indicated to a nearby cart.

She slid her hand from his then visibly relaxed.

Emiliano smiled. She didn't want to be seen holding his hand and he couldn't blame her. Catching up to her, he made sure to walk beside her in case the uniformed men were still nearby.

At the cart, Emiliano ordered two waters. The man sliced the tops off of two large, green coconuts, placed straws inside and handed them to Emiliano. Paying for them, he handed Iyanda hers then found them a seat on a nearby bench.

Taking a sip of the sweet water, he glanced at Iyanda. Her long lashes seemed to kiss the top of her cheeks. His eyes traveled to her sinfully, beautiful mouth curving around the straw. He envisioned the softness and the sweetness of her lips.

She frowned when she caught him looking at her.

"You're here with your family?" He needed to change the subject or she would leave.

She gave a small nod, her eyes full of doubt.

"Yesenia wanted some message paper for the festival," Emiliano explained. "My mother and her boyfriend came. I disappeared."

Her head leaned to the side.

"Needed to get away." He averted his eyes. The words to use to describe his money-grubbing mother and her boyfriend would be too much to explain and more than likely too much for her to hear.

She handed him a pad of paper.

"Me too," it read. A coy smile curved the corners of her lips.

"Since we're getting away," Emiliano said, "let's make the most of it."

He motioned for her to follow.

Walking off deeper into the market, they came across people selling cheap knockoffs of the Igbalaian fashions and plastic masks meant for the tourists to carry home. Emiliano tried on one of the masks. She covered her mouth, her eyes lighting up in amusement.

"You buy?" the man of the store asked in a rude tone.

Emiliano slid the mask off and looked at it. "I don't know whether to purchase or be insulted by this cheap imitation of Ori."

"You don't like, don't touch."

Iyanda moved to leave but Emiliano held her arm. He locked eyes with the man. "Careful, sir, or I could have this store closed before the end of business."

The man's steely eyes tried to call Emiliano's bluff but finally looked away in shame.

Emiliano escorted Iyanda from the store. She quickly scribbled onto her notepad.

"You shouldn't have done that," she wrote. *"These merchants can get violent."*

He stopped walking and looked down in her eyes. "I don't care. Let them. As long as none of them placed their hands on you, then they might get a chance to walk away."

"Why protect me?"

"What kind of man would I be if I didn't?"

Her eyes softened. Her fingers lifted to her lips, trying to conceal the smile lighting up her face.

"You hungry?" he asked.

She nodded.

He led her to the small food area, her hand safely wrapped in his.

* * * * *

Iyanda's pulse quickened as he led her through the crowd, his large, warm hand resting against the small of her back. His soothing scent of lemongrass calmed the quivering in her stomach.

They managed to make it to the front of the crowded area and order their food. He refused to have her pay for anything. She placed the money back in her bag, taking a deep breath to slow her heartbeat and calm her stomach flutters.

Holding on to their food with one hand, he led her through the crowd, making sure to use his body to shield her from the bumps and brushes of others. Squeezing out of the throng of people, they made their way to a nearby wall.

Iyanda unwrapped the paper-wrapped food, her mouth watering at the sight of the spicy fritter burger. Taking a bite, she closed her eyes as she chewed the warm, soft, homemade bread. She crunched down on the fried bean fritters, the spiciness of the peppers stinging her tongue. She didn't care. The last time she had the delicious burger she was fifteen and her brother Naade.

"You make the sandwich look more delicious than what it is," Emiliano said with a light chuckle.

Air burned her moistened eyes when she opened them. She lowered them.

"Hot?" He handed her a small bottle of water.

She sipped the room temperature water. She needed to gain control of her emotions. Now was not the time to think of her brother. He was no longer there. He didn't come back for her like he promised. She handed Emiliano back the bottle and took a deep breath.

"Better?" he asked.

With a quivery smile, she nodded. As good as she was going to get.

"Here you have something-." He wiped something from the corner of her mouth with his finger.

Iyanda froze, her drumming heart threatened to give away the blossoming sensations moving through her body. She melted into his exotic eyes, wanting to lose herself, if only for a moment in them. She lowered her gaze. She couldn't. Not now. Maybe in another time. Another life.

"I'm sorry." He handed her a napkin.

Before she could respond, she caught sight of her family inside the warehouse. She gasped.

"What's wrong?" he asked.

She squeezed her eyes shut, hoping it was just a hallucination. She peeked. It wasn't. Her grandmother and mother were looking in the store and stalls, probably searching for her. Iyanda indicated her family, using her hands to tell him she needed to hide. Thankfully he understood.

Emiliano grabbed her hand and led her down a path of more stalls and stores.

Her heart raced. She swore she heard her mother calling for her, getting closer with each step.

They slid down a narrow passage, his body pressed against hers. Crossing her arms across her chest to put a bit of space between them, she prayed her mother wouldn't catch them and he wouldn't get any closer.

He put his finger to his mouth and shushed her.

Iyanda frowned. If only she could reach her notepad, she would remind him she didn't speak.

Iyanda tensed at the sight of her mother. If only the wall would swallow her. Her heart raced. If Adeyemi looked in their direction, she would be dragged to the altar today to marry Mason.

He leaned close to her ear, his warm breath sending shivers through her.

"We're going to have to make out," he whispered.

She pushed him away and stared at him as if he had lost his mind. Did he not see her mother? She shook her head.

"Only pretend," he assured. "If they look this way, you and I are definitely in trouble. I'll just use my hands to hide your face like this." He demonstrated blocking her face with his hands. "And we'll get close, making it look like we're kissing. I promise I won't touch you, except on your face."

Her heart raced. Her mother asked a man if he had seen her and he was leading them back to where she and Emiliano were. Without another thought she grabbed his shirt and pressed her lips to his, turning him so his back would be toward the entrance of the passageway.

He grabbed her waist, bringing her in closer. His warm tongue dipped between the seam of her lips, parting her closed-mouth kiss, playing and enticing hers to dance.

She tried to pull away, but he held her lips captive, possessing them. His tongue, plunging deeper into her mouth, elicited a moan from her. Her cheeks grew hot at the sound. She had to get away but her body rebelled, relaxing in his arms.

Her heart skipped a beat when she thought she heard the sound of her mother's disapproving grunt. Had they been caught? She braced for the scolding she was sure to receive.

Hearing the sound of retreating steps, she pushed Emiliano away. Her fingers flew to her tender lips, still throbbing from his assault.

His brows knitted for a moment. "I-."

She pushed past him. She didn't want an explanation. Heat rose from her neck to her eyes. Keeping her face to the ground, she rushed through the crowd. It wasn't his fault, she had kissed him. But would it have hurt for him not to kiss back?

Even though her mother walked away, she swore Nana B had made eye contact with her. Her chest tightened at the thought.

She broke from the congested market house, inhaling the humid air. She squinted up at the late afternoon sun.

If Nana B did see her, would she tell Adeyemi?

"Iyanda, we've been looking all over for you," Adeyemi said.

Iyanda turned to face her mother. Tambara's hands were filled with bags and Nana B avoided her eyes.

Iyanda's heart dropped. The older woman did see.

"Where have you been?" Adeyemi asked.

"*I went to use the bathroom and got distracted,*" Iyanda signed.

"You're not a child," Adeyemi said. "Stay close next time."

Adeyemi and Tambara walked ahead. Iyanda glanced back before getting in step with Nana B.

CHAPTER 8

Iyanda watched as the candle flame flickered. It danced upon its wick, beckoning her to stuff Ms. King's mouth with the slices of fresh warm bread the waiter placed on the cloth covered table. The server poured water in her crystal glass before mumbling he would return for their orders. He rushed off, leaving Iyanda at the mercy of her fiancé and future mother-in-law. Both sat on the opposite side of the table, forgetting that Iyanda was still there. Ms. King wore a pricey dark blue evening gown, the bodice clung for life to the older woman's large chest. When she laughed, her dress sparkled brightly within the dim room.

"Mason, you know how to treat your mama!" Ms. King gushed. She pulled out a long strand of black pearls from a blue oval box. She showed them to Iyanda then gave them to Mason.

Undoing the clasp, he placed the necklace around his mother's plump neck. "Only the best for the most important woman in my life."

"One day you'll reach my status, Iyanda," Ms. King said.

Iyanda sipped her water, averting her eyes from the prideful display. She flinched at the loudness of Ms. King's conversation, their table receiving more scowls from the other diners in the restaurant. She was prepared to say no when Mason strolled into the store inviting her to lunch then Ms. King came in insisting Iyanda joined them, a threat behind the older woman's words.

Iyanda scanned the room for anything to avoid the boasting of her future mother-in-law. She froze at the sight of Emiliano. He walked in with the beautiful manager from the Portuguese restaurant on his arm. He held his head high, his steps in sync with the woman. Stopping to speak to a waiter, his eyes found hers. With an expressionless face, he made his way to his table, an older woman and gentleman following close behind. Iyanda took another sip of water hoping the painful tightness in her throat could be relieved. It couldn't.

"That is Quilla Petty and Aria Riviera," Ms. King said in a low voice. "If I'm not mistaken the younger man is Emiliano Petty, heir to the Petty fortune."

"And my competitor for the Chairman position on the Council," Mason said. He stabbed the salad on his plate with the fork before shoving it into his mouth.

Iyanda hung her head, hiding the water forming in her eyes from hearing his name. She peeked at Emiliano's table. He sat beside the beautiful woman.

Her heartbeat slowed. His eyes, unreadable locked with hers. Even when the beautiful woman touched his arm, he looked away briefly before finding Iyanda again.

"There's the bitch that disrespected me," Mason said.

Ms. King shushed her son. "That is Emiliano's fiancée, or so I heard. She left the island for a bit but she's back now. If you want to get far, you have to make the right friends."

"I'm about to be Council Chairman, why do I need friends in his position when soon he will not have one." Mason settled back in his chair, a hard smile on his lips.

Iyanda dropped her gaze from Emiliano's. Of course he was engaged. It was foolish of her to keep revisiting the kiss at the market. They were pretending after all. Her chest tightened. She left the table, rushing to the bathroom, ignoring Mason and his mother calling her. She needed to get away from Mason, his mother, and Emiliano's hard eyes.

Rushing into a stall, she closed and locked the door. Taking deep breaths, she willed the tears to stop falling. He is an engaged man. She, an engaged woman. Heat surged through her body. *How could I have been so stupid?* she thought. She struck the stall wall.

Iyanda took a deep breath. It didn't matter. Her fiancé was waiting for her at the table. She would make the perfume for Yesenia and then erase the Petty family from her mind. Drying her eyes, she left the stall.

Leaving the bathroom, she almost collided with Emiliano. He leaned against the wall, his intense eyes studying her. She exhaled and tried to walk away only to have her path blocked by him.

"I wanted to apologize for yesterday," he said.

Lifting her hands loosely with palms up, she gave him a polite smile. She prayed he couldn't see through her wall.

He reached up and closed his hand around one of hers awakening the swarm of butterflies in her stomach. Her mind screamed for her to pull away, to push him away and go back to her table.

She tried to back away from each step he took toward her.

"I shouldn't have kissed you," Emiliano said, stepping closer, "or rather I shouldn't have let you kiss me." A smile curved the corner of his mouth, a brow raised.

She snatched away and frowned. She refused to be the butt of his jokes. A simple Cove girl he conquered and played for a fool.

Iyanda shook her head. She wasn't her cousin.

She nudged him out of her way and returned to her table. Grabbing her bag, she left the restaurant without a word to Mason or his mother.

CHAPTER 9

During the scorching summer days of Igbala, the Petty women would sleep away the afternoon while the men worked. Today was no different except for the unknown absence of Yesenia and the lingering one of Senior Petty.

Emiliano sat at his father's desk, a small picture of Jack Petty watching him as he went over the quarterly reports. Taking up the reins of his father's import/export business since he was sixteen began to weigh on him. Eight years he swam in schoolwork and business, hoping to drown the pain of his father's death only to now glance at the older man's picture and feel a tightening in his chest.

When his mother tried to gain access to Petty Trading Company's finances, he knew he had been away from home for too long and needed a way for her to not see the business's day to day dealings. Thankfully the board had denied her access, but he never put it past his mother's manipulative ways. Speaking to some of the members, he had the IT department create an encryption to be used for when the day's work was done.

But work wasn't what kept traveling through his mind.

Iyanda had looked at him as if he were low. He pinched the bridge of his nose and closed his eyes. He shouldn't have teased her about the kiss. She was an engaged woman and she kissed him. The look of open mouth horror on her face that day at the market told it all. She had committed a wrong, in her own eyes.

Her eyes. The distant expression tugged at his stomach.

He didn't want to even be at the restaurant with his mother or Aria. Quilla had planned it. She made it seem as if it was an innocent lunch for him to get to know Edward then Aria showed up. The way his former fiancée smiled in his face and grabbed his arm, it was as if there had been no breakup. For a moment, he wanted to believe everything had been the way it was before she ran off with the other guy.

Then he saw her. Her brow knitted together above large eyes. Even when he took his seat at his table, his eyes didn't leave Iyanda's face. His stomach hardened at the sight of her trembling chin. He wanted to take away her reason for chewing her bottom lip.

Was the man at her table her fiancé? Emiliano scoffed. The way the other woman at the table was pawing and hugging on him, the man had to be a mama's boy. Not man enough for Iyanda.

Not man enough. Emiliano rubbed his face.

He wasn't man enough to keep his mouth closed about the kiss. His father had taught him never to embarrass a lady for it would make him no better than a man who strikes a woman.

He glanced at the photo. "Definitely failed you there, Baba."

Emiliano was finishing an email for a long time client when there was a knock on the door.

"I'm not staying for breakfast, Ana," he said without looking up.

"What kind of monster rejects Ms. Ana's fresh brewed tea and bread baked with grandmotherly love?"

Emiliano chuckled at the sound of the familiar voice. He looked up as Christopher Boyd came into the office and plopped himself on the reddish couch.

Christopher Boyd, Chris to Emiliano, had been a constant person in his life, one he knew he could trust and would always keep him straight.

Since diaper days they had been inseparable. Even when Chris's dad moved out and his mom remarried Alexander Riviera, Emiliano stood beside him. Quilla didn't care for the young man which made the friendship all the better.

"Someone whose stomach doesn't run their day," Emiliano said.

"How can anyone work when their stomach demands sustenance?" Chris grabbed his stomach and feigned weakness.

Emiliano rolled his eyes and hit send on the email then quickly went to work encrypting everything he had done.

"She still being a nosey bitch?" Chris asked.

"Hey." Emiliano stared at Chris. "That's my mother." He smirked. "Don't call her nosey."

Chris snickered. "Whatever you say, my longtime friend."

Emiliano glanced back at the screen. "What woman are you hiding from today?"

Chris sighed and put his hands behind his head. "Christopher Boyd does not hide from women."

"Christopher Boyd is full of shit. You only call me 'longtime friend' when there is a woman or her man you are hiding from and need my help."

Chris shrugged a shoulder. "Dude should know how to please his woman."

Emiliano sat back in the leather desk chair, eyeing Chris. "And what do I get out of this?"

"I'll keep my sister away."

"You have found a way to freeze hell and make yourself king?" Emiliano asked, his question thick with sarcasm.

Chris sat up. "Fine. I'll buy breakfast."

"Breakfast and lunch."

"You drive a hard bargain, Petty. A game first."

Emiliano, satisfied with the encryption, shut the computer down and stood.

"It's been a while since I kicked your ass." Emiliano walked out of the office. "Extra clothes in the guest house."

Moments later, Emiliano and Chris met on the basketball court Jack Petty had built in his younger days. Emiliano loved the game but not as much as Chris did. The latter ate and breathed the game his stepfather considered to be a poor man's sport.

They played hard against each other, both breathless and drenched in sweat before the sun rose high in the sky. Emiliano was losing. It was down to the last point in the game and he had the ball. His fingers rubbed the small bumps on the orange sphere as he stared down a confident Chris. Emiliano looked at the distance he would have to go to get around the faster man and his outstretched arms.

"Today, Petty," Chris jeered.

Emiliano smirked at his friend. "I can't wait to dunk on that stupid smile."

"I can't wait until the day you dunk."

Emiliano moved his right leg causing Chris to shift in the same direction. Emiliano, taking the small window, went to the left bouncing the ball to the hoop.

Emiliano's heart pounded, threatening to leave his body if he didn't stop. He pushed harder, hearing Chris gaining on him. Nearing the basket, his muscles tensed, preparing for the leap. Holding the ball between both hands, he pushed himself off the pavement toward the basket. He sailed through the air, his heart pounding.

He held his breath. This was the moment he always wanted, to be able to dunk on Chris in the hundreds of games they played.

Chris jumped up and knocked the ball out of his hand.

Emiliano landed on his feet, rolling his eyes at Chris's taunting and the frustration he was feeling. Walking over to a metal bench on the sidelines, Emiliano picked up a towel and tossed it at Chris.

"Where to for breakfast, longtime friend?" Emiliano asked, his pride sore.

"Julie's."

Emiliano scoffed. A small cafe in Pleasant Heights, known for its delicious, high-priced meals and beautiful high-class young women. One in particular, Julie, the owner.

"I'll skip on watching you embarrass yourself," Emiliano said, wiping the sweat from his bare chest.

Chris picked up a bottle of water and opened it. Flopping down on the bench, he took a swig of the warm water.

"She doesn't know what she's missing out on. What do you suggest?" Chris asked.

"Stingray Cove."

Chris frowned. "Where the hell to?"

Emiliano smirked. "Figure it out." He made his way back to the mansion, his mind finding Iyanda in his memory.

After freshening up, Emiliano and Chris sat outside a small cafe adjacent to WAISTED and Iyanda's EWE. With each bite of his scrambled eggs, Emiliano glanced at Iyanda's store.

"Is something in your eggs?" Chris asked.

Emiliano stared down at the plate, using his fork to move the cooked egg, tomatoes and onions around.

"No," Emiliano said.

"Then why the hell do you keep looking over there as if you are on something?"

Emiliano sucked his teeth. "Whatever, Bro."

"I mean, what's over there?" Chris pointed at the shops across the street.

Emiliano sat up straight when Iyanda's store door opened. She stepped outside with a shorter woman. In her yellow blouse and matching skirt, Emiliano imagined she made the sun jealous at the moment.

She smiled at the woman. What he would give to bask in the brightness of that smile.

Chris chuckled. "I see why you wanted to come here."

"And the reason I lost the game." He couldn't peel his eyes away from her.

Chris shook his head. "No, that's just you."

They watched as Iyanda conversed with the customer.

"I wonder if she has a cute little body under all that tribal stuff," Chris said. "Face is average but doable."

Emiliano's jaw tightened. In all the years they had known each other, Emiliano had never wanted to hit Chris square in the jaw.

"Who is she?" Chris asked.

Emiliano clenched his teeth as he watched Chris's thirsty eyes ogled her. He was thankful she finally walked back into the store.

"Out of your league," Emiliano said.

Chris made a buzzing sound with his lips. "Nothing in the Cove has a league. These women are always looking for men like us."

"She's different. And engaged."

"Engagements mean nothing to girls like them. Different, huh?" Chris chewed on his lower lip. "Let's see." Chris shot out of the plastic cafe chair and made his way across the street.

"Chris," Emiliano hissed.

He nodded to the diners looking in his direction before turning his head in time to see Chris disappear into the store. Taking a sip of coffee, his eyes never left the forest green door.

He knew it was a risk to allow Chris to talk to Iyanda. But deep-down Emiliano wanted to know if she was who he thought she was.

Trying to control his leg from bouncing, he shifted in the hard chair as the seconds passed. Why was Chris taking so long? Emiliano rubbed at his jaw, hoping to ebb the pain from his clenched teeth. What if Chris was right? Emiliano shook his head. Iyanda was different. He could feel it.

He stood up ready to cross the street when Chris came out of the store. His friend kept his head down as he walked to the street, making it hard for Emiliano to find any signs of success. Emiliano's chest tightened with each step Chris took. When Chris flopped down on the chair across from him, Emiliano slowly took his seat, searching his friend's unreadable face.

Chris picked up his fork and stirred his food on the plate, destroying the omelet into smaller pieces. Stabbing a piece of egg, he forced it into his mouth.

Emiliano's soft laugh turned into an uproar as his friend continued shoveling food into his mouth. His chest relaxed, his heart dancing at the failure of Chris's attempt.

"Real deal?" Emiliano asked.

"She's all right. First time a Cove girl looked right past me." He devoured another forkful of food. Pointing his fork in Emiliano's direction, he said, "If you let her get away we are no longer friends."

Emiliano resumed his soulful laughter. Chris sat back, his lips pressed tight, averting eye contact.

"We go to Julie's for lunch," Chris said.

* * * * *

Iyanda watched the man walk to the cafe across the street. He came in eyeing her and rubbing his thumb across his moistened lips. He wanted to know what herbs would help him sustain in bed, his lust-filled eyes undressing her. After telling him that she didn't specialize in those types of herbs, he proceeded to question her relationship status and if she was serious about it. He asked her how long she had been healing and to complain about an ache he had and that maybe she could help. Iyanda pressed her lips together, not wanting the man to know she wasn't oblivious to what he was talking about. After giving him a herbalist who would be better suited to his needs, he downed a cup of mint tea then left without another word.

She squinted against the sun's glare. The man who had entered her store sat down across from another man who looked identical to Emiliano. Was the man sent over? If he was, why?

"Did he leave?"

Iyanda walked to the counter and nodded at Yesenia. The young girl came from the back room clutching a jar of herbs. She had only been there for a couple of hours for her first lesson before the man entered the store. Iyanda suspected Yesenia knew him from the way she flew to the room before he barely made it across the street.

"He is so annoying. What did you say to make him leave?" Yesenia asked in Portuguese.

Iyanda handed her the chalkboard.

Using a translation application on her phone, Yesenia translated the words. "One does not consume salt according to one's greatness." She frowned. "What does it mean?"

"Too much of a good thing can be dangerous."

Iyanda's eyes widened. She turned to Gaiana standing with her hands on her hips.

"What are you doing here, Miss?" Gaiana asked Yesenia, the Portuguese words spoken so smoothly, one would have thought Gaiana was a native speaker.

Iyanda felt the young girl's eyes burning into her, pleading for the right answer to say.

"Iyanda?" Gaiana's brow raised.

"I'm teaching her about herbs," Iyanda signed in Yoruba.

"Are you crazy, Iyanda?" Gaiana asked in a hushed tone. She rushed over to them. "You could get in trouble for this."

"I know, but-."

"But nothing. What if your mother or aunt had come in? Or Tambara. Or worse, her mother."

"I know that word!" Yesenia chimed in. "Don't tell my mother!"

"Little Miss, this conversation is not for you," Gaiana said in Portuguese.

"Why?" Yesenia asked. "It's about me. I asked Iyanda to teach me. She said no but I persisted. If we get caught, I'll take the blame."

Gaiana scoffed. "It doesn't quite work like that, Little Miss."

"Why doesn't it?"

Gaiana sighed. "Iyanda is considered different because she won't talk."

Iyanda avoided Yesenia's eyes.

"Can't or won't?" Yesenia asked.

"Won't," Gaiana translated for Iyanda.

"And because she won't," Gaiana said, "many see her as a burden on her family. It doesn't help that she lives here in Stingray Cove. People like her have to watch their step or be punished."

"It doesn't have to be like that," Yesenia argued.

"But it is, Little Miss," Gaiana said in a calm tone.

The pained expression on Yesenia's face stabbed Iyanda's heart. The young girl lived a life of luxury, shielded from the real Igbala and its greedy government. She would never experience the abuse bestowed upon the lower class by the men in uniforms.

"I don't want to hurt you, Miss Iyanda," Yesenia said. She sniffled.

Iyanda sighed. She looked at Gaiana. *"I'm going to continue teaching her,"* she signed.

"Iyanda!" Gaiana protested.

"What makes me any better than those people sitting in their offices and telling us what we can and cannot do?"

"You're following the law, that's what will make you better."

"Gaiana-"

"No! If your mother catches you-."

"Then I'll deal with her. You nor Yesenia will get in trouble. Please. Let me do this. All I ask is for this one thing."

Gaiana eyed her and Yesenia. She groaned. "Fine. I'll keep your secret. But if you get caught," Gaiana paused and warmly smiled, "I'm taking the blame with you."

Iyanda returned the smile.

"I can stay?" Yesenia asked, her face brightened with hope.

"Yes, Little Miss."

Yesenia threw her arms around Gaiana's waist.

Iyanda touched Yesenia's shoulder. She scribbled on the chalkboard and handed it to her.

"How do you know the man who came in here?" Yesenia read.

"He's Emiliano's friend," Yesenia said. "Those two go everywhere together."

Iyanda gazed at the windowed door, gripping the board to her quickening heartbeat.

CHAPTER 10

Emiliano leaned against his car in front of the Petty mansion, waiting for Yesenia. The day before, Ana the housekeeper informed him his little sister did not take the customary afternoon nap. When the girl's laundry was done in the evening, bits of plant matter escaped from her pockets. With just a sniff of the fragments, he knew where she had disappeared to.

The front door opened. He covered his mouth at seeing Yesenia tiptoed out the door and slowly closed it.

"When did you start sneaking out of the house?" he asked. She stopped mid-stride. He coughed, trying to maintain his stern expression, her wide eyes tickling him.

"Brother!" Yesenia said in a high pitch voice. She gave him a tentative smile. "You're here early."

"Want to make sure you get to where you're going."

She laughed nervously. "I'm not going anywhere."

"You're dressed and you have your bag."

"I'm taking the trash out."

"Taking the trash out?" Emiliano smirked. "Where's the trash can?"

Yesenia's eyes searched for the trashcan. Not seeing it, she let out an impatient snort and stomped over to him.

"Fine. You caught me." She batted her eyes at him. "Don't tell Mom, please."

He smiled. "Only if you tell me where you're going."

"I-I can't."

Emiliano shrugged. "I'm sure Mother is looking for a reason to turn your party into a function centered around her," he said, pulling his phone out of his pocket.

"Not my party," she pleaded, rubbing her palms together vigorously.

Emiliano chuckled as she covered his phone.

She frowned. "You're not calling her, are you?"

Emiliano shook his head.

"I have to meet a friend," Yesenia said.

Emiliano reached inside his shirt pocket and showed her the plant fragments. "I would like to see this friend, again." He opened the passenger door for his sister. "Let's go see her."

Yesenia rolled her eyes and climbed inside.

Following the coast and Yesenia's directions to an unfamiliar part of the island, the twenty-minute drive under the warm morning sun relaxed Emiliano. The beaches' legendary black sand stretched for miles, contrasting with the crystal clear blue and green ocean. He inhaled the salt air, wanting to jump into the peaceful water and allow it to soothe his mind. Emiliano pulled to a stop in front of a small white house with a blue roof. Children of various ages chased each other within the fenced yard.

"What is this?" he asked.

"An orphanage," Yesenia said. "Gaiana said Iyanda comes here at least once a week."

"Why?"

"Why don't you ask her?" she pointed.

He looked in the direction Yesenia indicated. His heartbeat quickened. Iyanda's face bore a soft, calm expression as she watched the children playing. A small child ran up to her and tugged her hand, leading Iyanda to the game of soccer.

"Get out of the car, Brother" Yesenia said, her head poking inside the car window.

Emiliano broke his focus on Iyanda and chuckled. Turning off the car, he climbed out and followed his sister through the gate into the yard.

An older woman wearing a white head wrap met them, giving them a slight bow of the head. "Welcome, Young Miss," she said to Yesenia in English. "She said you would be joining us today," "I am Lolade. You may call me Auntie."

"Hi, Auntie Lolade," Yesenia said. She bounced over to Iyanda, leaving Emiliano with the elder.

Emiliano gave a tentative smile. "She's my sister," he said, eyeing his sister's back.

"Hmm," Lolade said, raising a brow. "You're here to help Iyami?"

Emiliano frowned.

The woman smiled. "It's a name the children have given her. It means 'my mother'."

He watched Iyanda as she greeted Yesenia and allowed the children to introduce themselves. "It suits her," he mumbled.

Emiliano strode over, his eyes charting Iyanda's curvaceous backside before she turned and locked eyes with him.

She looked between him and Yesenia.

"I followed her," he said in a joking manner.

Iyanda gave a tight smile. Heat rose from his neck to his face. Would she see the joke or would she think he was stalking her? When Iyanda walked past him, he dropped his chin. .

Yesenia covered her mouth, her eyes looking at him in amusement. "Smooth, Brother." Yesenia then followed Iyanda inside the building.

Emiliano gritted his teeth. "Get it together, Petty," he muttered. He dragged his feet behind the last of the children entering the house.

* * * * *

Iyanda sat on the black sand of Bela Beach, watching Emiliano and Yesenia amuse themselves in the ocean waves. After being at the orphanage for two hours, Yesenia requested to come to the beach.

She wriggled her toes in the sand, the day running through her mind. When Emiliano showed up at the orphanage, Iyanda's heart skipped a beat but she refused to allow him to see the effect he had on her. She had to erase the feelings. She would be married in two weeks.

She grinned. The way Emiliano held the little boy Tiago's hand while she applied a poultice to his arm, forced her to see a different side of him. At lunch time, a couple of the boys wanted him to sit with them. On the floor he seated himself among them, captivating them with stories and jokes. Some of the stories were familiar myths and tales of the island, but others she herself stopped to listen to.

Emiliano emerged from the waves. Iyanda's eyes widened. Her cheeks warmed as his muscular, bare chest glistened under the sun. The tip of her tongue licked her bottom lip, wanting to taste the beads of water traveling down his rich, tawny brown skin to his swim trunks, which forgot to leave anything to the imagination. She inhaled sharply when he looked in her direction, flashing a set of white teeth as he raked his locs back, a glint of mischief in his eyes.

She exhaled, attempting to steady her racing heart and cool her body of the rising heat.

"Don't swim?" he asked.

Iyanda shook her head. Swimming wasn't the issue, the way he made her feel was. She was engaged to another, to a man who's good standing in the community could wipe away the shame from hers. She had to stay focused on her family and what they needed. She couldn't afford taking a dip in the ocean with Emiliano, even if she wanted to.

He sat down beside her and wiped his face with his shirt. She slid over to put a bit of space between them. He watched Yesenia as a few teens came over to talk to her.

"I've missed this," he said. "We used to come to the beach all the time. My dad would help Nia collect shells and I would see how far I could swim out before my dad would make me turn back around."

Iyanda's throat ached. She knew about Jack Petty's death. She didn't know about his family life. Most of the prominent men in Pleasant Heights didn't have time for their family. Obviously, he had been different.

She thought back to her own father. They had only been to the beach together a few times when she was younger, but he chose to sulk under in the shade while Naade taught her to swim. Nana B used to say Iyanda's brother was a spitting image of their grandfather and she believed he would grow into a good man as well.

She had only heard tales of Elder Bankole and how he announced to the community that a daughter was better than ten sons, claiming he was truly blessed for he had two. She used to dream of marrying a man like him and being as happy as Nana B had been. Even now she was content, knowing a real man, as she would say, loved her one time in her life.

Emiliano said nothing more and they stared at the crashing waves together.

Iyanda watched the water ebb and flow, wishing she could take away his pain, something one of her herbs couldn't do. She unclenched her fingers. She hesitated, before touching his well-built forearm.

He glanced at her.

She mouthed, "I'm sorry."

He gave her a small smile and placed his hand on hers, the fluttering butterflies awakening once again in the depth of her stomach.

"My grandmother used to say my father found the most peace at the ocean," Emiliano said. "She believed she was given the privilege to bear the son of the Mother Goddess. He was different, maybe too different."

His eyes became distant, as if mesmerized by the swish of the surf. His fingers gently stroking hers.

"I don't know if I can be like him," Emiliano said. "I want to do what is right for the people, like him. He wanted to take away the pain and suffering of everyone: men, women, children, give them an opportunity to build something for themselves and feed their families. He knew he had a few enemies, but he didn't care. He said, it wasn't right for his family to live safe and comfortably while others couldn't. And he was a big opponent against the marriage laws and how girls were treated. After Yesenia was born, he fought harder, wanting her to have a say when it was her time to leave home. Sometimes," he chuckled, "I think my grandmother was right. My father wasn't of this world." He hung his head. "Maybe that's why he died. The good ones always do."

Iyanda gave his hand a gentle squeeze. He turned his face away, his shoulders hunched. Her chest tightened. There wasn't an herb strong enough to mend his pain. She wished she could only make it so.

＊ ＊ ＊ ＊ ＊

"They need a garden," Yesenia said, her hand riding the waves of air.

Even though they had dropped Iyanda off at her herbal shop ten minutes ago, her presence lingered for him.

"Who?" Emiliano asked.

"The orphanage. The lady, Auntie Lolade said if they had a garden growing the needed herbs, Iyanda wouldn't have to use her own supply."

"Does she charge them?"

"Auntie Lolade said they tried to pay her once but Iyanda refused. She wrote the children were more important than payment. I think she deserves a garden. Maybe one bigger than a small orphanage. One where she would never run out of herbs."

"You really admire her," he said.

"I do." Yesenia turned toward him. "Don't you?"

The corner of Emiliano's mouth turned up. He did more than admire her. "Anyone that can make my little sister see past her own social circle has more than my admiration."

Yesenia rolled her eyes and turned forward. "Whatever, Brother."

"Auntie Lolade told me of a goddess who protects orphaned children," Yesenia said.

"Oshun, if I'm not mistaken."

"You think Iyanda could be her?"

Emiliano chuckled. "I don't believe they have anything in common."

"Why? They both love children. They both want to help people. They both heal in their own way. And," Yesenia's lips curled into a smile, "they're both beautiful.

"Oshun is beautiful and Iyanda is-." Emiliano couldn't find the words.

Iyanda was pretty, maybe not Oshun beautiful, but a beauty that shone from the inside out.

"Just admit it, you like her."

Emiliano sighed. "She's engaged." The words leaving a numbness within him.

"Then change her mind."

Stopping at a stop sign, Emiliano turned toward his sister. "This isn't some reality tv show. You can't just hop from one person to the next just because you want to. It's wrong. Omidan Iyanda isn't that type of person. She keeps her word and I won't take her away from it."

Yesenia slid down in the seat and looked down at her hands. She nodded her lowered head, a slight quiver in her chin.

Emiliano turned back to the road. He wanted to believe Yesenia was just being a dramatic teenager, but his gut told him it wasn't an act. She really liked Iyanda and wanted her to be part of his life. He pulled off past the sign. Plus, he was lying. He couldn't allow Iyanda to walk away unless she made it clear she wasn't interested.

But he had to hear her say it.

CHAPTER 11

The early evening light chased the last of the customers out of the herbal shop. Iyanda exhaled. Closing time, her favorite time of the day. She closed the door behind the last shopper and leaned against it, surveying the store. The warm scents of the herbs gave her a second wind. Dunni once told her the herbs awakened when non-healers weren't around, for their secrets were for only the healer's ears. Grabbing a notepad from the counter, she walked among the shelves, making note of what was needed in inventory and listening.

Her mind lingered on Emiliano. He was unlike any man she had met. He was warmhearted toward his sister, rare for someone in his class and yet, there were moments he seemed similar to Mason.

And yet, he wasn't.

Mason never cared for his father and only cared for his mother as long as the older woman fawned over him. And to walk into an orphanage and help children was out of the question for Mason King.

Emiliano's eyes still burned into her soul even though he wasn't present.

And the kiss at the marketplace.

Warmth started from her chest, diffusing to the rest of her body.

She stopped writing, closing her eyes. She tried to block out his glistening body from her mind. The way his powerful legs walked up the hill of sand to get to her. And the bulge revealing shorts…

Iyanda fanned herself with the pad of paper.

The sound of broken glass made her jump. She looked around for the source. A vial of balsam apple extract seeped into the wooden floor.

Iyanda frowned at the shards of glass. What could have made the bottle fall?

She paused.

The air in the room shifted. It reached out to her, sending a different warmth through her body. A familiar one.

Looking up, she came face to face with a man and a woman. She recognized them both from pictures at home. They wore the traditional clothes of Igbala and smelled of earth after a fresh rainfall and plumerias. She wanted to reach out and touch the dark brown skin to see if it was real but decided against it when the man's empty eyes stared at her. The woman's gaze bore into Iyanda.

Iyanda dropped to her knees, sitting back on her heels with her head and eyes to the floor. *"Grandfather. Great-aunt Bimpe,"* she signed.

"Stay away from him. He will bring change to this family," Great-aunt Bimpe said.

"I-I do not know who you mean." Iyanda's heart raced.

"You lie to me with your hands, but your heart cannot. Stay away from the Petty boy or there will be much change."

"Is change so bad?"

Great-aunt Bimpe sucked her teeth. "This child will not use her tongue to speak," she said in a sharp tone, "and yet she insults us. You will do well, Iyanda, to honor us by following these words."

"Forgive me, Great-aunt, Grandfather. I will honor you today and for the rest of my life."

There was silence. The air slowly normalized.

Iyanda lifted her head.

The figures were gone.

Did she dream it? Her mother said she had been working too hard. Standing, she looked around for any sign of them.

There was none.

But it didn't mean they had left.

She picked up her notebook and went back to taking inventory of the herbs, her shoulders tense, and her eyes constantly searching for their return.

Later in the evening, after WAISTED and the EWE were closed for the day, Iyanda went to the back room of her store. Donning her apron, she offered an offering to Osanyin before continuing her work on Yesenia's gift.

The stillness was comforting. With the soft pounding of the pestle, Iyanda was able to take steady breaths. There was no threat of her mother coming in and demanding her to play nice with Mason or to be extra courteous to others, in fear Iyanda's lack of speech might offend someone. She planned to stay for a while before hurrying home to Nana B.

The older woman's pain had increased as of late and her appetite had not been the same since the doctor's appointment. When Iyanda asked for the results, Nana B cut off Adeyemi and told Iyanda not to worry, her tea was working.

She felt her grandmother was lying, but she knew better than to question the older woman.

She paused at the sound of the door chime. She must have forgotten to lock the door. Who would come out this late for anything?

"Omidan Iyanda!" Emiliano called.

Iyanda's hair on her nape stood up, warmth radiating through her body. Was it his voice? Her stomach leapt when he called out to her again. It was him. Wiping her hands on her apron, Iyanda tentatively made her way to the front. Why would he be in Stingray Cove at this time of night and at her store?

He stood on the other side of the counter, smiling warmly and holding a covered basket.   Iyanda's heart drummed against her chest. She looked down, taking a breath, needing to calm the smile that threatened to escape. Lifting her head, she stared at him with as much as a straight face she could muster.

"My housekeeper thought I needed to have lunch," Emiliano said. "I told her it was too much. Have you eaten yet?"

Iyanda shook her head, her brows knitted together. It still didn't explain why he was in Stingray Cove and not Pleasant Heights.

"I was at a council meeting at the government house," Emiliano explained.

Iyanda breathed a silent sigh. She indicated for him to wait. Rushing to the back room, she grabbed a small blanket. Coming from behind the counter, she spread it on the floor then took the basket from him. Opening the top, she pulled out the dishes of honeyed fruit, fried meat pies, spiced beans, and a covered dish that Emiliano quickly grabbed.

"A surprise," he said.

He joined her on the blanket, sitting on the other side of the laid-out dishes. Reaching inside the basket, he pulled out a glass bottle of dark pink liquid. Popping the cork, he poured some in a clear cup and handed it to her.

The tartness of the drink told Iyanda it was hibiscus, cold and refreshing tea made with tender love and care. And made from the highest quality. The label of the bottle read Bese Saka and had the familiar drawing of cola nuts in a flower pattern stamped on it. The company was known for its fresh ingredients but also for their steep price tag. Placing the cup down, she sat back.

"Ana makes the best empanadas on the island," Emiliano said, offering one of the fried meat pies to Iyanda. "When my mother came here from Colombia and couldn't find anyone to make her childhood food, she begged my father to bring someone here from her home."

Iyanda took a bite. The taste of beef cooked to perfection, spiced soaked potatoes, and a spice she had never experienced but gave the meat pies the perfect kick, communed on her tongue, overpowering her taste buds. She could see why Mrs. Petty would have missed such a dish.

"On his next business trip," Emiliano continued, "he searched for a woman from my mother's hometown that specialized in empanadas. Of course, many women came and allowed my father to try them. The married women were turned away before they could even start. Women with more than one child were sent home. Only one stood out. Ms. Ana was a widow and had been a grandmother."

Iyanda stopped chewing and focused on Emiliano, her eyes asking what he meant by 'had'.

"Her family was wiped out by a local gang fight. Her oldest son had angered the leader and while he, his siblings, and their children were at a picnic, there was open fire. Ms. Ana barely made it. When the coast was clear, she crawled to help. She stayed in the hospital for almost a month, part of that time grieving for what she had lost."

Iyanda stared at the half-eaten pie, her heart heavy for the creator of it. How strong would her own grandmother be if the entire generation of her bloodline was wiped out by anger and bullets?

"Seeing that she had no reason to stay behind, father brought her home and my mother refused to allow her to leave. Honestly," Emiliano shrugged, "I think Ms. Ana has adopted us as her own family and won't leave until the day she passes."

Iyanda glanced up at Emiliano, a small smile on her lips. She took another bite of the pie, chewing slowly, her eyes welling up with tears.

"Tell me about you," Emiliano said. "I've been opening myself up to you, but I know nothing about you."

Iyanda grabbed the chalkboard and scribbled, *"Like what?"*

Emiliano shrugged. "What's your favorite color?"

"Green."

"Food?"

"Chin-chin for snack and egusi soup, just the way Nana B makes it."

Emiliano gave a slight nod. Then, with a sideways smile, he gazed at her. "Why don't you speak?"

Iyanda's heart dropped to the pit of her stomach. The question had been asked before, but those people were gathering more kindling for their taunting while others looked upon her with a mixture of pity and frustration.

His eyes were sincere and bright with curiosity that for once made him seem down-to-earth.

She scribbled, "It's a long story."

"Take as long as you need," he said, indicating the board.

Getting up, she went behind the counter and pulled her notepad and pen from her bag. Reclaiming her spot on the floor, she embarked on writing about the incident. Her heart raced as each word was etched, her mind screaming for her to stop reliving the moment. She ignored them. He wanted to know. She needed to tell it.

He wandered around the store, never venturing too far from her. A warm sensation flowed from her stomach to her neck whenever his eyes assessed her. From the corner of her eyes, she could see he thought he was stealing secret glances. She held in her amusement.

Finally when she was finished, she laid the notebook on his side of the blanket then picked up a honey drenched mango piece and popped it in her mouth, licking the sticky residue from her lips and fingers.

He sat down and picked up the notepad and lightly chuckled. "It's not that long."

"My father hated my voice. When I spoke, he would glare at me or yell at me to shut up. He did it so much, I became scared of speaking when he was around. I would wait until he left for work to speak to my family. My mother would tell me father was having a hard time at work. After a while, I stopped believing her. He never spoke harshly to my brother, only to me and her. My brother would teach me some English when father wasn't around, claiming he was going to take me to America so I could be free from Igbala's oppressive ways. I thought he was dreaming. Anywhere I went, I knew people would force me to stand out, wanting to put me in their categories."

"One day, I was telling my grandmother and brother about the Rebellion, a story I knew she knew but I wanted to tell it to her while she made waist beads. My mother was inside cooking dinner. I didn't hear my father come in the house. I had got to the part where General Boaventura and her followers had cornered the Portuguese landowners on the hill for days when we heard a scream from the kitchen. We rushed inside. My father had struck my mother to the ground and was standing over her threatening to do it again. Thankfully, my brother was bigger than him and pulled our father away from her. I knelt in front of him, blocking him from her, apologizing for being a disobedient daughter. It was my fault not hers."

Iyanda wanted to soothe Emiliano's furrowed brow. She kept her hands in her lap, resisting the urge to snatch the notepad away.

"My father stared at me as if I was a stranger, an animal that had offended him for walking into his home. He shoved my brother to the side and struck me so hard I bit my tongue. He told me if I ever spoke to him again, he would tear my tongue from my head. He left. He never returned but I still wouldn't speak. By the time my brother left for Nigeria, I had forgotten how to use words. But Dunni and Nana B wouldn't give up on me. Dunni taught me sign language and Nana B continued speaking to me, believing that one day I would find my voice."

Iyanda bit her lip. Emiliano stared at the ceiling, the notepad still in his hand. What was he thinking? Probably that her family was the worst, a typical Stingray Cove poverty pot of abuse and runaway men. She wouldn't be surprised if he packed up his food and never showed his face around there again, possibly even cancelling Yesenia's order.

He looked at her, his sunset-colored eyes glassy. He reached up, his warm hand cupping her cheek. "If anyone ever hits you again," he said in a low, soothing voice, "they will have to answer to me. You speak when you want. If someone has a problem with it, send them to me."

CHAPTER 12

Today was a special day, like it would be for most children. It was the third day of Yesenia Petty's birthday celebration and thankfully, Iyanda had finished the order.

Igbalaian birthdays were a six day celebration with the third day being the largest event. If one's family was able to afford it, like Yesenia's, then it would be talked about for centuries. If not, then close friends and family would bring special food dishes and handmade gifts for the birthday child.

Gaiana placed the delicate package containing Yesenia's order inside Iyanda's shoulder bag and closed it. She took a few deep breaths and straightened the counter.

"What's wrong?" Iyanda signed.

"I'm nervous for you," Gaiana said.

Iyanda gave a tentative smile.

"I feel as if something is going to happen once you go to this party," Gaiana said. "I know you're just dropping off an order but it's going to change everything."

Iyanda thought of the small picnic. After she told her story, Emiliano made sure to brighten the mood once more. He wanted to feed her some of the fruit but when his eyes traveled to her hair, he placed the morsel back on the fruit dish. For a second he looked defeated until he looked at the covered dish. His attitude brightening back up, he revealed the two dishes of sweet coconut rice pudding. Her sweet tooth had been teased and satisfied all in one night. She blushed at the memory of his sin-filled eyes watching her delighting in the treat.

"Let me go," Gaiana said, coming from behind the counter and standing before her "It's not proper for an engaged woman to go to the house of a bachelor. Even if you don't see him, this one action could change you."

Iyanda bit her lower lip.

The other night, Nana B dreamed about a faceless family member changing form. She described a dark garden with a small light being held by another being. Iyanda thought nothing of it until she received a visit from her deceased relatives.

"Stay away from Emiliano," Gaiana said. "You don't know if he's really interested. You don't want to mess up your engagement."

Iyanda's eyes widened. Words similar to her great-aunt's. She closed her eyes and took a breath.

Looking at a worried Gaiana, she signed, *"Don't worry. Osanyin will protect me. I know Emiliano is not interested. He's just being nice because of Yesenia."* She hugged her friend, holding on longer than usual. She was nervous. Not about Emiliano. She refused to look too deeply at his intentions, believing it would pass once she finished the order. No, she was worried about herself around him.

Letting Gaiana go, she smiled, then walked outside to the bright sun before her friend had a chance to protest more.

She rode to Pleasant Heights on Gaiana's yellow scooter. The warm breeze made her sweaty palms more slippery as she gripped the rubber covered handlebars. Gaiana's words shook her. It couldn't be a coincidence. All signs pointed to her keeping her distance from Emiliano.

The memory of his warm smile and bright eyes relaxed her grip on the handlebars. A blush rose from her neck to her cheek. She quickly shook off the feeling. Emiliano Petty could never be in a serious relationship with someone like her.

Plus, she was to be married in a week.

After a forty-minute long ride, Iyanda was relieved to see the wrought iron gate. The elegant mansions were tucked away in a gated community within the village of Pleasant Heights, hidden from the mediocre and poverty. Iyanda supplied plenty of herbal remedies to some of the residents, but like surgeries and illegitimate children, her deeds would be kept a secret.

She pulled into the semi-circle driveway of the Petty residence. Town cars and luxury vehicles lined the driveway. Loud music came from the large mansion. People standing outside paused their conversation to eye her. Under their sneers and whispers, Iyanda wanted to ride away and never return.

A young man, wearing a red vest, rushed out to her and nudged Iyanda out of the way. She pushed back, guarding the scooter. She eyed him with an unspoken promise of harm if he touched the bike again.

"What the hell?" the man in red exclaimed. "Something wrong with your head, o?"

Was something wrong with her? She didn't approach him without speaking and try to take his property. Ignoring the profanity, he spewed at her, she walked toward the door. Looking back, she narrowed her eyes at the small boy like man, then made her way up the porch steps to the door.

Ringing the doorbell, she rocked on her heels as she waited. Clutching the handles of her homemade shoulder bag, her insides fluttered at the thought of the door opening and seeing his face.

The door opened. She breathed a sigh of relief when it wasn't him who answered.

Yesenia's beaming face greeted Iyanda. The young girl pulled her inside the house, bouncing on her toes.

Iyanda stood at the door, staring in awe at the high ceilings covered with blue and white balloons. High school girls and boys talked in groups or danced on the makeshift dance floor. The girls wore skirts shorter than anything Nana B would have allowed her or Tambara to wear at that age. She watched as they grouped together, talking more with their hands and facial expressions than with their lips. The young men watched the group of girls from the other side of the room, like hunters watching prey.

"Iyanda! You came!" Yesenia gave Iyanda a tight hug then released her after giving her waist a final squeeze. "Did my brother invite you? Of course he did." She squealed, bouncing on her toes. "Did you bring it?"

Iyanda nodded.

Yesenia squealed with excitement again and held out her palm.

A small group of girls crowded around them. Reaching inside her bag, Iyanda pulled out the brown package and handed it to Yesenia who immediately tore off the wrapping, revealing the small glass bottle. The group of girls stared at it in admiration.

"What is it?" one of them asked Yesenia.

"Something to catch the boys."

Iyanda covered her mouth to hold back the laughter.

The girls giggled as Yesenia opened the bottle. They all leaned in to catch a whiff, the scent bringing a smile to the receiver's face. Placing a small drop on her wrist, she rubbed it into her skin before inhaling the strong fragrance.

"Nef is going to love it. He is so going to notice you," another girl said.

"I thought you said she was deaf," another girl said, eyeing Iyanda.

"She's mute, Mara," Yesenia said.

"Then how is she able to see what she's putting in the bottle?"

* * * * *

Emiliano's gaze followed Iyanda from the moment she walked into the house. His eyes followed her every movement. Admiring her thick calves that peeked from under the yellow skirt, he envisioned his fingers exploring the length of her beautiful, brown legs.

Her eyes searched for an escape as Yesenia and her friends crowded her. He strode over, making his way through the group of girls, stopping short of Iyanda.

"She's not blind," Emiliano said. He stared at Iyanda, her large dark eyes watching him.

"Right. She doesn't speak," Yesenia said.

"That means she probably can't taste her food," Mara said in a sympathetic tone. "You know, since you need your tongue to speak."

Emiliano eyed his sister. She shrugged.

"Go play," Emiliano said, shooing Yesenia and her friends away.

"Mute people are so cute," one of the girls said as they walked away.

"I'm going to see if my dad will buy me one of my own," another said.

Emiliano grimaced.

The private schools of Pleasant Heights were advertised to be the best place for a child's education. His father foresaw the deterioration of the precious academies when the parents began making final decisions for the curriculums. They decided the history of Igbala was not as important as etiquette and dating within one's class.

"Nothing good comes out of being ignorant of history and common sense," the late Jack Petty once said.

Iyanda turned to him and held out her hand, pointing to the flat palm with her other finger. She wanted to get paid.

If he knew no other sign, he knew this one. He worried payment would give her a reason to leave and he wasn't ready for her to go. He shook his head as if he didn't understand.

She did the sign again, this time with more emphasis on the palm stabbing.

He studied her slender fingers, admiring the beautiful way they spoke, wanting to place kisses on each tip.

She reached inside her bag and pulled out a small pad of paper and a pen. She quickly scribbled something down then shoved it into his hands.

He read, *"I need payment."*

Emiliano chuckled. He handed her the pad.

"I'll pay you," Emiliano said. "But you have to do something for me first."

Taking Iyanda's hand, Emiliano led her through the crowd, stopping to give a brief introduction to a few of the children's parents.

"Who is this pretty young woman, Emiliano?"

"She just delivered Yesenia's gift. This is Omidan Iyanda, Ms. Trappe."

Ms. Trappe raised a thin brow before extending her hand to Iyanda. "It's nice to meet you, Iyanda," she said in a frosty tone. "Who is your family?"

Iyanda motioned to her ears.

Ms. Trappe looked to Emiliano for an explanation.

"Music is loud!" Emiliano shouted. "We'll talk to you later!"

He led Iyanda through the kitchen to the backyard. Taking a nearby stone trail, they followed the slight incline to a small garden of manicured flowers and citrus trees on the other side of the house, away from the eyes and noise. He led her into the shadow of one of the trees and turned to her. Holding her hand, he caressed his thumb over her knuckles, staring down into her eyes.

"My father built this garden for my mother when she started to feel homesick," he said, his deep, pleasing voice rolling over her. "It was said, he and my mother would hide away in the shadows of these trees, stealing moments away from the rest of Pleasant Heights' society. Probably the only time my mother knew how to show someone other than herself some love."

His eyes explored the contours of her face. She didn't have high cheekbones like her mother, but Iyanda had beautiful thick lips that he wanted to sample again.

He brought her knuckles to his mouth and gently kissed them. Reaching, tracing a finger over one of her defined cheekbones.

"I don't know why, but I can't get you out of my head," Emiliano said. "I would never tire of your voice."

She lifted her face. Her cheeks flushed a warm scarlet as he devoured her beauty, swearing to memorize every curve and angle of her face. She lowered her gaze, but it was already too late, he had seen the need. He settled his hand in the curve of her neck, fingering the loose soft coils at the nape. Leaning in, a faint scent of licorice tickled his nose.

"I want to kiss you," he said, "but only if you ask."

She lifted her chin to him.

He lingered close, the memory of her soft lips exciting him. This time, he wanted to go slow. His bottom lip brushed against her top.

"Emiliano?"

They looked in the direction of the voice. He silently cursed when he saw Aria standing there.

Iyanda pulled away and frowned at him, her gentle eyes demanding answers.

Emiliano glared at Aria. "What are you doing here?"

"I was invited," Aria said. "Your mother told me to find you at the basketball court. Thankfully, I followed you out here."

He wanted to kick himself for not being more alert. Aria eyed Iyanda.

"Especially with you being with her," Aria said. She came closer to Iyanda.

"Why is that any concern of yours?" Emiliano asked, placing himself between Iyanda and Aria.

"I know you," Aria said. She smirked. "You're the girl that came to my restaurant."

"What are you talking about?" Emiliano asked.

"She came with some rude guy, Mason King, I think was his name. Isn't he the one trying to steal your father's seat?"

Iyanda looked down at her feet. Emiliano reached for her but she pulled away, making a hasty retreat to the large house.

Aria stepped in front of him, a smug look on her face. "Who would've thought a deaf girl would cheat on her boyfriend."

Emiliano glared at Aria before rushing after Iyanda. He searched the crowd, catching a glimpse of her going out the front door. Pushing past the hormonally charged teens and their snotty parents, he prayed he could make it outside in time.

Outside, he surveyed the area. Not seeing her, he asked one of the valets and they pointed toward the gate. He ran out to the gate just in time to see Iyanda speeding away on her scooter. His heart ached as her figure became smaller and smaller.

"Damn," he mumbled.

* * * * *

Iyanda moved along the rows of dried herbs, rechecking her order form. When the doors of WAISTED closed for the night, her mother and Gaiana came over and volunteered to stay.

She declined. She needed the time to herself.

Iyanda knew they were worried. When she returned to the store earlier that day, they hounded her, inquiring as to what happened at the party. Gaiana questioned where the payment was when she couldn't find it in Iyanda's bag, causing the other woman to eye her. She couldn't bring herself to tell her friend the reason she left without payment was because of Aria Riviera showing up.

Having to explain why the appearance of the beautiful woman and her payment were connected was something Iyanda didn't want to have to explain to her mother.

Iyanda's fingers delicately touched her lips.

He almost kissed her again. But then the beautiful manager interrupted.

She closed her eyes and let out a hard sigh, willing the memory to go away. When she opened them, she was still in her store with a deep longing for him.

She couldn't work like this. Grabbing her things, she walked out the door. Raising the key to the lock, she paused.

Why didn't she communicate what her heart felt? Why didn't she just kiss him?

Because you've been warned, she thought.

Iyanda locked the door, her hand lingering on the key.

She had been warned and didn't listen. If she had allowed Gaiana to go to the party in her stead, her heart wouldn't be fighting with her head at the moment. Turning to leave, she shuffled back at the sight of Emiliano standing close, blocking her path. Her belly fluttered as she stared into his gentle, deep-set eyes behind his thick locs. His scent of lemongrass threatened to take away what little logical sense she had left. Wanting to stay strong, she shook her head and pushed him away.

He held up a single plumeria with a deck of big index cards. The white floral symbol of beauty and love beckoned for her to accept his gift. But she couldn't, it was wrong. Wrong for her to want him or anything he offered. And yet she needed to know why he was there and not with Aria. She snatched the index cards, stepping back, watching to make sure he didn't try to move towards her.

Lifting the first card, it read, *I'm sorry.*

Iyanda pressed her lips together and tossed the card at his feet. She lifted the next one.

I didn't know she was coming. My mother invited her. We were engaged once. Not anymore. She broke my heart.

Iyanda dropped the card, turning slowly away from his piercing gaze. She flipped through the next eight.

Since that day, I've had to speak to you. I want to explore and love every flaw about you. I want to get to know you. I want to protect you. Hold you. Kiss you. I want you to know me. No matter how long it takes.

She wrapped her free arm around her waist. Biting on her bottom lip, she read the next one.

But first I'll start with a kiss.

Iyanda looked up. Emiliano stood inches from her. She clenched the remaining cards between her fingers. Turning toward him, he slid the delicate white flower behind her left ear and lifted her chin. She tried to swallow her heart back into her throat.

His eyes told of his intentions, his thumb caressing her bottom lip.

She parted her lips. What was happening? She wasn't supposed to respond to another man like this. What if Mason or his mother found out? What about her mother?

He leaned in slowly.

She pushed away the negative thoughts. Some part of her craved him with an unreasoning desire. She wanted Emiliano to kiss her. Needed him to.

His lips softly brushed against hers, and she prayed no more beautiful women would get in the way before he pressed in to possess them. Why did he taste like sin and innocence rolled into one? A sensation, a hunger almost, washed over her, drowning out the mixed feelings urging her to move away.

The cards fell from her hands. The slips of paper floated to the ground, the light breeze scattering them like plumeria petals around their feet.

His hand embraced her waist, pulling her closer. Resting her hands on his biceps, she reached up for a deeper kiss. He gladly granted it.

CHAPTER 13

Emiliano slowly pulled away, making sure to steal one more kiss from her sweet, full lips. Their breathing synced in tiny pants as they tried to catch their breath. A sensation of light-headedness and warmth flooded his senses. He couldn't remember ever having a feeling like this before. And he loved it.

Iyanda placed her hand on his chest, sending a wave of tingles through him.

"Hey," he said, "I hear there's a street festival happening close to the docks." He caressed her face, leaning in again. "Or, I could kiss you again. Both I believe you would rather enjoy."

Iyanda let out an easy laugh, causing him to smile.

"Festival then?" he asked.

She bit her bottom lip, tentatively touching one of his locs. He wanted to wipe away the pained expression on her face. He imagined her concern was about her fiancé or her family, one of whom he didn't care for.

Finally, she nodded.

Taking her hand in his, he led her down the street for five blocks, never allowing her to walk close to the road.

Live music greeted them as they neared closer to the plaza. Stringed paper lanterns lit up the night sky, giving a relaxed atmosphere among the small crowd of people. Emiliano and Iyanda passed food vendors selling beverages, spiced nuts and meats, as well as grilled fruits.

"Want something?" Emiliano asked Iyanda, his own stomach grumbling.

She gave a slight nod, staring at the cooking meat.

They approached a vendor selling grilled food. Emiliano ordered suya and roasted plantain with mango juice to wash it down for them both. Finding a nearby bench, they took a seat to enjoy their meal.

The spices of the meat were mild compared to the tingling warmth surging through his chest. He stole glances of Iyanda, only to catch her checking him out as well. They coyly smiled at each other before looking away.

He stared at the cruise ship. Bright lights illuminated the large, white vessel as its flags flapped in the island breeze. The company Boaventura Cruize was the brainchild of the Governor of Igbala, believing it would bring more tourists. And it did.

The Governor's wife, believing it to be similar to a yacht, took a three-day holiday only to come back ranting about how the food and entertainment were poor imitations of luxury, not meant for citizens of high standing. In other words, too low for the high class.

His mother was one of the many wives of Pleasant Heights to use their power of persuasion on their husbands, preventing the children of their social circle from ever boarding one.

"I wonder what's like to travel on one of those," Emiliano said, "to be able to go from port to port and meet new people. We used to sail on the family yacht, but it's not the same. Usually you're on board with people who have the same privileges and you don't go further than Igbalaian waters."

He looked over at her. "Maybe one day we'll take a cruise."

Iyanda lowered her gaze, her cheeks reddening. Lifting her hand, he waited until she looked at him before lightly kissing her knuckles

"Let's dance," he suggested.

Emiliano led her to a nearby dance floor. She looked nervous standing among the other dancers. Tourist couples danced slowly, their feet shuffling awkwardly to the slow, sensuous rhythm of the drums and other instruments. But Iyanda's eyes settled on the Igbalaian couples. Many danced the Kizomba, a dance that had been introduced to the island years ago.

She pulled her hand away, cradling to her chest, biting at her lower lip.

"Do you know the steps?" he asked, assuming her nervousness was about the dance.

She shook her head. She surveyed the floor, her eyes lingering on the Igbalaian couples again.

He understood, at least he hoped he did. "No one will see us. If they do, we can say your fiancé needed me to be a stand-in dancing partner for you until he returned from the restroom."

A small smile curved her lips, waking a joy in him that he had forgotten after Aria broke his heart. He lifted her chin up so she could meet his eyes. "You have a beautiful smile, Omidan Iyanda."

Taking her hand, he placed it on his shoulder and wrapped her other in his. She tensed when he curled his arm around her waist. Now was not the time to make her uncomfortable. "Sorry," he said, moving his hand up to the middle of her back.

They mirrored the dance of others, him leading and her following. She moved stiffly, refusing to allow her body to feel the music. Emiliano didn't blame her. The dance was an intimate one and could cause misunderstandings between the participating parties. Their bodies were to be pressed together while moving in rhythm to the music, but she kept a distance between them, allowing air and light to pass between them. Iyanda kept looking around nervously.

"Whatever happens," he said, getting her attention, "I will make sure nothing happens to you. No one will hurt you nor shame you. I'll keep you safe."

Emiliano buried his face in her neck, the sweet scent of licorice from her skin intoxicating him. Pulling her closer, her body relaxed under his touch, her hips finding the rhythm to the music and him. Iyanda's fingers rested on the nape of his neck, stroking the roots of his locs.

He inhaled sharply, as the tingling sensation traveled down his spine then branched out to the rest of his body. He had to keep his cool. His hand slid to the small of her back, resting just above the curve of her round bottom. With the flavor of her kiss still on his tongue, he resisted tasting again. He ignored the stirring in his groin, mental images of the things he wanted to do to her weren't appropriate for the dance floor or for her relationship status. Clenching his fingers, he resisted the temptation of cupping the perfectly swollen bottom.

Thankfully, seconds later the music ended. He breathed a sigh of relief. Righting himself, he eased his hold on her waist and hand.

Iyanda stood on her tiptoe and kissed him softly on the lips.

Damnit, he thought, gritting his teeth. He needed to get them away from the dance floor. Taking her hand, Emiliano led her away from the plaza to the moonlit beach.

When they reached the water's edge, Iyanda slipped off her sandals and waded into the lapping ocean. She skimmed the clear, light blue surface with her fingers, making circular patterns then straight ripples across. Emiliano opened his mouth, ready to ask what she was doing when he saw movement coming her way. He rushed out to her, putting himself between her and the dark shadow. The creature took off, frightened by his loud approach.

Iyanda gave his arm a reassuring squeeze then bent back over the water and performed the same finger dance on the surface. Moments later the shadow returned, now a bit more hesitant. Peering closer, Emiliano saw it was a stingray. His mouth fell open.

"How-what did you do?" Emiliano stammered.

Placing her hand on top of his, she guided him to gently stroke the beautiful sea creature. When more stingrays joined the petting fest, Emiliano raised his brows. "Feels like smooth rubber," he muttered. He tried to give each of them love but soon there were too many. "Hey, hey, I only have two hands, guys. Form a line," he joked.

He remembered his grandmother telling him the stingrays were sacred not only to the true natives of Igbala but also to the descendants of the Yoruba captives. Each life loss on the journey to the island became a stingray and brought a message of love and encouragement to each generation. Maybe one of them held a message from his grandmother or father.

Iyanda waded back to the shore, glancing over her shoulder at him.

"Have to go," Emiliano said to the stingrays. "Hope we see each other again." He then followed Iyanda back to the beach.

* * * * *

Iyanda cringed when she saw the inside lights on. She couldn't remember a time she was out till two in the morning. The neighborhood was still. Emiliano had asked if she wanted him to stay. She didn't want him to go but sticking around would have caused issues for both of them. Taking a deep breath, she turned the door handle. Iyanda stopped dead in the doorway. She lowered her gaze from Adeyemi's disappointed expression.

"Where have you been?" Adeyemi asked.

"I was at the store," Iyanda signed.

"Do you know what time it is?" Ola asked. "You had your mother worried. You had all of us worried."

"I'm sorry." Iyanda's humble eyes pleaded for Adeyemi's forgiveness.

"Where did she get the flower?" Tambara asked.

Everyone in the room looked at Iyanda's hair. Adeyemi grabbed the flower, a symbol of courtship on the island, and held it out to Iyanda, who shook her head in denial.

"Who did you get this from?" Ola asked.

"No one."

"Then why put it behind your left ear?"

Iyanda looked to her mother, her eyes begging for the older woman to save her from Aunt Ola's questioning.

"You lie to your mother? After all she's done for you," Ola said. "What kind of daughter does this to her mother? Tell the truth, Iyanda! Nana B has been worried. She has been praying to the Ancestors and refuses to move until you come. Look at the trouble you've caused."

"Enough, Ola," Adeyemi said.

Ola looked at Adeyemi. "What do you mean enough? You have spoiled her. Now she acts like a rich brat. She comes and goes as she pleases. What do you think people will say?"

"Ola," Adeyemi's tone warned her younger sister to stop while she had a chance.

"All because she can't speak," Ola hissed. "She wouldn't be like this if you had not chased him away with your evil ways."

Adeyemi struck Ola's cheek. Ola's hand covered her stinging face, her watery eyes wide and resentful. Tambara rushed to her mother's side, ready to defend no matter the cost. Tambara glared at Iyanda.

"I will discipline my child," Adeyemi said in a steady voice.

Ola glared at her sister then stormed back into the room she shared with her husband and daughter.

Adeyemi looked at Iyanda with defeated and tired eyes.

"Iya, I'm sorry," Iyanda signed.

Adeyemi stared at the flower before slowly crushing it in her hand. "No more working late. We leave together."

As if aging before Iyanda's eyes, Adeyemi shuffled back to the room she shared with Nana B. When the bedroom door closed, Iyanda flopped down in the armchair. She was relieved her mother hadn't scolded her but the tightness in her chest made her wish she had.

She and Emiliano had gone to the tourist town part of Stingray Cove. The lit paper lanterns relaxed the tension she felt walking out in the open with him however, she couldn't shake the feeling they were being watched. Emiliano never released her hand from the protective cocoon he swaddled hers with. As they danced, she couldn't stop searching the streets for a sign of anyone familiar.

She closed her eyes. A shiver slithered through her body at the memory of his warm hands resting on the curve of her waist. Her heart pounded. They'd danced only for a moment, but in his arms time didn't matter. She hated it when it ended.

Afterwards, they had stopped at the beach to watch the stingrays rest and hunt small fish in the moonlight. Their hands brushed against each other, the desire to steal more kisses growing between them.

He had wished her goodnight. When he leaned over, her heart pounded in anticipation for another possessive kiss. Instead, he placed a gentle kiss on her cheek so close to her lips and another on her forehead.

She wished she knew what he had been thinking. Probably about her fiancé. Would he see her differently because of who she was engaged to?

Why should it matter?

At the end of the day, she was engaged and he was free to be with who he wanted. She couldn't afford messing up the match she had with Mason, no matter how she felt about Emiliano.

Pushing herself out of the sinking cushion, she made her way to the room she shared with her grandmother and mother.

She vowed that tonight was the last night she would allow herself to be vulnerable around Emiliano Petty. She had to focus on her goal and stop chasing fantasies, for the good of her mother, her family, herself.

CHAPTER 14

Emiliano rubbed at his tired eyes as he looked over his father's investment portfolio as well as the weekly reports of the business. He usually would do such checks on Monday, but he had two hours to kill before he and Yesenia would go to the afternoon Bones Festival and Parade in Stingray Cove.

He smiled.

In two hours, he would see Iyanda. He could still taste her soft, dark brown sugar lips. He wanted to sample them again. Needed to. Not wanting to rush her into anything, he didn't partake in the deliciousness when he dropped her off earlier in the morning. She was still engaged and even though he wanted to take her for himself, he didn't want to do to her fiancé what had been done to him.

Even if her fiancé was Mason King.

Quilla's steps coming toward the study interrupted his thoughts. The clicking of her heels crushing the peace within the room.

She stopped in front of the desk. His eyes remained glued to the screen.

"Have you no manners?" Quilla asked in Spanish.

"I do, just didn't learn them from you," he replied in English.

"I'm going to ignore that." Quilla walked closer to the desk. She tried to peek at the computer screen before it went black.

Emiliano leaned back in the leather desk chair.

"What can I help you with, Mother?" he asked.

"You've been avoiding Aria."

"I haven't been avoiding her. I'm ignoring her," he replied with a smug smile.

Quilla hit the top of the desk with her palms and used them to lean on the desk. "Aria Riveria's stepfather is one of the richest men on the island."

"Third."

"What?"

"He's the third richest. We're second."

She threw her hands in the air. "And we could be first with his money and influence!"

Emiliano remembered his father showing him their rank on the island. They were below Mr. and Mrs. Trappe by just a few cents. He instilled in Emiliano to not let such things determine how he treated others.

"Father never cared about being first. The poorest man can have the most influence," Emiliano said.

"Your father was a dreamer," Quilla said with a grimace.

Emiliano picked up his phone, flipping through his social media accounts. "That was obvious when he married you."

"Just like that African girl is to you."

Emiliano stared at his mother's lofty eyes and smirking lips. She was fishing for info. She probably heard about him leaving Aria by herself to chase after Iyanda.

He didn't care what she thought. What he did was his business. He was a grown man. And unlike Aria, he cared how others were affected by his actions.

"Aria has African blood as well," Emiliano corrected.

"No, she doesn't. That blood has been diluted with pure Spanish blood, like mine. You know exactly what I'm talking about. You've been ignoring Aria for a poor girl that plays with grass."

"She heals with herbs."

"And from what Yesenia has told me, the girl is mute. Not only do you ignore a woman of high society, you chase after a deaf girl."

"She doesn't speak."

"As if there is a difference."

Emiliano rolled his eyes. "It doesn't matter who I talk to."

"It does. I refuse to have stupid grandchildren with dark African blood. Can you imagine what others would think?"

"What do you think others will say knowing I took Aria back after she ran off with some other man?" Emiliano stood to leave.

"Aria is going to the parade with you," Quilla stated.

"Maybe we'll see each other in passing."

"I don't think you understand. You are taking her with you. You will make up with her. Put the past in the past. You will forget about that girl."

"Or else what?"

"Don't test me, son. Don't test me."

Quilla turned and left the room, without another word. Aria walked in, a wry smile on her lips.

* * * * *

"So, you kissed him?" Gaiana asked, handing a jar of dry herbs to Iyanda.

Iyanda carefully lined up the jars on the shelves. She was thankful Dunni was able to order the herbs for her. Her heart grew heavy at the thought of possibly never being able to gain her onisegun license.

Iyanda nodded, a smile hid in the corners of her mouth.

"Why?" Gaiana asked.

"Why not?" Iyanda signed.

"Because you have Mason."

Guilt tugged at Iyanda's conscience, but she quickly unraveled its fingers.

"Only half the time," Iyanda signed. *"Mason has not once tried to communicate with me. He's never cared for what I have to say."*

"And Emiliano does?" Gaiana raised a brow.

"Yes. Well, at least I think he does."

"And you got all this from a kiss?"

Iyanda gently shook her head, amused by Gaiana's question. *"It was much more than a kiss. There's a connection. Something I've never felt with anyone."*

"So, where did you go?" Gaiana asked.

Iyanda's hands dropped back into the box, sorting through the assortment of herbs. How could she tell her friend what she and Emiliano had done the previous night? To do so, would only bring more questions, questions Iyanda wasn't sure she was ready to answer.

"Gaiana."

Gaiana and Iyanda turned to the familiar voice of Ola.

"Yes, ma'am," Gaiana said.

"Have you seen Tambara?" Ola asked.

"No, ma'am, not since we opened this morning."

Ola asked Iyanda the same question. Iyanda shook her head.

Ola eyed Gaiana and Iyanda.

"What are you doing over here?" Ola asked Gaiana.

"Talking to Iyanda."

"We pay you to talk to customers. You wait until your day off to talk to your friends." Ola went back into WAISTED, leaving the door open.

Gaiana gave Iyanda a weak smile then reluctantly followed Ola back to the other side, closing the door behind her.

Getting off the floor, Iyanda walked behind the counter. Reaching underneath, she pulled out a folded red handkerchief and placed it on the countertop. Carefully unfolding the delicate material until it revealed a flattened plumeria flower, she caressed the soft petals, imagining they were the gentle hands which had placed the flower in her hair.

Startled by the shadow cast upon the counter, she shielded the treasure with her hands. Looking up, Mason stood on the other side of the counter. She snatched the handkerchief and its contents then stuffed them into her skirt pocket.

She gave him a tentative smile. She prayed he didn't notice the flower.

"We're leaving," Mason said.

Grabbing her chalkboard, she wrote, "Leaving? What do you mean?"

Mason looked down at the words, rolled his eyes, and slid the board away.

He pointed at his mouth, his mouth widening with each word. "Don't you understand? Let's go."

He motioned impatiently for her to follow him.

She looked down at the black slate. He hadn't bothered to learn any other way to communicate with her except with anger and irritation.

Iyanda asked for one minute then walked briskly into WAISTED. She asked her mother to watch the store for her.

"Where are you going?" Adeyemi asked.

"Mason wants me to come with him."

Adeyemi beamed, nodding her head in approval. "You stay close to him. He'll keep you safe at the parade."

Iyanda didn't agree. She smiled, giving a slight nod then made her way outside.

The air was warmer.

Natives of Igbala danced down the street dressed in their ancestral garb and face paint.

The percussion of the Batá drums found the rhythm of her inner being. With eyes closed, her head swayed. Her hips rolled and gyrated to the beat.

Mason grabbed Iyanda's arm, yanking her out of the trance the drums commanded. She stared up at him, confused. Giving her a dirty look, he shook his head, then dragged her away from the crowd following the drums.

Iyanda sulked as she followed behind Mason. This was one of the few celebrations the island held during the year and the most important.

She hated the person he had become. Before he left to travel around the world, he believed in the Ancestors and knew they were the reason he existed.

Not anymore.

Since his return, all he talked about was how everyone on the island was closed-minded and needed to let go of the old way of thinking or face the risk of extinction. As if they were animals.

Many tourists came to watch and engage with her culture without respecting or being part of it, and the residents, wanting to profit from these visitors' enjoyment, willingly conformed to their whims. Is that what Mason meant? Had the place she loved, home to rebellious slaves who fought to win their freedom, now come under another form of slavery? Would this one be so easy to break away from?

Iyanda's heart grew heavy. The movement and festivities rushed by in a blur. She opened her mouth to scream out to her people. Nothing came out.

They wouldn't hear even if she made a sound. They had lost their ability to hear long ago.

The vibrations of the Bátá drums changed.

Time for the parade.

Three rows of dancers dressed as stingrays floated down the blackened road, the seven egunguns following close behind. The latter's raffia attire rustled as their knees lifted high with each beat and step.

The egunguns represented the ancestors, the elders of the seven tribes established on Igbala. They called out, the descendants responding back. The stingrays were the messengers from those lost at sea. Their wings help them glide through the oceans to deliver strength, stories, and wisdom to those survivors. Reminding them to never forget home, for one day they would return.

Iyanda cringed at the tourists' attempt to mimic the replies.

Mason's upper lip raised in disgust as he watched the celebration. He gave Iyanda's arm a tug. She gave a longing glance at the parade then followed him through the crowd.

When they emerged from the sea of people, Iyanda touched Mason's arm. She motioned to him that she was thirsty. He looked around at the various stands. Spotting a palm wine vendor, he left her side.

She breathed a sigh of relief.

She watched the parade, wishing she could get closer. The man-made floats represented each tribe, their history, and the great rebellion that had freed their ancestors.

Since Naade left, the festival was never the same for her. Her mother would make a fuss about her going by herself, which in the end would dampen the cheerful mood for Iyanda and she would resign to staying inside the stores. She would listen to the festive music and excited voices of the crowd from the safety of her shop, longing to taste the food of the vendors and smell the mingled fragrances of body odor, smoke, and spices.

Iyanda had become so focused on the parade that the light touch on her arm startled her.

Yesenia smiled up at her then wrapped her arms around Iyanda's waist. Before Iyanda could react, the young woman took her hand and led her past the stall Mason was waiting in line for. The girl's quickened steps helped them weave through the throng of people but threatened to drag Iyanda across the litter-filled ground. She was more than thankful when they finally stopped so she could catch her breath.

"Look who I found, brother," Yesenia said.

Iyanda's heart quickened when she locked eyes with Emiliano, the memory of his kiss imprinted on her lips.

"Iyanda," Emiliano said as if exhaling.

Her cheeks blushed hot as his deep voice rolled over her, tugging at the desire she was determined would stay concealed. She hated how his presence made her resort to a schoolgirl talking to her crush. She struggled to steady her breathing as he stepped closer to her. The Batá drums and her heart found a common rhythm when he stopped an inch from her.

Iyanda's body relaxed as he reached for one of her warm, moist hands, her heartbeat shooting to the heavens.

His hand was slapped down, breaking the trance for them both.

Aria's narrowed eyes glowered at Iyanda, her thick lips pressed tightly together.

A cold sensation sank to Iyanda's belly upon seeing a cowrie shell necklace gracing Aria's throat. A love token. Iyanda looked away and took a step back.

He told her Aria was the past and she had been naive enough to believe him.

Shaking her head in disbelief, she turned to leave. Emiliano grabbed her hand, but Aria broke the connection once again, this time possessing his arm against her chest.

Iyanda blinked rapidly, not wanting to cry in front of the other woman or him

"Iyanda, wait," Emiliano said, taking a step toward her.

Mason stepped between them, blocking any access Emiliano could have.

"What gives you the right to touch my fiancée?" Mason asked.

"I was just talking to the lady?" Emiliano stated, looking Mason square in the eye.

"The only talking you need to be doing is to the Head of Council or lose your father's chair."

"The Council would never give such an esteemed position to one," Aria sneered her nose up at both of them, "so lowly."

Emiliano brushed her hand away before stepping into Mason's space. "If the mention of my father's chair ever comes out of your mouth again-."

Aria touched his arm.

"Go ahead. Finish." Mason smirked. "I would love for the Council to hear how their star is nothing more than a spoiled bastard."

Iyanda took a step forward, wanting to stand between Mason and the now enraged Emiliano. Thankfully, Emiliano's eyes looked in her direction. The murderous rage that had been there calmed a bit. Aria pulled Emiliano back, caressing his jaw. The motion stabbed Iyanda's heart.

Mason grabbed her arm and led her away. The back of her eyes burning, she didn't dare look back.

CHAPTER 15

Iyanda dragged her feet behind Mason into Juanita's Tasty Fare, an Igbalaian restaurant on the other side of Stingray Cove and took a seat across from him at an empty table.

The peppery smell of chourico bread and tomato beef stew made her stomach grumble. She forced herself to ignore it.

Time and her heart came in sync, both slowing to almost a painful halt.

Emiliano was with Aria Riviera at the festival. The smile of satisfaction on the other woman's face as she gripped Emiliano's arm made Iyanda wince. He told her there was nothing between him and Aria. Then why was she wearing a love symbol around her neck? Even Mason had not given her one in all the years they had been together. He claimed the tokens were outdated, superstitious, and that a man in his position needed a woman who didn't get all simple about such things.

Iyanda didn't want to go to the stingray ceremony. Her family would be there expecting her to send off messages and love to the Ancestors. But she couldn't bear to watch Emiliano and Aria together.

Her eyes watered. It was painful swallowing the lump in her throat.

Mason grabbed her arm with a vise grip. Her wide eyes looked up at him in confusion.

Had he been talking?

"I've seen that bastard kiss you!" Mason accused.

Mason's words felt like a large stone crushing her chest. So he did follow her that night. And he had seen them. She tried to get up from her chair, but he forced her down, his hand heavy on her shoulder. She looked around, hoping others would intercede. Many of the diners did not look in their direction or ignored the scene.

Why was he outside her store at a late hour? How long had he been doing that?

She squirmed, trying in vain to get away from the growing pain he was inflicting on her shoulder.

"You must be stupid too!" Mason shouted. His eyes were filled with rage.

She had seen those eyes before. A swift hand usually followed.

He pressed down more on her shoulder. "My luck, I get a fiancée who's not only a cripple, but stupid as well."

Iyanda cringed at the word 'stupid'. How many times had she heard it while in school when she stopped talking?

She braced for him to raise his hand but before he could, he was tackled to the ground.

Iyanda sat stunned for a moment.

Emiliano.

A brown-skinned waitress motioned for Iyanda to come to her. She still wore the tribal make-up from the festival.

Standing next to her, Iyanda studied the woman's face. The high cheekbones, thick lips, and darker skin broadcasted her African roots. Her bone straight hair was brushed back in a high bun, a bun Iyanda could almost remember playing with. She knew this woman, but from where?

A slap stung Iyanda's face causing her eyes to water. Nursing her cheek, she caught a glimpse of Aria glaring at her, her chest heaving as the waitress stood between them.

Heat rose to Iyanda's face. Her muscles tensed. Everything within told her to return the attack. But she couldn't.

With the laws, Aria could beat her and would not receive a charge, maybe a stern lecture, but then would be sent away with a pat on the head, while Iyanda would be placed under the jail for harming a daughter of an upstanding family.

Plus, she didn't want to.

She wanted to go home and forget about the day ever happening. She wanted to find the peace she had when she was in her store, when she was with Nana B. Before she met Emiliano Petty.

Aria walked to the other side of the room, glaring at her.

The waitress looked back at Iyanda. "Are you okay?"

Iyanda gave her a small smile.

The two women stared at each other. Iyanda knew who she was. She had seen her before, talked to her before, loved her before. Her brother once loved her before. Iyanda wanted to tell the waitress she was the little sister of Naade. If she did, then maybe the orishas would grant her a small piece of her brother to hold.

But before she could, men in green uniforms rushed in, separated Emiliano and Mason, then roughly pinned them down.

She rushed to them, only to be blocked by the brown-skinned waitress. Iyanda's heart raced, threatening to explode as the officers handcuffed Emiliano.

She needed to get to him.

"Get back, Iyanda," Emiliano said, his head pressed to the table.

Iyanda tried to pull her arm out of the waitress's strong grip. Her eyes locked with Emiliano's as the police escorted him and Mason out of the restaurant. Her knees weakened, threatening to give if she made a step toward him.

Hot tears clouded her vision. She tried to wriggle herself free to get to Emiliano. He shouldn't be going with the police, she was to blame for this, not him. The officers shoved him and Mason into separate vehicles then slammed the doors. Emiliano looked at her mouthing no, concern etched on his face.

When the police cars left, the waitress released her grip.

Iyanda stared at the spot where the cars had been. She couldn't stop her body from shaking or the tears from rolling down her cheeks.

She glowered at the smirking Aria. *How could anyone smile at a time like this?*

Iyanda's head began to swim. She had to get to Emiliano.

Taking a step toward the door, she fell to her knees. She was the cause of all of this. If she had never kissed him or helped his sister, none of it would have happened.

She tried to stand, her legs like fresh cooked noodles. The police needed to hear that the fight was because Mason was mad at her and Emiliano was trying to help.

Taking a step toward a nearby chair, she stumbled then everything went black.

* * * * *

Emiliano was fingerprinted, photographed, then tossed into a holding cell neighboring Mason's.

"Do you know who I am?" Mason shouted at the officers. "I will have your badges and everything you own! By the time I'm through with you, the streets will be too good for you to sleep on!"

The officers left the room without a word or acknowledgment to Mason.

Emiliano chuckled. "I don't think they're worried."

Mason gripped the bars that separated their cells. "You need to be. When I get out of here, I'll make you regret you even looked at her."

He eyed Mason. One side of the other man's face was beginning to swell. "Her name is Iyanda."

"I didn't ask you for her name. She will be whoever and whatever I want her to be."

Emiliano's jaw tightened. He closed his fingers into tight fists.

"I am her fiancé," Mason said, "and when I'm through, I'll be her husband."

"Her family would never allow it."

Mason chuckled. "I'm Mason King. Their family is a bunch of poor women led by an old woman with a lot of mouth. They need my money. Plus, I've already paid the bride price. She's mine."

"Money is not what she wants," Emiliano said. His fingers dug into his palms more.

Mason pressed closer to the bars, his brown face becoming red and distorted.

"Do I look like I give a fuck what the cripple wants? She's lucky I notice her. If I wanted, I could bang her whore of a cousin while stupid is having my babies and no one would bat an eye."

Before Mason could enjoy the taste of the last word, Emiliano had his hand wrapped around his throat. Mason struggled to move away, causing Emiliano's grip to tighten.

"I'm sick of social climbing shitheads like you," Emiliano said through clenched teeth. "You believe money gives you the right to whatever and whoever you want. Treating those with less as if they owe you something. If it wasn't for these bars, I would kick every cent out your ass again. But I'm going to do one better. Iyanda will be mine and I'm going to protect her from people like you."

Mason's eyes bulged as Emiliano's grip tightened. Emiliano had never killed anyone, wanting to live as peacefully as his father did. But as Mason gasped for air, Emiliano was willing to make an exception. He was risking his father's chair but at the moment, he just wanted to close the mouth which had insulted Iyanda.

Remembering how Mason grabbed Iyanda just as he walked into the restaurant brought his other hand to Mason's throat.

What right did this bastard have touching her?

"Let go of my son!"

Emiliano's hands were snatched from Mason's throat by the officers.

Mason nursed his neck, coughing and sucking in air. He was led out of his cell to a tall, slender woman with a haughty nose and the beautiful woman whom Emiliano recognized as Iyanda's mother.

Emiliano's heart leapt when Iyanda walked in behind them.

"How dare this thug touch my son," the tall woman spat. She glared at the officers.

"Emiliano Petty is no thug, madam," Edward said, walking into the small space.

Upon seeing his mother's boyfriend, Emiliano's eye twitched. Of all people to come bail him out, why couldn't it have been his mother?

The woman, who Emiliano guessed was Ms. King, sneered at him. "I'm aware of who he is. Does it excuse this behavior?"

Wide-eyed, the officers looked at Emiliano, then lowered their heads, bowing at the hip in apology.

Emiliano held up his hand. "It's fine. No harm done."

"Why are you worried about harm being done to him? My son is future Council Chairman and you allowed this criminal to hurt him," the woman accused.

"The fact that Young Master Petty has not pressed charges on your son is anything short of a miracle," Edward said.

The tall woman sneered at Edward. "Are you his lawyer?"

"No. Close friend of the family."

Emiliano choked on his laughter, then straightened his expression when Edward and Ms. King looked in his direction.

"I don't care if you're the butler," the woman said to Edward. "He attacked my son for no reason."

Iyanda rushed to her mother, frantically making hand gestures. She gripped the older woman's arm then spoke with her hands again.

The tall woman tapped her foot on the cold concrete floor. Mason's face reddened with each hand movement.

"Are you sure?" Iyanda's mother asked.

Iyanda nodded.

The now nervous woman looked at the police chief. "My daughter said Mr. Petty attacked Mr. King because Mr. King grabbed her by the arm and was going to hit her."

Iyanda gave Emiliano a small smile which he returned.

"Like I'm going to take the word of a cripple," the tall woman said, her face scrunched in disgust. "She couldn't hear what was going on."

"She can hear just fine and feel too," Iyanda's mother defended.

Ms. King glared at her, making the beautiful woman close her mouth and gripped a bell-shaped pendant she wore around her neck.

"And she can see," the police chief said.

The older man looked at Emiliano. "We're sorry, Young Master Petty, you may go."

Ms. King blocked Emiliano's exit.

"I'm pressing charges," she said.

"Then we have to press charges against your son as well," Edward said. "And I'm sure if we examine the young lady's arm, there will be more charges trumped against him."

Ms. King glowered at Iyanda and her mother. Iyanda was unmoved, but her mother tugged at the pendant on her necklace.

"Imagine how embarrassing it will be for you. Your son not only attacked a woman but the son of one of the wealthiest families of Igbala. I can promise you," Edward said, "that by the time the news and the Internet have had their fill, you and your son will be chased into poverty if not off the island."

Ms. King's eyes narrowed. Edward did not falter.

The police chief moved Ms. King to the side, allowing Edward and Emiliano to pass.

Emiliano locked eyes with Iyanda, begging her to come.

She shook her head.

He wanted to reach out and take her with him, but her mother held onto Iyanda's arm with both hands, as if reading his mind.

Emiliano followed Edward out of the police station.

On the steps, the cool, night air greeted them. Emiliano's jaw clenched. He wanted to go back in and bring Iyanda out. Protect her from the abuse, he knew, she was about to endure.

Edward stood beside him. He wore an expression of undeserved, supreme confidence on his face.

"You're welcome," Edward said.

"Don't remember asking for your help."

Emiliano looked up at the stars, connecting them to make her face, and to avoid eye contact with Edward.

Edward chuckled then sighed. "Young Master Petty, Emiliano, if I may?"

"You may not," Emiliano responded.

"We could be quite the team if you would give it a chance. That poverty-stricken girl, who is rather pretty I might say, could be our little secret."

Emiliano eyed the British man. "Secret?"

"I know your mother wants you to deal with the Riveria girl. Knowing her son is still seeing someone lower on the pole would send her into a rage."

Emiliano cocked his head to the side, his eyes trying to blink away the sight of red as fast as he could. Many people, including his mother, tried to get money from him all the time. But no one had ever dared to blackmail him.

He took a breath, the color red going away. He smirked.

"And what keeps you from telling my secret?" Emiliano asked.

Edward polished his nails against his shirt. "Your mother gets access to the family accounts."

"Correction, you get access." Emiliano stood nose to nose with Edward. "As long as I'm alive, she will never get her hands on that money. Even when I'm dead, she'll never see a single dime. And you sure as hell will never come within reaching distance of what my father worked for. Take your deal and shove it up your ass. Get out of my face, leech."

Edward blinked rapidly, a slight twitch in the corner of his mouth. Taking a step back, he gave Emiliano a slight nod then walked down the stairs to a waiting car. Edward climbed into the back of the car then rode away.

A cool breeze stung Emiliano's moistened eyes. He quickly looked around then made a hasty retreat down the street. He would have to walk a few miles before he reached his car on the other side of Stingray Cove.

He needed the walk. Maybe he would catch the stingray ceremony and send a message to his grandmother and father, requesting their wisdom, something he was in need of right now.

Jack Petty had known the true heart of his wife. Emiliano looked back on the day they took their last lunch together. His father had been preparing a trip to Colombia to meet with his import/export partners.

It would be his last trip.

Emiliano and Jack had lunch at a small African restaurant in Stingray Cove far from Pleasant Heights' eyes.

Emiliano tried to block out the memory of the folder contents.

His father had explained the suspicious account activity and the photos of his mother with countless men. Men who lived in Pleasant Heights.

"I hired an investigator some months ago," Jack Petty had said. "I became suspicious when she came home from a beauty appointment and her hair wasn't freshly done. She claimed the stylists was taking too long. Your mother doesn't understand waiting. Others would've been pushed to the back."

"Why not ask her about this?" Emiliano had asked.

Emiliano wanted to believe his rigid mother would never hurt his father, her husband. And certainly not steal from him.

"Don't have to. Son, I know it's hard to believe, but I've known for years that your mother has never loved me. She married me to get out of poverty, out of Colombia. After you were born, I hoped she would change her mind. For a while, she seemed content with being a wife and mother until your sister was born. Maybe she hated my skin or her own but seeing that little coco baby reminded her of her origin, locking her heart from me forever."

Emiliano noticed the blatant favoritism she had for him. Their nanny was not allowed to tend to Yesenia first until Emiliano was happy and content.

Jack Petty had slid another folder to him. He intently looked into his son's eyes.

"Emiliano." His tone had been comforting and steady, "listen to me carefully. If anything ever happens to me, know that everything, accounts, businesses, investments, land and property, has all been signed over to you. Even Yesenia's trust fund has your name on it. Your uncle will be acting guardian, if need be."

"What about mom?" Emiliano had asked.

"What allowance she gets will be solely up to you."

Emiliano stopped walking. He rubbed at the tightness in his chest. Did his father know it would be the last time he would see his son, see his home? He didn't take the chance to tell his dad he didn't want the responsibility, that he wanted to go with him.

He looked up at the night sky.

Iyanda's face wasn't there.

No face was. Just stars struggling to shine brighter than the island's lights.

CHAPTER 16

The glaring sunshine warmed Iyanda's face as the morning birds called for her to rise. She stared up at the frames of the weathered treehouse which still stood just as her brother had erected them years ago. Using the hard floor planks to lift up onto her elbows, she winced. The pain was coming from her left arm. Examining it, she felt bruises on her elbow and upper arm.

Mason.

Last night, Adeyemi refused to believe her and didn't defend her against those two. Her mother's defeated posture in the vehicle told Iyanda she was alone in the fight. Ms. King was upset because she couldn't press charges against Emiliano.

Iyanda sat up, folding her legs under her buttocks. She sighed.

Emiliano probably went home to Aria. He claimed they weren't together, but she saw differently.

"Iyanda!"

She tensed at the sound of Mason's voice.

"You know I'm a patient man," he called up to her. "I forgive you for getting me locked up."

Iyanda quietly scoffed.

"We'll talk about this over breakfast," he said.

Her cheeks grew warm. She had allowed Emiliano to kiss her. Would she be his secret, destined to the seclusion of Stingray Cove?

"You have two minutes to get down here," Mason threatened.

A ladybug crawled along the wooden boards, unfazed by the large shadow cast over it, walking over and under the leaves in its path.

Alone.

Adeyemi was abandoning her, claiming Iyanda needed a better life. What was a better life? Iyanda was content with Nana B, her store, Gaiana, her family, and friends. Even Tambara.

Iyanda smiled, a single tear falling to the floor.

"One minute!" he hollered.

Her brother would never allow this. He would be back. Sometimes it was difficult for people to come back from Nigeria. She had given up the hope that her father would ever come back but not Naade. Naade would never leave her for so long. She was his little sister.

He was in a rush that day and couldn't wait for her to get home from school. She knew when he returned, he would bring her gifts and chase away Mason and his mother.

She closed her eyes, trying to remember Naade's face, the way he sounded, the way he smelled. She couldn't. She rubbed her chest, trying to ease the ache. It was becoming hard to breath.

"To hell with you!" Mason stormed away, muttering under his breath.

The tears rolled down her cheeks in steady streams, wetting her arms and hands. Her brother would be back. She took a shallow breath.

* * * * *

Emiliano was awakened the next morning by his mother storming into Chris's guest house. Upon seeing Quilla, he wrapped himself back in the blanket and closed his eyes.

"How the hell did you get arrested?" Quilla shouted.

"It's quite easy," Emiliano said. "Keep standing here long enough, and I'll call them for you."

"Real cute. While you're recusing beggars, your face is plastered all over the news!"

Emiliano opened his eyes and sat up. How did he forget to lock the door last night? He didn't want to go back to the mansion because he didn't want to hear his mother's screeching and he couldn't go back to the emptiness of his own apartment.

"What about her?" he asked. "She's not on the news, right?"

"Aria knows how to keep herself out of trouble."

"I don't care about her. I mean Iyanda."

"Her? What about her? You're dragging your baba's name through the mud and you're worried if her face is on the news! What have I done to deserve this?"

"Besides storming into private property," Chris said. He walked in the guest house and took a post at the dining table, eyeing Quilla.

She pointed a finger at him. "You're the cause of this."

"How is he the cause of this?" Emiliano asked.

"If it wasn't for his woman chasing ways, you would see this girl for who she is."

Emiliano stood before his mother. "And who is she?" His voice laced with a threat. Quilla scoffed. "You would hurt your mother like you did Mason King for that girl?"

He glowered at her. Her eyes dared him to make the first move. He turned away.

"Stay away from that girl, Emiliano," Quilla said. "Before she ruins everything your baba built. No more playing with toys."

Before Emiliano could open his mouth to retort, his phone chimed. He peeked at it and smiled. He smirked at his mother.

"You're right, Mother, I'm done playing with toys. Time for me to make some manly moves."

He gave her a kiss on the cheek, ignoring her protests, then rushed out the door.

CHAPTER 17

Iyanda washed and dried the dishes as Tambara went on about a man she recently met.

"Aren't you worried about Aunt Ola finding out?" Iyanda signed.

"Mama needs to catch up," Tambara said. "People don't wait for their parents anymore. If we did, we would be waiting forever and never get a chance to experience anything."

Iyanda wanted to agree with her cousin, especially after meeting Emiliano, but she couldn't. Honoring one's elders being an inherited Igbalaian custom, Iyanda knew Tambara dishonored the family and the Ancestors by giving herself freely to any man of her choosing. But did she not do the same with Mason?

No, it's not the same, she told herself. *Mason was someone they always approved of.*

Tambara knew but never cared. She wasn't brave enough to say it to the older women of their family though.

"And I need to get Emiliano's attention," Tambara said.

The mention of his name grabbed Iyanda's attention.

"What do you mean?" Iyanda asked.

"He's obviously interested. The way he looked at me. Such passion, like he wanted me right there."

Iyanda stifled a laugh.

"Bless you," Tambara said, oblivious to the amusement on Iyanda's face. "He'll be the reason I get out of this shithole," Tambara continued.

Iyanda frowned. *"Don't say that. Nana B has made a home for all of us here."*

"You can sit here and call it a home if you want to but there are bigger and better things out there and I intend to get them."

"Through a man?" Iyanda asked.

"Some of us, little cousin, don't have special skills like healing to make a living."

Before Iyanda could ask Tambara what she meant, Uncle Onuoha came into the kitchen to inform Iyanda she had a visitor.

The young women rushed out to the living room.

Emiliano stood in the middle of the room, his charming smile making Iyanda's heart dance in her chest.

Tambara swayed her child-bearing hips as she walked in Emiliano's direction.

"Tambara, stop being loose," Uncle Onuoha scolded in Yoruba.

Tambara pouted. Turning, she dragged her feet in her father's direction, bumping Iyanda on the way.

Iyanda wanted to rush to Emiliano, to feel his thick lips on hers, his large, gentle hands on her waist. But Aria's face haunted the moment. Iyanda eyed him. She glanced at the beautiful dark-skinned woman standing next to him.

"I'm Blessing," the woman said. "I'm Yesenia's language tutor. Emiliano hired me to translate in sign language."

"Hired you?"

Blessing signed, *"I told him I would do it for free. I love a love story. But he insisted I stay for the entire date."*

Iyanda shook her head. *"I'm not going on a date with him."*

Blessing interpreted.

Emiliano's intense eyes focused on Iyanda.

"Is this about Aria?" he asked.

"She said you lied," Blessing interpreted.

Tears welled in Iyanda's eyes.

"I didn't lie," Emiliano assured. "We are done. We've been done. My mother forced her on me. She would have-."

"I don't care. I'm tired of everyone's lies. I don't need anyone else in my life who is going to lie to me."

"You didn't tell me you were engaged to Mason King."

"I didn't lie! You never asked."

189

Emiliano scoffed. "Why didn't you tell me?"

"Would you have stopped chasing me? Would it have stopped you from kissing me?"

Emiliano softly chuckled and shook his head. "If I really wanted Aria, would I be here with an interpreter?"

Iyanda glanced at Blessing, searching for an alternative answer to what she already knew.

"He's right," Blessing signed. She gave a smile of encouragement. *"Give him a chance. Yesenia tells me she knows her brother really likes you. She said, he never acted so goofy when he was with Aria."*

Iyanda turned her head, trying to conceal her blush.

"Just give me the day," he said.

He came closer to Iyanda, and a rush of heat flooded through her being. His gentle sunset eyes gazed into hers.

"If I'm not the one you want," he said, "then I'll leave you alone. I'll even leave the island, so I won't be tempted to see your beautiful face again."

She studied his eyes. To go on a date with him would be going against her mother, Mason, and Ms. King. But if she let him walk away, she would be going against herself.

"Why are you doing this?" Iyanda signed to Blessing.

Emiliano caressed Iyanda's cheek and her heart threatened to leave her body.

"I want you. I want to know you. And I believe," he lifted her chin, "you do too."

Iyanda lowered her eyes. Was she crazy? Her duty to her family warned her to pull away while Mason still wanted her.

Cocking her head, she caught him gazing at her with a tenderness she never received from Mason. Her heart and mind feuded with each other, the latter stressing the importance of her engagement. But Iyanda wanted to explore the depths of what Emiliano was offering until she could see him the way he saw her. And she wanted to do it before it was too late.

She looked at Blessing. *"Tell him to give me a few minutes to clean up."*

Blessing clasped her hands together and bounced on her toes. "Wonderful!" she said in excitement.

Moments later, they left the Bankole household in Emiliano's R8 Spyder. Wearing a flowered *Buba* and matching ankle-length *Iro* with flat sandals, Iyanda took her place in the front seat beside Emiliano. She ignored the insistent questioning in her head; she didn't want to know how many times Aria sat in the seat she now occupied.

They left the familiar salty air of Stingray Cove, drove through the heavy burnt smell of Talaka Village, and into the fresh, floral aroma of Pleasant Heights. All different signatures of the beauty and ugliness of the island.

Iyanda frowned as they drove through Pleasant Heights. There was only one other community on Igbala, grander and more exclusive than Pleasant Heights. She nor anyone she knew had ever been there.

Bunkum Colina.

It had been the home of the richest slave owners. During the revolt, the richest three families were trapped on the high hill. The revolting slaves waited at the bottom for five days before the families jumped off the cliffs to the jagged rock-filled ocean below. The three generals of the uprising, one being the legendary Adetowumi Temitope Boaventura, and their families the inhabited houses after they were ritually cleansed by the newly appointed Priests. The revolution commanders became the chiefs for the people, defending the island from Portuguese reinforcements and other European powers returning. But for their descendants, a more challenging adversary, the American peaceful invasion, rendered the families to just figureheads.

Iyanda admired the lushness of the area with wide eyes.

The paved road was evidence the jungle had been taught not to branch out too far, while still trying to maintain its wild beauty. The tops of the trees intertwine their branches over the road forming a green canopy. As they drove through, Iyanda could hear the pounding of ancient drums coming from the green thicket.

What she wouldn't give to walk among the cool earth with bare feet to feel and see what the Ancestors did.

Coming to a clearing at the top of the cliff sat three 17th century-style mansions, each wearing a fresh coat of paint to hide the corrosion of time and salt. The fenced-in gardens of two of the houses threatened to join the jungle in its plot to reclaim the land.

Emiliano parked the car in front of the house at the end of the road, as an older, salt-and-peppered hair man rushed to help Iyanda and Blessing out of the vehicle.

Iyanda gazed up at the towering castle. How many rooms did such a house contain?

Emiliano took her hand, and they followed the older gentleman up the three porch steps and into the house.

Sunlight poured into the wide windows brightening the foyer and a royal red rug led into a large room with doors and a corridor leading to more doors. The grand staircase led to the second floor. A balcony with arches gave one the luxury of watching others in style.

"Where are we?" Blessing interpreted as Iyanda drank in the house's wonders.

Before Emiliano could respond, an older woman entered from one of the corridors.

Her somber, wrinkled face possessed a haughty nose and yet her dark eyes shone with friendliness. Her salt and pepper hair was brushed up and pinned back to create a smooth pompadour. She held her chin as her regal walk was guided by a silver cane.

The woman nodded at them. "Glad to know there are young people who know how to be on time," she said, her tone steady and each word fully pronounced. "Welcome to my home. Who is Iyanda?"

Emiliano nudged Iyanda forward.

Iyanda dropped to her knees and bowed her head.

The woman's figure cast a shadow over her. With a crook of her finger, she lifted the younger woman's chin and studied her for a moment.

Iyanda slowly raised her lashes, looking directly into the darker woman's eyes.

The older woman's brows furrowed. A small smile curved her lips softening her wrinkles.

"You are everything I've been told and more," the woman said in a low voice.

The woman took a step back, giving Iyanda room to stand.

Emiliano rushed over to the older woman's extended delicate hand and tucked it safely in the crook of his elbow. She indicated for Iyanda and Blessing to follow.

She led them to a pair of double doors where the salt-and-peppered hair man from earlier held a tray. He opened one of the doors to the outside as Emiliano opened the other.

The small group walked out onto a sandstone porch with sun-faded steps.

Iyanda pressed her hands to her chest, a mixture of emotions stirring within her as she stared at the overgrown garden. She inhaled the familiar herbal and floral scents on the light breeze.

"You grow herbs here?" Blessing interpreted for Iyanda.

"Yes." The cane clicked as it came closer. The woman stood beside Iyanda, staring at the garden. "But I don't have the time I used to take care of them. Many gardeners know how to tend to flowers or cut grass. Giving true care to these herbs is something not many are blessed with."

Iyanda looked up at her. *"What will you do?"*

"Tear them down," the woman said.

Iyanda turned to Blessing, her hands frantically signing. "She says, you can't do that. The garden is important," Blessing interpreted.

"In all my years, young lady, no one would dare tell my family what we couldn't do," the woman said, her smooth molasses skin darkening.

Iyanda bowed her head. She took a breath, remembering she was speaking to an elder.

"You shouldn't tear them down," Iyanda signed.

"What do you suggest?" the woman asked.

Iyanda stared at the large garden. Such an abundance of herbs and medicinal plants could supply not only her store but also the orphanage. To keep it, she would have to take care of it. Her mother would worry about the extra responsibility she added for herself, but if she didn't, how many people would miss the care they needed?

Of course, her marriage to Mason could hinder the attention needed for the healing oasis but that was an obstacle she would figure out how to clear when it came time.

Iyanda glanced at Emiliano. His intense eyes observed her.

He brought her to this place. He easily could have ignored her interests or, like Mason, given her a patch of dirt to start her own garden. Emiliano went out of his way to find this woman and this garden, he must have wanted her to have it.

She cast an uneasy glance at Blessing, receiving the assurance she had come to trust in that short amount of time. Taking a breath, she lifted her chest before making eye contact with the older woman.

"I will take care of it," Iyanda signed.

"No."

Iyanda frowned. *"What? Why?"*

"I don't want to hire anyone to take care of it. I'm tired of possessing it. It's time for a woman my age to tend rose gardens."

"I'll buy it."

The older woman's eyebrows raised. "Are you sure?"

"Yes. How much?"

"Thirty thousand."

Iyanda gulped. She didn't have such an amount. She would have to borrow more money along with the bit she did owe for her part of the building her family's businesses were housed in. She looked back at the garden.

She squeezed her eyes closed and inwardly groaned before looking back at the woman.

"I will pay tomorrow," Blessing interpreted.

"I've been informed of your family's financial struggles. How do you intend to get the money?"

"I'll find a way. Even if I have to work for you to pay for it, I will do it."

The woman smirked. She motioned to the butler. He presented a silver tray with a paper, a pen, and an envelope with Iyanda's name on it.

Iyanda's eyes scanned the paper.

"What is this?" Iyanda asked.

"An ownership contract," the older woman said. "Once you sign, you will be the sole owner of the garden and everything that goes with it. In the event of my death, my great-niece will uphold this contract and place the garden under the protection of the Boaventura Foundation, in honor of my Ancestor's dream to keep her people alive."

Iyanda's heart pounded. She looked at the older woman. *"But I haven't given you the money yet."*

"Payment has been made," the woman said, picking up the envelope and handing it to Iyanda.

Iyanda opened it and pulled out a check. The amount of thirty thousand was paid to Cynthia Boaventura from Emiliano Petty. She held the check out to Emiliano only to have him push it back to her. Shaking her head, she held it out to him again.

"This is a gift," Emiliano said. "The only thing I ask in return is that you don't let go of your dream of healing others."

Iyanda studied his eyes. Why was she hesitating? Mason.

Everything Mason ever gave her had a string attached to it, including the small garden, one she never had the intention of pulling in the first place.

Emiliano wasn't Mason.

She placed the check back on the tray. Taking in a deep breath, she picked up the pen and signed her name.

* * * * *

Iyanda took a bite of the sandwich Emiliano purchased.
The juices of the pineapple and mustard covered chicken
mingled and danced on her tongue.

They had stopped in front of Juanita's Tasty Fare
and Emiliano asked if she was hungry. Waiting in the car,
she thought of sneaking away, fearful she would be seen
by family friends or acquaintances, but her heart forced
her to stay.

Thankfully she did or she would have missed the
view of the afternoon sun hovering just above where the
ocean and the sky met. As well as the delicious sandwich
she was now savoring with a bottle of ginger beer to
wash it down.

They had dropped Blessing off an hour earlier,
wanting to finish the date alone. The day played over and
over in her mind radiating warmth through her body.
She quivered at the plan of providing the orphanage with
their own small medicinal garden from the seeds.

They sat on the rocks of Yi Pada overlooking the
black sanded beach, their silence overpowered by the
laughter and the chatter of distant tourists and Igbalaian
children. She was accustomed to Mason not saying much
on the date unless it was about him. This was different.
She was enjoying herself. For a moment guilt made the
bread swell in her mouth, taking away the sweetness and
spiciness of it.

"Do you love him?" Emiliano asked.

He was asking about Mason. Saying yes would forever lock her in an eternal lie. The opposite would give him permission to pursue creating complications.

The waves crashed on the shore, leaving their white foam on the sands.

Her family and community were the waves, demanding and beating her to submit under their power while she was the grain of sands.

"You don't have to answer," he said.

She closed her eyes. An army of wandering ants tickled her skin. She brushed them off, only to have their reinforcements take their place.

"My father used to say, 'truth lies in a woman's silence'." A tiny smile appeared on his lips.

Iyanda's eyes fixed on him, the smile fading. He flexed his jaw.

"He died," Emiliano started, "eight years ago. Airplane accident. They claim it was engine failure. Sometimes, I wish it had been a conspiracy, like someone had planned it. Maybe then his death, his absence, wouldn't still hurt."

Iyanda laid her hand on his.

He placed a notepad and a pen on her lap. She raised a brow.

"Had it the whole time," he said. "Thought you would be more comfortable with Blessing around. Plus, I wanted to be able to stare at your face, not your hands all day."

She lowered her eyes with a coy smile crossing her lips.

Opening the notepad, she wrote, *"Thank you."*

Then she wrote underneath it, *"Mother?"*

Emiliano frowned. "What about her?"

"I'm sure she misses your father as well."

Emiliano scoffed. "I don't really care if the woman had golden tears flowing from her eyes right now."

Iyanda frowned. *"How could you say that? She is your mother."*

"A snake is a better mother." He took a swig of the cold ginger beverage.

"You must show her the respect and honor that is due her."

"*Ife mi,* you don't understand. Quilla Petty does not need nor would she want you defending her. She wants everything my father has worked hard for so she can spend it on her boyfriends."

"It doesn't matter." Iyanda shook her head. Did he not understand? Had he forgotten his roots as well? *"The woman carried you then birthed you from her womb. She is your mother, no matter how imperfect."*

Emiliano stared at the words she wrote then stared at her, his top lip twisted up as if the mingling of the air and his mother were offensive.

She stared back, undaunted. She didn't agree with what his mother wanted to do. But Iyanda's filial heart wouldn't allow it to be any other way.

He averted his gaze to the beach below.

"You defend her as if you know her," he said coolly. "Do you suggest, in showing her respect, I should hand my father's assets to her as well?" His tone daring her to go against his reasoning.

She wrote, *"He gave you his memory, so you must carry it on. But do not disrespect your mother for it shows how you feel about women. Think of Yesenia. Think of me."*

His brows raised, a crease forming in the center of his forehead. He stared back at the ocean. Drawing a sharp breath, his mouth opened then shut close before he finally said, "One day, she'll receive my forgiveness. Time to go home."

Emiliano stuffed the empty sandwich papers into the white paper bag and collected the glass bottles. Helping her to her feet, his fingers entwined with hers as they made their way to the car.

Iyanda took a final glance at the sun. The sand was shifting.

CHAPTER 18

The late afternoon drive back to Stingray Cove was a quiet one except for the pitter-patter of the light rain. She held out her hand, allowing the cooling water to wet it before flicking droplets at him. Faking anger, he did the same to her causing her to giggle. When the drizzle ceased, Emiliano held her hand, massaging her knuckles with his fingers. When they reached her herbal store, he gave her a sweet, lingering kiss, chasing away any thoughts she had about Aria and him.

She waited until he pulled away before she walked inside where Gaiana was waiting. And so was Mason.

Grabbing the broom Iyanda began sweeping the floor.

Gaiana touched her shoulder. *"I know you said you didn't want to talk to Mason,"* she signed.

Iyanda rolled her eyes.

"But he said he has something really important to say," Gaiana continued.

Iyanda's lips pressed together, she glanced at Mason. Cleaning the store would have been better than listening to Mason. Being scolded by her mother and listening to Tambara babble was better than listening to him. Anything was better than listening to Mason or his excuses.

She gave a slight nod.

He came and stood beside Gaiana, flashing his barrier melting smile.

"Iyanda, I forgive you for getting me locked up. I know you didn't know any better."

Iyanda cocked her head to the side. Mason was arrogant but she never imagined he would be an egotistical ass.

"Now," Mason continued, "I'm willing to take you back if you behave like my woman and not some whore."

"Whore? Behave?" Gaiana snapped. "Is she a dog? She is a person, not a pet for you to control. And my friend is far from a whore unlike those little girls you play with!"

Mason smirked and waved Gaiana off. He looked back at Iyanda. "I'll still give you the luxury of being my wife. I'll even let you be my guest at the Council Ball."

Iyanda's eyes narrowed. Did he believe he was doing her a favor by not calling off the wedding?

A thump from WAISTED caught the attention of Iyanda and Gaiana. Hurrying toward the sound, they found Nana B unconscious on the floor.

They rushed to her. Not seeing her grandmother's chest rising and falling, Iyanda rushed back into her store and grabbed a small satchel from behind the counter. Hastening back, she reached inside the pouch and placed a pinch of cayenne powder on Nana B's tongue. Seconds later shallow breaths were heard from Nana B but she still didn't wake up.

"It's rude to walk away from someone who is talking to you," Mason said. He grabbed Iyanda's arm and lifted her to her feet. His eyes spoke of his impatience. "I would like my answer now. I have other important things to do."

"Don't you see her grandmother on the floor?" Gaiana asked. Grabbing the phone, she dialed for help.

"The old woman has always been a bit dramatic," Mason said. "She can get back to the drama queen when she has answered my question."

Iyanda shoved him away, glowering.

His hooded eyes burned with a jealousy she had never before witnessed. For a moment, they threatened her. She didn't care. She was ready to do whatever was necessary to get her grandmother some help.

He stood back, the intensity of his glare cooling.

Iyanda knelt back down beside Nana B, trying to rouse her as Gaiana called for help.

* * * * *

Only five hours passed, but it seemed like days for Iyanda. Her family sat in the hallway of the hospital, waiting, dreading the news they might receive.

Gaiana had closed the store for them and joined them an hour later. Now, she comforted a sobbing Tambara on the floor.

Adeyemi clutched to the bell pendant she wore around her neck as if it would take away the ticking seconds of the hospital's clock.

Ola's complexion was paler than usual. She kept her fist clasped to her chest as she rocked silently in a chair. Onuoha stood beside Ola's chair, his arms folded across his chest, his face unreadable.

Iyanda watched Mason with narrowed eyes. He leaned against the wall across from her, checking his phone every few minutes. With each heavy sigh that escaped his lips, she opened and closed her fists, ready to restrict airflow if he did it again. His phone beeped a notification. Glancing at it, he smirked. His fingers moved rapidly as he responded to the text. A few seconds later, he received another notification. Iyanda assumed it was another woman. It wouldn't be the first time. And she assumed it wouldn't be the last.

She glanced at Gaiana who raised a brow.

She saw it too.

Iyanda shook her head. She didn't need Gaiana, or anyone else causing a scene. She honestly didn't care but at the moment her grandmother's health was more important.

She looked the other way, needing a distraction from Mason. Her eyes widened at the sight of Emiliano rushing toward them.

She yielded to him taking her protectively in his arms, ignoring the whispers of her family, finding comfort in the calming scent of lemongrass.

"I came as soon as Lily Poe called me." His warm breath sent shivers down her spine.

Mason pushed Emiliano away, his chest out and ready to fight the bigger man again.

Iyanda stood between them, her back to Emiliano. She frowned at Mason and shook her head. Indicating to his phone, she tried to tell him it was over between them.

"What do you mean it's over?" Adeyemi asked.

"I don't want to be with Mason," Iyanda signed. *"He is not a good person. He didn't even care that Nana B had passed out. He was too worried about me apologizing to him."*

"Did you?"

Iyanda's mouth fell open in disgust. *"Of course not! I have no reason to! He needs to be apologizing to Nana B. He has no respect. I'm calling off the engagement."*

"The Petty boy is no good for you. You have to stay away from him. He'll use you."

"And Mason hasn't?"

Adeyemi grabbed Iyanda's arm and forced the younger woman to stand beside her. Her narrowed eyes focused on Emiliano.

"You need to leave," Adeyemi said.

"I'm here for Iyanda," Emiliano said.

"You're not here for my daughter! She is not for you."

"And he is?" Emiliano pointed at Mason. He lowered his voice. "I'm not perfect, but I would never hurt your daughter the way he does."

Adeyemi's eyes shifted to the onlookers.

Iyanda tried to pull away from her mother, but the woman's grip tightened.

"She is engaged," Adeyemi stated. "You will no longer come around her." She turned and walked over to Ola, dragging Iyanda with her.

Iyanda watched, helplessly, as Emiliano walked away with his head lowered.

"Mama, why? I am not a child."

"You and Mason are engaged."

Iyanda pushed Adeyemi's hand off. Standing back, her breathing rapid, she looked between her beautiful mother and a triumphant Mason.

"You have signed my death." Iyanda asked.

"Iyanda-," Adeyemi started but Iyanda quickly held up her hand.

Tambara and Gaiana gasped. Ola and Adeyemi stared at her through narrowed eyes, a stare death himself would run from.

Iyanda didn't care. *"I am not marrying Mason! I will never marry him. I will never let him touch me again. How could you think this is what I wanted? Do you not love me, care for me? Have I become such a burden to you?"*

Adeyemi struck Iyanda's face.

Iyanda inhaled, the sting bringing tears to her eyes. She nervously glanced at her mother.

Adeyemi's narrowed eyes dared her to speak again. "You have never been a burden. I just want what's best for you."

Iyanda choked on the lump in her throat, backing away from the group. She rushed down the hall, silent tears rolling down her cheeks.

* * * * *

Emiliano stared out of his apartment window at the setting sun. His locs, now released from their restraint, brushed his face. It should be her hands.

Iyanda's watery eyes and trembling chin haunted his memory. He squeezed his eyes shut trying to block out the vision.

He knew of her engagement. What did he think would change?

Her family had arranged the marriage. It wasn't the first on Igbala and hers wouldn't be the last. An archaic tradition passed down from the Portuguese and their own Ancestors that Jack Petty had wanted to change.

Emiliano clenched his fingers into fists.

Even if his father had managed to pass it, those in Iyanda's class would not follow. Tradition was important to them, no matter how harmful it could be.

He pounded the side of his fist against the window. He tried to control his breathing as he thought of the future laid out for Iyanda if she were to marry Mason King. He promised no one would harm her. Heat flushed through his body. He had to calm down. For her.

His phone ringing brought him back to earth.

Seye. Emiliano prayed for good news.

"Seye," Emiliano answered.

There was a pause then a sigh. Emiliano's chest tightened.

"It's not looking good, Young Petty," Seye said.

"What do you mean?"

"The Council is convinced you would not be the best choice."

"And that boy is?"

"You got arrested."

"So did he!"

"There is rumor you started a fight with King over a domestic situation. You have to realize, many of the men on the Council, myself included, are of an older generation. Getting involved in a man's marital dispute is out of line."

"They are not married."

"From what I heard, him and the young woman in question are engaged and have been for some time. There are also rumors of you being seen with her, alone."

Emiliano grit his teeth. Mobolaji was going out of his way to make sure his choice stole Emiliano's rightful spot. How many people had the usurper hired to spoil his reputation? And these individuals who were going out of their way to ruin Iyanda was a call for him to wrap his hands around the pompous man's sweaty neck.

"Seye, I-."

"I will do my best to convince the Head otherwise. Keep *your* head down. Focus on your plans for the chair. And for the love of Igbala, stay away from the girl. I feel these are more than rumors and frankly I don't care. I, and a few of the others, have been known to have a beautiful woman or two on the side-."

"She is not like that."

It got quiet on the other end. Seye was probably smiling his wide toothy smile.

"You sound like your father," Seye said. "We all knew your mother was no good, but he refused to get another woman. He used to tell me, 'She's different. My love is just for Quilla. She deserves nothing less'."

The corners of Emiliano's mouth curved at the compliment.

"Just keep your distance from her," Seye said.

"I can't promise anything, Seye."

Hanging up the phone, Emiliano stared at the screen. He wasn't going to lose his father's chair to Mobolaji or his coterie. And he would be damned if he lost Iyanda to Mason King.

Scrolling through his phone, Emiliano clicked on Lily Poe's name. He listened to the ringing, hoping it wasn't too late to speak to her. He sighed in relief when the phone picked up.

"I was just getting ready to go to bed, Emiliano," Lily Poe said.

"I need a favor, old friend."

CHAPTER 19

Emiliano gave the wrapped box a squeeze. Standing outside Nana B's hospital room door the next morning, he steadied his breathing. After the conversation with Seye, he needed to speak to Iyanda. But it was impossible.

Calling her house was futile.

Gaiana refused to interfere with family affairs. In addition, knowing someone could be watching his every move from the Council didn't make seeing Iyanda any easier.

He knew it was a long shot to speak with Nana B but talking to the elder of the family was his last resort.

Holding his breath, he knocked on the door and waited for permission before entering.

Upon opening the door, Emiliano was greeted by the scents of cleaning supplies and flowers as well as Lily Poe's small smile. She had given him a quick refresher the previous night on what he needed to say to Nana B if he wanted her blessing.

Morning light peeked into the white room's window blinds. The heart monitor connected to Nana B by a finger clip beat steadily, printing out results that piled on the floor next to the bed. Closing the door behind him, Emiliano tensed at how loud the echo of the sterilized room was.

Propped up by pillows, Nana B's once dark, alert eyes were now weary. They fixed on him, causing beads of sweat to form on the back of his neck. She twisted her mouth and sucked her teeth, a sound his grandmother called kissing one's teeth.

He gave a slight bow then quickly came to the bed, offering her the wrapped gift. "Beaded shoes from Nigeria," he said in Yoruba.

She stared blankly at the purple wrapping paper before she focused back on him. For a moment he believed he glimpsed a twinkle in the dark eyes but chalked it up to the morning sun.

"You must know some powerful people to get them here so quickly." Nana B accepted the box, thumb brushing against the edges.

Emiliano winked at Lily Poe. If it hadn't been for her, he would have arrived empty-handed. Lily Poe managed to get the shoes to him at two in the morning. He owed her big. She reminded him of the offense he would have committed by visiting an elder without a gift. Insulting Nana B was the last thing he needed at the moment.

"How is your health, Nana B?" he asked in a concerned tone.

Nana B stared off at the other side of the room.

Wanting to follow the proper etiquette, he replayed his words, dissecting them for any hint of disrespect. He believed he had done everything but lie face down on the floor, and he was willing to do that too, if need be.

He glanced at Lily Poe, who gave him a slight nod.

"I have some things to take care of." Lily Poe stood to leave. She bowed her head in Nana B's direction. "If you need anything, I am available." She walked around the bed, stopping at Emiliano's side. Briefly, she touched his shoulder then walked from the room and closed the door behind her.

The room seemed bigger and emptier with his friend gone.

Nana B still looked straight ahead, not acknowledging him. He debated whether to ask again.

"I hope everything is well," Emiliano said, a little less confident.

Nana B gave a shaky sigh. "I'm dying and my granddaughter will be alone."

It felt as if the air had been knocked out of him. "Are you sure?" he asked.

"I've known for a while. The doctors verified it's stomach cancer. Very aggressive, they say." She finally looked at him. "Sit down. I know why you're here."

Emiliano walked around the bed and claimed Lily Poe's seat. He studied his clasped hands, not daring to look Nana B in the eye.

"You have caused much confusion in my family," Nana B said in English.

"You know English?" he asked in disbelief.

"I know five languages. I choose Yoruba, the tongue of my mother, it sounds better."

Emiliano softly chuckled. No disagreement there. Leaning forward with a bowed head, he said in Yoruba, "Auntie, I came to see you about Iyanda."

Nana B huffed. "She is to be a married woman soon."

"Yes, ma'am, I know what her mother wants." Emiliano gazed at the blinds, powerlessness at that knowledge. He took a sigh. "But it's not what Iyanda wants."

"Are you saying her mother does not know best?" her voice accusing.

His head spun around, his tongue stumbling over his words. "No, ma'am. I know she does-."

"Do you?" Nana B interrupted.

Emiliano glanced at the elderly woman's face. Her tight lips and analyzing stare made him drop his eyes back to his hands.

"I love her," he confessed, "and can give her a better life."

Nana B sucked her teeth. "You young people are so quick to love but never think about what it means. Everyone wants to live this fairytale. Does the fairytale chase away poverty or disease? What about the pretty faces? A man who really loves a woman will make sure he can provide a lifestyle she is used to or one that is better. His hands will caress her. His words will treasure her. Young women, our women, are forgetting this. I don't want this for Iyanda."

Emiliano looked up. Nana B's glistening eyes were staring at the white wall across the room as her chin slightly quivered. Not wanting to embarrass her, he averted his gaze before catching a glimpse of her swiping at her cheek.

"I have bought your granddaughter an entire garden of herbs and flowers," Emiliano said, "more than she could ever need. Not only can I give her the lifestyle she wants and deserves but I will give her anything better than a fairy-tale. Never will my hands or words strike her. I will not only take care of her but also her family for as long as I live and after."

Pulling in a deep breath, a feeling of weightlessness and invincibility came over Emiliano at his last words. Never had he said those words for another and felt this way. He meant it. She would be protected, no matter the cost. He sighed. Wiping at the tears that hadn't fallen yet, he sniffed then sat up with a soft chuckle.

A light knock was heard at the door before it was opened. Four women dressed in white doctor coats walked in and stood beside Nana B's bed. She studied them, wrinkles of uncertainty forming on the older woman's forehead.

"These are the best doctors from Nigeria," Emiliano said. "They studied there as well as in Europe. They're here to help you with your condition."

"You knew what was wrong with me," Nana B stated.

"I've known for a while. Your granddaughter has been concerned for your health. I spoke to your doctor. After reasoning with him, he agreed that anything could help." Emiliano rubbed his thumb against his index and middle finger indicating the money he had to pay to get the information.

"You bribed him?" Nana B's disapproving frown made the doctors exchange awkward glances.

"Look at it as I've paid for your health, buying it from one who doesn't care for it."

Nana B looked away, the corner of her lips curled up. She nodded her head as if answering an unheard question.

"At the moment," Emiliano said, "I can't see her but if I have your blessing, I'll stay true to only her."

She sat up straight. "I can't promise you anything." She paused before finishing with an unwavering tone. "Protect my granddaughter, Emiliano Petty. I leave her well-being in your hands."

Emiliano nodded, the tension now lifted from his body. He turned his attention to the doctors. "Take care of her. If there is anything she needs, contact me."

Nana B gripped his arm. "If you hurt her, no amount of money will protect you from me."

Emiliano gave a small smile. "Auntie, I would harm myself before I ever hurt Iyanda."

She gave his arm a final squeeze before she released him.

He left the room smiling at the elderly woman's command to the doctors not to be treated so delicately.

* * * * *

Iyanda watched people passing by her shop, searching for him. It had been two days since she had seen Emiliano or even heard about him. Yesenia reassured her it was because he was focused on the next council meeting. Claiming his father's chair was important to him and Iyanda was willing to do whatever was needed so he could achieve it. But she missed him.

She debated about going to the market and purchasing the items needed to fix asun for him. A few days prior, Yesenia informed Iyanda about Emiliano's childhood love for the spicy roast goat dish. Iyanda never cared for it herself, but she was willing to prepare it, knowing it would give him peace of mind.

Yesenia came from the backroom carrying a box of freshly jarred herbs. She placed the box down in one of the aisles and knelt beside it. Her groan caught Iyanda's attention. The young girl held her stomach, her face scrunched in pain. Iyanda rushed to her side and touched Yesenia, concerned about where the pain was coming from.

"I'm fine," Yesenia said between breaths. "I just don't feel so well."

Wrapping one arm around the girl, Iyanda helped her over to the step by the counter. Kneeling before her, Iyanda felt Yesenia's cheeks. Damp and overly warm. When she tried to lift one of the young girl's eyelids, her hand was brushed away.

"I'm fine, Iyanda. I just need to go home to lie down." Yesenia tried to stand, only to fall back down with a groan.

There was no way she was going to allow the young teen to go home in such a condition. Quilla Petty would cause an uproar through the island until she received Iyanda's head. She didn't want to disturb Emiliano, but this was more important. She motioned to Yesenia to stay put then rushed over to WAISTED.

Thankfully the store was quiet, except for Tambara's sewing machine in the back corner. Adeyemi and Ola were probably at the hospital with Nana B, leaving Gaiana in charge of the store for the moment.

Iyanda tiptoed through the store to the glass counters. Tambara was hard at work, her headphones making her oblivious to anyone's presence. Spying Gaiana flipping through a catalog, Iyanda crept over to her

A small gasp escaped Gaiana's mouth and she shuffled back a step. "Iyanda!"

Iyanda motioned for her to lower her voice.

"What's wrong?" Gaiana whispered.

"Something is wrong with Yesenia. She doesn't want me to help. She wants to go home," Iyanda signed.

"I knew it was a bad idea to let her come here. What are we going to do?"

"Take her to Emiliano."

"Emiliano?"

"Yesenia said he's been at his apartment lately. If we take her there, then maybe we won't get in trouble and maybe she'll listen to him."

Gaiana cast a glance at Tambara who was still focused on the dark blue project at hand. She looked back at Iyanda. "Fine. But I seriously want you to rethink teaching Miss Petty."

They glanced at Tambara. She was now engrossed in her cell phone. They would have a couple of seconds before the young woman would look up and try to find a reason to sneak out.

"I'm taking an early lunch," Tambara said in a singsong voice. She grabbed her yellow purse and rushed out of the store without waiting for an answer from anyone.

"The Ancestors must be looking out for you," Gaiana teased.

They hurried to the herbal shop. Yesenia's head leaned against the wall, her eyes closed. It pained Iyanda to listen to the young woman's labored breathing but there wasn't much she could do for someone who didn't want her help.

"Miss Petty?" Gaiana knelt before Yesenia.

Yesenia responded in a groan.

"We're going to take you to your brother," Gaiana said.

Yesenia nodded weakly.

Each taking a side of Yesenia, Gaiana and Iyanda wrapped their arms around the tiny girl and assisted her outside. They shuffled across the street to where Gaiana's compact, blossom purple car was parked. After helping Yesenia lie down, Gaiana ran to the driver's side.

Iyanda closed Yesenia's door and stood back. Gaiana frowned.

"What are you doing? Get in," Gaiana urged.

"Someone has to watch the store," Iyanda signed. The truth was, her stomach fluttered at the thought of seeing Emiliano.

Her friend gave a slight nod of understanding. She hopped into the seat, then drove toward Pleasant Heights.

Iyanda hurried back to the store, anxious about her mother and aunt walking into an empty establishment. The cool air of WAISTED cooled the beads of sweat on her forehead and neck. They had not returned. Iyanda untensed her shoulders.

She walked back to her herbal store, planning to close for a couple of hours to watch WAISTED. She was startled to find Mason standing at the counter holding a black envelope. Refusing to allow him to control her emotions at the moment, she steadied her breath, then strolled over to the counter, avoiding eye contact with him.

Mason chuckled. "You can save that act for someone else. Ignore me if you want but after the wedding, I won't tolerate it." He tossed the black envelope on the counter. "In two days, I will expect you ready to come with me to this. I'm a future Chairman and if you don't want the position of Chairman's wife to be taken by someone else, I would advise you to be ready to go. My mother will take you shopping tomorrow and is willing to do your hair."

Without another word or even waiting to see if she had anything to say, he left the store. Iyanda stared at the black rectangle. Chairman. To make him part of the Council could threaten the traditions of the Igbalaians. Attending the party would show her support for birth rights being stolen from others. Silence against such things would award greedy individuals power over those who were helpless.

But it would also allow her to see Emiliano.

She would go.

She brushed the envelope off the counter.

But not for Mason.

CHAPTER 20

Nana B sat on the porch swing in front of the house, stringing the last bead on a string full of red, glossy beads. The fragrance of damp earth and freshly watered plumerias relaxed her body. Small birds bounced in the dew-drenched grass, hoping to catch the worms that hadn't been quick enough to go back underground. It was her second day home and she was thankful to be out of the hospital, to once again feel the sun kissing her unsandaled feet. The doctors Emiliano Petty provided were willing to do everything possible to fight the cancer without resorting to invasive measures.

A small smile appeared on her lips when she saw Dunni walking toward her house, carrying the familiar large shoulder bag. It had been Adeyemi's first sewing order for WAISTED. After twenty-two years, Dunni pridefully carried around the faded purple tote, testifying that it was still sturdy enough for the work needed to be done.

The porch step creaked under Dunni's foot.

"Why don't doctors say what they mean? Invasive measures. Just say 'surgery'," Nana B said.

Dunni smiled. "Maybe they believe it sounds better."

Nana B stared at the string of beads in her lap, rubbing the last one between her thumb and forefinger. Making an internal prayer for the future wearer, she placed them on top of three other strings of beads and closed them up in a purple Adire bundle.

"Like the onisegun school being on break?" Nana B eyed Dunni.

"Since I've started the school, we've never taken a break. But you already know this, old friend."

"Then explain my granddaughter spending more time at home and in her store, risking everything by training the Petty girl."

Dunni frowned. "I thought you were aware of Iyanda not coming anymore. She said you would not be able to complete payments for the rest of her training. And I was not aware of her training anyone illegally."

Nana B averted her eyes, her jaw clenching and unclenching. Iyanda never kept secrets from her and even though the young woman tried to convince her everything was okay, Nana B knew differently.

"How is your health?" Dunni asked.

"I am dying. Cancer." The word leaving Nana B numb.

"I-I'm sure something can be done. There is an herb-."

"I know of it. My granddaughter has tried to make me take it. That Petty boy has sent in doctors for me." Nana B shook her head. "I don't want either."

"You want to die?" Dunni took a seat on a nearby rocking chair.

"No one wants to die." Nana B swallowed the lump in her throat. "I'm ready to join my Ancestors but only if my granddaughter's future is good. I fear I'm leaving her by herself."

"She's never alone." Dunni laid her hand on top of Nana B's. "I'll be here for her."

Nana B gave a slight nod. "I want to pay the amount for the rest of her training and her licensing for Igbala."

"Yes, ma'am."

Nana B reached inside her skirt's pocket and handed Dunni a folded envelope. Looking inside, Dunni's eyes widened.

"This is more than enough. There will be much left over," Dunni said.

Nana B nodded. "Good. I have been saving it since she could walk. Tambara has some as well, but Iyanda needs more for what she would accomplish."

Dunni placed the envelope in the bag. "I will give her the extra."

Nana B reached inside her pocket and pulled out a purple bundle. She gave it a squeeze. The click of the beads triggered tears to form. She blinked rapidly, hoping her lashes could cool the heating behind her eyes.

She handed the bundle to Dunni. "After my death, give these to Iyanda."

Dunni looked down at the purple bundle. She opened her mouth then quickly closed it as if the words would offend Nana B. She carefully placed it in the bag then bowed her head.

"Nana B, may your health be long."

Nana B's dark lips curved up. If it were possible, she would welcome it. But now, it was time to ready herself to join the Ancestors.

* * * * *

Emiliano's steps echoed in the Petty mansion as he made his way to the kitchen. He brought Yesenia home after his sister had stayed at his apartment for almost two days. She didn't want to come home, but he needed to prepare himself for the Council Ball. When Gaiana had dropped her off and explained what happened, he called a private doctor. The man assured him it could have been something the young girl had eaten.

As his sister rested, his mind wandered to Iyanda. What was she doing at the moment?

Telling himself he didn't want to jeopardize his father's seat, he avoided seeing her. But he was determined to keep a personal promise to never keep himself from her again once everything settled. If she wasn't married by then.

Every minute he fought the urge to be by her side, never wanting to leave. But he couldn't risk the authorities arresting her for immorality or labeling her family as shameful women. He promised to keep her from harm, and he intended to keep his word, even if it meant having to wait to claim her as his own.

He walked into the kitchen to grab himself a bottle of water. Shooting some baskets would temporarily clear his mind of Iyanda. Deep in thought, he didn't notice his mother and Edward sitting at the breakfast table.

"Welcome home, son."

Emiliano's jaw clenched at the sound of his mother's voice.

They smiled at him. Their eyes told him that he had been the topic of their recent conversation. He wasn't interested in what they had to say.

Though he was curious to how Edward managed to stay around. By now his mother would be sporting a new model, sometimes a bit older than Edward. To ask would be playing into a discussion his mother was obviously eager to have. Heading for the refrigerator, Emiliano grunted a response. He grabbed a cold bottle of water and headed for the back door.

"It's rude not to greet your mother," Edward voiced.

"Not my father," Emiliano shot back.

Edward stood, blocking the door. "I can be more than a dad. I can be a close friend. I thought we established something at the jail."

Emiliano stopped in his tracks and looked at the older man. "That suave English role works on my mother, not on me."

"Emiliano, I want to talk to you about something," Quilla said, regarding him.

Clenching his teeth, he returned to the kitchen and leaned against the counter. Edward claimed his seat next to Quilla.

"I know things around here have been tense with Edward being introduced into the picture," Quilla said with a smile, "and with you picking up where you left off with Aria."

"Nothing to pick up." Emiliano took a sip of water.

Quilla brushed a lock of hair behind her ear. "School will start next month and I'm sure you'll want to prepare to go back to the mainland."

"I'm not returning to school this semester," Emiliano stated.

Quilla's smile became strained. "I wasn't told this."

"Because it wasn't for you to know."

"I'm your mother," she said in irritation.

"And I pay my tuition."

Quilla tilted her head, letting out a heavy sigh. "You will let go of the Cove girl," she said.

Emiliano smiled. "No."

Quilla sneered. "I'm not asking, I'm telling you."

"And I am telling you, no." Emiliano stood to leave, tired of his mother's nagging.

"She is not the one for you."

Emiliano scoffed. "And I can see where Aria would be my soulmate."

Quilla closed her eyes and took a deep breath. When she looked at him again, her face was relaxed, but her eyes spoke of pain he would receive if he didn't yield. "Sarcasm is beneath us."

"And yet," Emiliano responded with a smirk, "you've made yourself queen of ridicule." He feigned a bow causing her to make a tsk-ing sound.

Edward held up one of his hands. "Let's be civil about this. Emiliano, your mother is just concerned for your future. You already have school and your father's business to handle. A thing with a poor girl is not something else you need to add to your plate. And she got you arrested." Edward touched Quilla's hand. "Isn't that right, dear?"

Quilla glowered at Emiliano. "Yes, papi," she replied in a strained tone.

"I don't know what the hell makes you think you can talk to me as if I'm your child," Emiliano snapped at Edward. "It's Mister or Master Petty to you. And who I see," he glowered at his mother, "is my damn business, no one else's. I will marry her before I marry Aria." Emiliano walked to the glass French doors.

The chair clanged on the floor as Quilla stood up. She glowered at Emiliano. "Over my dead body will that girl be part of this family!"

"Then prepare your funeral soon." He placed his hand on the door handle.

Quilla exploded. "She will bring this family to ruin!"

Emiliano spun on his heels. In a couple of steps he towered over his short mother. She appeared unfazed, her chin still in its haughty position. "How? How, mother?" he spat, each word laced with anger. "What has she or any of her family ever done to us?"

"She is a reminder!" Quilla sighed, then lowered her voice. "A reminder of where we used to be."

"What? Poor?"

"African."

"You married a Yoruba descendant. Your mother was African!" He towered over her. "Sorry to inform you, mom, but your skin is as dark as hers."

Quilla slapped Emiliano. Her chest heaved as she glared up at him.

Nursing his cheek, he looked down at her. He didn't care that he had struck a nerve, she had struck her fair share. He brushed by her, making his way to the front door.

"Stop seeing her," Quilla said.

"Bye, mother."

"I will take away everything from her."

Emiliano halted in his tracks. He looked back at Quilla. "What are you talking about?"

She smirked. "By the time I'm through with her, she'll wish she never met you."

He turned to her, an amused grin on his face. "And how will you do that?"

"The building her family is renting is owned by Edward's friend and colleague. If you don't stop seeing her, I will have them evicted."

Emiliano's heart dropped to his stomach. She couldn't be serious. He knew his mother could be petty, even conniving. But would she really go out of her way to destroy a family that she herself claimed was beneath her?

"And my friend has been made aware not to sell it to you and or your friend," Edward added.

Emiliano avoided his mother's eyes. "What do you want?" he asked.

A relaxed smile crossed Quilla's face. "Ignore her. When she tries to contact you, make it clear you are not interested in anyone like her."

He glared at her. "I'll find a way to get around this. And when I do, I'll make sure you suffer for this."

Quilla shrugged. "Not in this lifetime. Go enjoy some basketball. Don't forget about the Council Ball tonight. Aria will be ready at seven."

Taking Edward's hand, she led him out of the kitchen with an extra bounce in her walk

* * * * *

The night stepped in with the click of heels on hardwood and the rustle of dresses on the dance floor. Waiters weaved through the crowd, carrying trays of bubbly champagne and lobster pâté. Rich music from the live orchestra bounced off the high walls and vaulted ceiling of the historical Grand Salão.

All of this became background noise to Emiliano when Iyanda descended the spiral staircase.

His gaze devoured her beauty as she glided through the room. Her champagne-wet lips, tinted a ruby red, curled into a friendly smile as she shook the hands of people. How he wanted to claim them, smear the lipstick barrier to get to the sweetness of her full mouth. The dark burgundy, floor-length, evening gown exposed her creamy, sepia shoulders. He thought the bell-shaped sleeve hems made her look silly, like one of those flamenco dancers in the old movies.

Heat burned his cheeks as he watched Mason wrap his arm around her.

They walked across the room, Iyanda's chin high, her back stiff as if afraid to disturb the matching Gele on her head. Emiliano's heart ached as they disappeared further into the throng of people. More likely, they were meeting Mobolaji and the nest of snakes.

"The water one is destined to drink never flows past him or her," Seye said in Yoruba. He handed Emiliano a flute of champagne.

"She shouldn't be here with him," Emiliano said.

"Who's to say she's supposed to be here with you? You are focused on a token when you should be focused on the prize."

Emiliano took a sip of the bubbly liquid. He knew Seye was right but he refused to allow the older man to know. The room was full of old money and politicians. Many needed to be convinced of why his birthright shouldn't be taken away by someone not even worthy of breathing in the same air his father once breathed.

Taking a deep breath, he followed Seye. He shook hands and laughed with elders of old Pleasant Heights families. His glass had been refilled three times but still the drink did nothing to fill the gap he felt. Many of them asked about Aria and when the wedding would be. He smiled and gave a short answer of women not ready to leave their families, receiving hearty chuckles from the seasoned men.

Quilla insisted he attend the ball with Aria, even going so far as informing him of what time to pick her up. Seven o'clock came around and Emiliano came straight to the Grand Ballroom, without Aria.

"Jack Petty's son." Chief Njoku's large hand encased Emiliano's in a hearty, firm handshake. "The prodigal son has returned."

Emiliano and Seye chuckled.

"Yes, Olóyè," Emiliano said, "there is no place like home."

"Too bad many of our youth don't have the same sentiment." Chief Njoku eyed Emiliano.

"Young Petty breaths Igbala, Olóyè," Seye added.

Chief Njoku smirked. "You don't have to sell me on Jack's son. I don't care for the King boy. A social roach, as my wife calls him."

"Then maybe you put in a good word-."

Chief Njoku held up his hand, halting Emiliano's words. "Tonight is about much more than politics, my boy."

Emiliano frowned at the comment. Tonight *was* politics. Every man in the room had their hands deep in the dealings of the government. Many were there to make the right connections for their own selfish endeavors.

Chief Njoku placed his hand on Emiliano's shoulder and led him and Seye through the crowd. "Can you tell me what happens to men who work all day and do nothing else?" Chief Njoku asked.

"I imagine it would give them the opportunity to finish what they've started, Olóyè," Emiliano answered.

"Not even close." They stopped before an elegantly dressed ebony-skinned woman. She smiled at them before focusing on Chief Njoku. He kissed the back of her hand before grinning. "You get more beautiful each time I leave your side, my Bride."

Emiliano and Seye bowed their heads. "Olorì," they said in unison.

"I swear the honey tree couldn't produce anything as sweet as your tongue, my love," Olorì caressed Chief Njoku's cheek.

Chief Njoku glanced at Emiliano. "They become dried up raisins of the men they used to be," he said, answering his own question. "There are things more important than work and chairs." His eyes looked to the left.

Emiliano turned his head in the direction the man was looking. His heart danced when he saw Iyanda. She held her champagne flute in both hands, her eyes surveying the room as Mason and the men he laughed with ignored her.

"I'm aware of your rendezvous with the young lady," Chief Njoku said. "She is lovely."

Iyanda's dark eyes locked with his. His heart threatened to pound out of his chest.

"One dance has never hurt anyone," Chief Njoku urged.

"Olóyè, I wouldn't advise Young Petty to do that," Seye said. "Young men can become territorial when it comes to young ladies."

Chief Njoku gazed at his wife. "What say you, my Bride?"

She gave Emiliano a gentle smile. "What can a dance do that words have not already done?"

Without a second thought, Emiliano strode across the room and stopped a respectful distance from Iyanda. Mason and the Council Members glared at him.

"I was wondering if the lady would like to dance," Emiliano said.

Mobolaji gripped Mason's arm.

Iyanda's downcast gaze shifted to Mason before looking up at Emiliano. She nodded.

Holding out his hand, he led her to the large dance floor. Putting her glass on a waiter's passing tray, he wrapped his arm around the petite indent of her waist and pulled her close. He inhaled her alluring scent of licorice.

"Iyanda, look at me," he said.

Her cheeks reddened but she kept her eyes downcast.

"Nothing will happen to you as long as you're with me."

She cast a glance to the sideline. Mason glowered at them. If it wasn't for the large man holding him back, Emiliano knew he would have to fight.

Taking the crook of his finger, Emiliano lifted Iyanda's chin. "I show no shame here. It's just a dance, right?"

Her lids slowly lifted, her large eyes softening when they looked into his. She gave a small smile and placed her hand on his shoulder.

Emiliano looked over at Chief Njoku. The older man winked then laughed a hearty laugh.

CHAPTER 21

A week had passed since the ball and Iyanda had not heard from Emiliano. She felt numb. After being swept across the floor in Emiliano's strong arms, Mason dragged her from the room to the carpeted foyer and verbally lashed out at her. He reminded her she was there to be his obedient fiancée, not a flirtatious whore for Emiliano Petty, then kept her at his side for the rest of the evening.

Now a day did not go by without Mason calling the store or coming by to "check on her". She knew he was making sure she had had no interaction with Emiliano.

The relationship with her mother was strained since the day at the hospital. To make matters worse, since the incident the previous evening, the wedding date was moved.

Three days.

A date her mother made with Ms. King without Iyanda's consent. Three days and she would have to let Emiliano go and resort to being at the mercy of Mason and his meddling mother.

The tea kettle's whistle broke the trance. Grabbing the handle, she poured the boiling water into a waiting teacup then placed the pot back on the stove. Picking up the tray with the cup and a bowl of soup, she made her way to the front porch.

Nana B sat on the porch loveseat, stringing an order of waist beads. Iyanda placed the tray within reaching distance on a small circular table. She picked up the cup and gingerly held it out to Nana B.

The old woman shook her head. "Put it back down. Too hot."

Iyanda gave a patient smile. She placed the cup down and picked up the bowl. Black-eyed peas and locust beans danced in the reddish-brown liquid. Gbegiri soup was one Nana B used to give her as a child when she didn't feel well.

"I'm not hungry, either," Nana B said. She continued stringing the golden beads.

Iyanda put the bowl back on the table. She knelt in front of Nana B and looked up at the older woman.

"Nana, you have to eat," Iyanda signed.

"No, you are trying to make me take medicine."

"My medicine is in the tea."

"Too hot."

Iyanda shook her head, slightly amused by her grandmother's stubbornness. She knew the woman would never take any of the doctor's medicine, she didn't trust them. And for her to reject Iyanda's was almost expected because of the bitterness of the herbs.

"Help me with these beads," Nana B said.

Sitting flat on her bottom, Iyanda grabbed a piece of freshly cut white string, a bowl of beads, and went to work on creating a masterpiece equivalent to Nana B's.

For two hours they worked on the order in silence. The tea and the soup were now cold. Nana B told Iyanda not to bother making more.

Iyanda's fingers slid the seed beads down the white cord but her mind stayed busy on other things. In two weeks, she would have been starting preparations for becoming an onisegun.

She stopped beading and stared at the diamond ring on her left finger. Mason had gifted it to her the night of the ball, claiming it was time everyone knew who she belonged to. It was just another way to show off his mother's money. She closed her eyes, willing the hot tears to stay back.

How did this happen? Why was she still engaged to Mason?

Damn her father. He was the cause of all this. He left behind a burden of shame they were forced to carry for the last seven years, leaving it up to her to lift it off her family's shoulders through a marriage she didn't want.

Her hand dropped to her lap. She hung her head to hide the tears rolling down her cheeks.

Nana B's warm, heavy hand touched the top of her hair. Iyanda scooted over and laid her head down on her grandmother's lap. She closed her eyes as the comforting hand stroked and caressed the confusion and heartbreak away. The hand slowed to a stop then lifted her chin. Iyanda looked into the piercing eyes of Nana B.

"You can't let others decide your life for you," Nana B said.

Iyanda frowned.

"Those days are over," Nana B continued. "If you don't take charge of your life, someone else will. Don't dishonor your grandfather, don't dishonor me, by letting this happen."

"Nana B, I can't-," Iyanda's hands stuttered, *"I can't go against mama."*

"You must! I won't always be here to protect you. Love your mama. Honor and respect her. But you are different. Stronger. Don't let your strength be taken."

Nana B caressed the bamboo knife resting on her other leg. "You know there was a time when the children of Igbala lost their senses. I made this knife when I was just fifteen, a mere girl. My parents were killed and I had no brothers to protect me. All I had was two little sisters. The government forgot the men, so the men forgot us. Igbalaian women and girls became the victims and the prizes of such a foolish rebellion. I refused to be either."

"I provided food for us, sometimes going hungry myself just so they could eat. At night, I stayed up, guarding them with just this knife I carved from a bamboo plant my mother grew in the house. This went on for months, but each day felt like years. Finally, the government regained control and we were safe. Not once did I have to use my weapon, but I was ready to, if need be."

Nana B looked Iyanda in the eyes. "And so should you. Don't be a prize to foolish men. Be a gift to a real one."

It was strange for her grandmother to tell her to go against her own mother. It had been ingrained in her from childhood to follow Adeyemi's wishes and to go a separate path would be like slapping her in the face. Nana B was the one who taught her and Tambara this. A knot formed in Iyanda's belly.

"When I leave this earth, you leave this place. Follow your heart and your dreams. Take care of the family but don't become the family," Nana B said in a hushed tone.

Why was Nana B talking about leaving? It's not time yet. I won't let her. Iyanda thought.

The people Iyanda knew she could stay with had issues of their own and having an extra mouth to feed was not a strain she wanted to add.

Plus, in three days she would be married.

"Don't go with Mason," Nana B stressed. "You go where the Ancestors will guide you. Where I will guide you."

"What do you mean?" Iyanda asked.

Nana B sat back. "Go get me a drink, omo."

Iyanda nodded. She stood and turned to leave then paused. Everything in her screamed she should stay close to her grandmother, but she wanted to obey the request. She looked back. Nana B's eyes were closed and she was taking deep breaths. Iyanda debated whether to follow her instincts.

Not wanting to argue with the older woman, she went inside the house.

A moment later, Iyanda returned with a glass of cool water. Stepping onto the porch, she found Nana B slumped over.

The glass slipped from Iyanda's fingers, the crash mirroring her heart. She rushed over to her grandmother, shaking her, pleading for her to wake up. Holding her hand to Nana B's chest, she waited, feeling for any movement.

Nothing. An ache gripped Iyanda's heart.

Nana B's body, threatening to fall to the porch, was guided by Iyanda's hand to the wooden slabs. She gave Nana B's shoulders a gentle shake.

Nana B didn't stir.

Iyanda prayed, pleading with the Orishas to breathe life back into Nana B's body. They were alone. She threw herself onto her grandmother's chest, her body racked with weeping and sobbing.

Even that was silent.

* * * * *

Iyanda sat on top of her legs, numb, staring at the closed door, hoping her grandmother would walk through. But she wouldn't.

It had been five days since her death and the women of the family were in the mourning room. It was the third day of mourning and Iyanda couldn't weep. External tears wouldn't shed. She blocked them. She didn't want to cry anymore.

She surveyed the other women in the room. Many of the women were cousins and great-aunts Iyanda hadn't seen in a while. They all faced the door, crying out their loss. Tambara and Ola's lamentations outdoing everyone's. Their bodies rocked back and forth in sync with the others.

Adeyemi knelt on the floor next to Iyanda. Her eyes closed as her face looked up at the ceiling, lips moving. She was praying.

To whom, Iyanda wasn't sure. She knew her mother explored the gods of Christians and the god of the Muslims. Adeyemi claimed she needed more options when it came to her prayers being heard.

Since they entered the room, Adeyemi had not shed a single tear. Iyanda's body heated at the thought.

A couple of days ago, her mother told her they would see Nana B again when it was their time.

Iyanda frowned at her mother.

How could she be so cold? Nana B would come back through their bloodline not floating in some clouds like the Christians said.

Iyanda touched Adeyemi's shoulder.

"What are you doing?" Iyanda signed.

"I'm praying."

"To who?"

"To whatever god will listen."

Iyanda frowned. *"What is the point of your prayers? She is dead and has been for five days."*

"Don't be disrespectful, Iyanda."

"You are being disrespectful to the òrìṣà by praying to foreign gods. Did Nana B know what you were doing?"

"Iyanda," Adeyemi said in a warning tone.

The room's air had become stale with tears and body odor. At sunset they would be allowed to leave the room to bathe and eat but Iyanda felt as if she was going to scream before then.

Her mother demanded her obedience and respect, yet she couldn't give the same treatment to her own mother. How many secrets did Adeyemi keep from Nana B? Would these secrets have killed the elderly woman all over again?

Iyanda unclenched her sweaty hands and stared at her palms. Nana B had said she was stronger. How? She crumbled under her mother's stare.

A commotion outside the room brought everyone's wailing to a halting silence. Adeyemi gripped Iyanda's arm.

"What is it?" Iyanda asked.

Adeyemi shook her head. Her eyes, as well as the other women's, were glued to the dark brown wooden door.

Tambara timidly walked to the door and took a peek outside. Her mouth dropped open before she hastily left the room. The other women rushed after her with Iyanda and Adeyemi bringing up the rear.

Iyanda and Adeyemi maneuvered their way to the front.

Uncle Onuoha was being arrested.

Ola tried to reason with the officers before resorting to stomping her foot and demanding they release her husband. A wailing Tambara wrapped her arms around his father's waist, trying to prevent the handcuffs from being clamped down on his wrists.

Uncle Onuoha wore a stone face. His eyes spoke of the fear and worry he had about being carried away by the island police. They were never gentle, whether native or foreigner, male or female; all were criminals in their eyes.

Iyanda swallowed hard. She hoped he would walk out in one piece or at least alive.

Two of the officers dragged Ola and Tambara away from Uncle Onuoha, causing the other women to come to their aid. The two women had no choice but to stand back and watch as the four officers hauled him outside.

Adeyemi rushed after them then moments later came back in.

The women asked how the officers could be disrespectful at someone's funeral.

Adeyemi made eye contact with Iyanda but spoke with everyone in the room. "A dancer at his club is charging him with sexual assault and battery."

The room was in an uproar of questions and confusions. Some of the women tried to comfort Ola and Tambara.

Ola glared at Adeyemi. Breaking free from the women, she pounced on her older sister.

Iyanda's feet froze to the ground. She watched her mother and aunt fight, clawing at each other's clothes and face. She knew she should rush over and help the other women break them apart.

She couldn't.

She had seen the way her uncle was aggressive toward other women especially toward her mother and aunt. The charges had to be true.

She took a step forward but paused when a movement from the corner of her eye caught her attention.

It was Emiliano.

He was dressed in traditional dark blue funeral attire. His locs, tied back under the matching fila cap, made him look more like the respectable Igbalaian man she knew him to be.

Her heart skipped a beat as he walked to the door. His eyes widened then scanned the crowd for her. A sense of relief took over his demeanor when he locked eyes with her.

She glanced back at the fighting women. She needed to get away while she still could.

She made her way to him, grabbed his hand, and led him to his car.

He helped her into the car then climbed into the driver's side. Within seconds they were on the main road.

CHAPTER 22

As if knowing she needed peace, he said nothing the whole car ride, just stroked her hand with his thumb. The lowering sun cast a shadow over Emiliano's penthouse building as they arrived. When the elevator reached the top floor, the doors opened into a spacious living space. A big round rug consisting of smaller circles graced the floor before two white beaded chairs and a matching C-shaped couch. The decor of the room was composed of Yoruba beading, tribal Igbalaian and African art, much of it not Yoruba. Stepping inside, she removed her sandals, allowing the hardwood floor to cool her feet.

A sunset view of the ocean greeted Iyanda. Her fingers pressed against her cheeks, her breath catching as she became lost in the view. She walked to the five tall windows and watched as the sun slowly lowered itself behind the ocean's horizon. Nana B used to love sunsets.

Iyanda's eyes watered. She had just witnessed her family falling apart and there was nothing she could do or wanted to do. She wanted *that* day back. She wouldn't have left Nana B alone, she would've listened to her instincts. She wiped at her cheeks, brushing away the pain that wanted to escape.

Emiliano's fingers wrapped around her shoulders. She leaned back into his chest, allowing the sight of the waves crashing on the shore to soothe her.

He kissed the top of her head, making her warm all over. She turned and looked up at him. Standing on her toes, she gave him a soft kiss.

Pulling her hands up to his mouth, he kissed her fingertips with a familiar tenderness then led her to the couch.

"You thirsty?" he asked.

She nodded. He walked into the kitchen as she allowed the soft couch to swallow away the day.

She watched as the sky grew dark before she closed her eyes. She didn't remember falling asleep, but she thought she heard Emiliano whisper in her ear the words, 'I love you' before she drifted off into the dream realm.

The familiar smell of fried plantains and eggs awakened her. She sat up and stretched. Looking around, she remembered she left with Emiliano the night before. Walking to the counter, she inhaled the delicious aroma.

"Morning," Emiliano said. Turning off the stove, he placed a plate on the counter.

"Morning," she said. She bit her bottom lip as her eyes roamed over the deliciously defined muscles of his chest down to the waistband of his shorts.

They paused, their wide eyes meeting.

She had spoken. She giggled, before releasing an ear-shattering squeal that made Emiliano chuckle.

"You spoke," Emiliano said. He walked around the counter, stopping inches from her.

"I did, I spoke," she said, feeling breathless. She rubbed her hands over the side of her hair, resting them on her cheeks. Warm tears cascaded down her face, her tongue tingling from the words. Her insides felt as if they were vibrating. It had been so long since she heard her voice, she didn't realize how much she missed it. She wished Nana B or Gaiana was there to share this moment with.

She paused and scrunched up her face in worry when she looked up at him. "You don't like it?"

Emiliano chuckled. "Like it?" He grabbed her waist, pulling her close. "I wouldn't have it any other way," he said in a low voice.

He kissed her. Wrapping her arms around his neck, Iyanda pulled him down for a deeper one. Their tongues danced, caressing and exploring each other. He pulled her closer by the waist, his warm hands sliding over her buttocks and squeezing them hard. She moaned.

Duty screamed to her to stop before they went any further, but the magic of his lips made her silence the voice.

Breaking the kiss, she bit her lip before saying, "I'm hungry."

"Let me fix you a plate," his deep voice sending a shiver up her spine. He attempted to straighten up.

Iyanda pulled his head back down. "How about dessert first?"

He frowned, his head tilted to the side. "You mean-?"

She nodded.

Giving her a sinful smile, he scooped her up in his arms and carried her to his room.

A red sheer canopy fell on all sides of the four poster, king-size bed. The room was as big as the living room with Yoruba art on the walls. It held a perfect, if not better, view of the ocean.

At the room door, Emiliano stopped and allowed her feet to drop to the floor. His arm lingered around her waist. He frowned.

"What's wrong?" she asked.

"This damn halo."

Releasing her waist, his hands unraveled the braid. Thick, black coils falling slowly around her face. He stroked the softened strands.

"Better," he said. "The next time you wear this damned style, it'll be for me."

Iyanda softly chuckled.

Tilting her head back, he devoured her soft lips with a deep kiss. Her mouth opened, inviting his tongue to dance with hers once again. He willingly obliged, pulling her closer, demanding more.

Placing a hand on his chest, she broke the kiss.

He raised his brows. "Am I moving too fast, ife mi?"

Iyanda lowered her gaze, biting her bottom lip. Her heart was racing. She wanted this, wanted to explore him. All the reasons to walk away scrolled through her mind but there was no use denying it any longer. She ached for more than just his kisses and touch, she wanted him to possess her, claim her, keep her, if only for one night. Shoving the nosey little voice of judgement aside, she walked over to the bathroom door.

"You don't wash before having dessert?" she asked, casting an enticing glance. Her insides quivered. She had never been with any man in the shower. She remembered hearing Lily Poe tell her and Gaiana that not only was it intimate, but it was the most fun she ever had.

His hungry eyes watched as she unbuttoned her blouse, revealing a simple black camisole. The way he stared at her stirred a desire within Iyanda that she never felt with Mason. If she was granted this one night with Emiliano, then she wanted to make it worth it. Taking his hand, she led him into the bathroom.

* * * * *

Iyanda's body still thrummed from the passionate lovemaking in the shower. She never knew it was possible to do so many positions standing up. Then not to interrupt their streak, he carried her to the bed, never breaking the kiss. There he explored her body with not just his hands, but his mouth and tongue as well, bringing her to call out his name in an uncontrollable wave of pleasure. Tucking her under the soft Egyptian cotton cover, he slid underneath the king-size bedding and pulled her close, burying his face in her neck.

The next morning, they hopped back into the shower to cleanse each other's body then they sat on the bed to share the now ice-cold breakfast. Iyanda borrowed one of his buttoned shirts, her bare crossed legs not hiding the lack of underwear.

The open window invited in the morning sounds of birds chirping and tweeting. Ocean waves crashed against the reef. They had missed the morning drums which started the day for the residents of Igbala.

"I'm sorry about your grandmother," Emiliano said.

Iyanda sadly smile. "I don't think her passing is what upsets me the most. It's the way no one cares. They expect me to be excited for a wedding I don't want. I just-I know if she were alive, she would find a way to prevent this marriage."

His amorous, sunset brown eyes studied her.

"What?" she asked, a nervous smile in the corner of her lips.

"I have something for you." Climbing off the bed, he walked over to a tall dresser.

"I see what you can give me," she said, admiring his muscular buttocks.

Opening a drawer, he grinned. "Behave, woman, or you'll get more than you can handle."

Pulling out a small, velvet box, he walked back over to the bed and handed it to her.

Opening the lid, Iyanda fingers rose to her parted lips. Her heart fluttered at the rare black coral lining the cord then meeting a pendant-sized stingray egg case, or mermaid's purse, at the center. Emiliano flipped the pendant over to reveal a single white cowrie shell.

Tears choked her words. It was the most beautiful love token she had ever seen and expensive. Managing to swallow the lump in her throat, she said, "Thank you."

She allowed Emiliano to fasten the necklace around her neck. She shivered as the cold pendant rested between her breasts. She turned so he could admire it.

"Perfect," he said. His hands reached inside the shirt, sliding it off her shoulders. She trembled under his fingers as they trailed from her shoulders to the roundness of her breast.

Cupping her small, perky mounds, he bent his head and softly kissed her. She groaned as he kneaded the ripe flesh, melting under his touch once again.

She pulled away from the kiss. "I have to get home," she said, trying to catch her breath. His sinful lips, a whisper away, tempted her. She had to resist. She closed her eyes, needing strength at the moment.

"Stay with me." His kisses traveled to her neck. She rolled her head back, with a moan.

"I'm engaged to Mason," she said, her breath coming in tiny pants.

Emiliano paused. She lifted her head and looked into his inquiring eyes. "You love him?" he asked.

"I've known him for a long time," Iyanda tentatively answered.

"Knowing someone and loving them are two different things." Exhaling, he dropped his hands. "I understand if you have to go home. I mean, I don't. You're an adult."

She smiled. "And you think like an American."

Emiliano gave a wry smile. "I was born and raised here."

"But your mind and ways have become American. I'm an adult and could make decisions for myself but our traditions are what keep our people together. If I must marry a man of my family's choosing, so be it."

Iyanda flinched at the word family. Her family was broken because of the absence of Nana B.

He caressed her cheek. "Stay with me for three days." His finger traveled down to her chin, brushing her bottom lip.

She shivered.

"After the three days," his finger trailed to the meeting of her breasts, "you still want to go home and marry him," he moved down, following the trail to her quivering stomach, "I'll let you go and never bother you again." He stopped just below her belly button, a seductive smile curled on his lips.

How was he able to have so much control over her body? She bit her bottom lip, the wave of need and desire washing over her.

His finger continued the trail down.

Three days of passion and just being with him was all he asked. Would it be foolish to say yes again?

He opened the shirt she was wearing, revealing her rows of waist beads. Her body trembled from either the cold air or from his hungry gaze, she couldn't tell.

"I heard the beads sing when in the presence of a lover," he said.

"Depends on the position and the stamina of the lover," she said, her eyes wickedly caressing his body.

"Have yours ever sang?"

"Not yet," she said, a seductive look in her eye.

"Not even with him?"

She shook her head.

"I think they whispered this morning." His finger traced her trim waist, pausing on each bead.

Three days of beads singing was exactly what she needed.

"I know the perfect position to make them ring, let me show you." Iyanda pulled him onto the bed.

CHAPTER 23

Iyanda beamed with the morning sun as she watched Emiliano play dolls with a young girl sitting next to him. They were on their way to the marketplace in Stingray Cove and Emiliano wanted to take the public bus. Her heart warmed as he interacted with the people, not recoiling or sneering at their position, or for some, their extra smells.

The little girl sitting next to him, her two front teeth missing from a delightful smile, giggled at the voices Emiliano created for her two cloth dolls, making them dance, sing, and fall in love. The mother and a few nearby passengers chuckled at the play as well.

"Do you have any children, Sir?" the mother asked in Yoruba.

Iyanda blushed at the amorous gaze Emiliano gave her.

"Not yet," he said, "hopefully one day."

The woman gave a knowing smile to Iyanda. "I don't believe you will have a problem having many, Sir. May The Mother bless the fruit of your loins."

The bus came to a jolting halt a few steps from the market. Helping her down the rusted bus steps, Emiliano interlocked his fingers with hers and escorted her to the marketplace.

"What would you want for dinner?" Iyanda asked.

"I'm sure whatever you cook will fill my belly."

"What about asun?"

Emiliano eyed her. "You've been talking to my sister, I see."

"I hope that was okay?"

Emiliano smiled. "I love a woman who does her research."

Iyanda raised her brow in amusement. "And one who is fertile."

Looping his arm around her tiny waist, he pulled her close, pressing her body against his. "Being fertile isn't necessarily important. We could always adopt."

Iyanda's stomach fluttered at the thought of growing big with his child. "We?" Closing her eyes, she could see a rambunctious little boy with budding locs being chased by his father along the beach. He would be an eager student of herbal medicine, working alongside her in her store. She shook away the image. It would never happen.

Iyanda put her hand on his chest, pushing away. "Emiliano."

Releasing his hold on her waist, Emiliano shoved one of his hands in his pocket and rubbed the back of his neck with the other. Avoiding her gaze, he cleared his throat. "What else are we having with the asun?"

He was embarrassed. She sensed it was hard for him to admit his innermost desires, knowing she would belong to another soon. Unbeknownst to him, she was tempted to remain with him. He made her feel safe and stable with not only his actions but his words as well. And just like now, he shamelessly presented his heart to her while patiently waiting for her to open hers fully to him.

They purchased the freshest vegetables from a woman Nana B used to buy from all the time. The woman squinted to see them. Dunni once offered the elder a salve for her weakening eyesight. The woman refused and told them that if God wanted her eyes, then she was more than willing to give them to Him. The older woman recognized Iyanda. Sandwiching the younger woman's hands between her own, and with a sorrowful countenance she told Iyanda she carried the same spirit as her grandmother. The woman nodded at Emiliano with a small smile then went back to selling her wares.

After purchasing the needed spices, Iyanda made her way to Emiliano, who was haggling prices with the market butcher. The butcher's cheeks puffed and reddened each time Emiliano rejected the price offered only to give a lower price. At this rate, unknowingly to Emiliano, the butcher would reject his business altogether unless he found a way to calm the man down.

"Uncle," Iyanda said in a calm tone, "how are your children?"

The butcher looked between the two, his fiery eyes hooded by thick brows. "They are good. My son is now top of his class."

"Are you talking about Aaron, your middle son?"

The man gave a slight nod, his eyes shifting between the two of them.

"Nana B always said, out of all your children, Aaron was special and would take care of you in your old age."

The man focused just on Iyanda. "You are Nana B's youngest grandchild. Why did you not say so?"

"It's fine, uncle. My friend does not understand how certain things are done in the market."

"I see you are speaking now. Your grandmother knew one day you would. It is good to hear a soothing voice to these old ears."

The butcher went through his inventory of fresh goat meat, and picking the best slabs, wrapped them in white waxy paper. Coming from behind the counter, he handed the package to Iyanda, his hands lingering on hers.

"We lost a real Igbalaian woman," the man said.

Iyanda's eyes watered.

He cleared his throat. "She raised you well and we know you'll carry on her legacy. If there is anything the granddaughter of Nana B needs, do not hesitate. There are many in the market who respected and loved her."

Iyanda swallowed the lump in her throat. The man gave her hands a gentle squeeze and walked back into the store with hunched shoulders.

They left the marketplace, Iyanda's heart a bit lightened at knowing her grandmother's presence lingered with many there and made their way to the bus stop.

"Are you okay?" Emiliano asked.

She nodded.

"A few more moments and I would have had five pounds of goat meat at a low price."

Iyanda laughed. "You would've become the goat meat if he had anything to do with it."

A young man wearing faded clothes over sweat drenched dark brown skin stopped his bike in front of them. He focused on Emiliano.

"You Jack Petty's son?" the man asked.

Emiliano smiled. "I am."

"Here is a message from the people for your father." The man spat in Emiliano's face, the spittle barely missing Iyanda, then pedaled away.

Using his shirt, Emiliano wiped away the disgusting charge from his eyes while Iyanda quickly purchased a few bottled waters from a nearby vendor.

Opening one, she poured it over his face. "What was that about?"

Satisfied with the possibility of the spit being gone, she opened the other and rinsed his hands.

"Some people have been made to believe the suffering they are going through are the workings of my father." He stared at the back of the man riding away.

"Are they?"

He looked into her eyes. "Absolutely not. My father wanted to help, if not fix the problems of the people, but that meant reaching into pockets of some very important people. I have an idea of who started this slander on my father's legacy." He looked back in the direction of the bike man. "And I intend to correct it."

CHAPTER 24

Iyanda marveled at the view of the blue ocean from the floor-to-ceiling windows. Sitting with feet tucked under, she allowed the singing of Tiwa Savage to drift softly from the sound system, wrapping her in a state of euphoria. Three days had flown by. Iyanda's time with Emiliano was short and she was to return home the following morning. He tried to convince her to break off the engagement and just marry him. She couldn't.

And honestly, she didn't know why.

Mason would be a terrible man to be married to but a piece of Iyanda felt it was her duty to marry into a family who could erase her family's shame.

Plus, Emiliano at the end of the day, was still a rich boy from Pleasant Heights. A sweet talker who could eventually get bored.

Iyanda couldn't risk her family for temporary passion.

She touched the pendant. Would he give her such a valuable gift if it was temporary? She snuggled further into the overstuffed chair, stirring the scent of lemongrass from the fabric. Closing her eyes she imagined his arms bringing her closer to the warmth of his chest.

A jingling of keys at the door made Iyanda hop off the couch, her insides vibrating. She peeked at the time on the stove. He was home early.

Giving her thick coils a quick fluff, she unbuttoned the top buttons of the light green shirt she borrowed from Emiliano's closet. The smell of freshly cooked jollof rice and chicken pepper soup staying warm on the stove made her mouth water. Maybe they could have a bite before a sensual session.

She held her breath in anticipation as the door opened. But instead of Emiliano standing at the threshold, it was Aria Riviera. Iyanda's smile vanished.

Aria stormed in, making a beeline for the master bedroom before searching the rest of the apartment. With each door slam, Iyanda took a shaky breath. How was this happening?

Time slowed as Aria's heels clicked on the hardwood floor. She eyed Iyanda then smirked.

"When did the help start wearing their employer's clothes?" Aria asked. "Don't you have somewhere to be? Like a field of weeds or maybe at your own boyfriend's house?"

Iyanda bit down on her tongue, restraining her words. She couldn't stand up to her, not now. Anything she said and did could be twisted by Aria to the proper authorities and not even Emiliano couldn't protect her. Aria's expensive floral perfume assaulted Iyanda's sinuses.

"I don't know what Emiliano has told you." Aria sneered at Iyanda. "But let me clear all of this up for you. I've been his beginning and we-," Aria placed her hand on her stomach, "are his end. He might play with girls like you, but he always comes back to me."

Aria was pregnant. At least, that's what she was implying.

The very words wrenched at Iyanda's heart. It couldn't be true. Emiliano made it clear he and Aria were not together.

But Iyanda saw them together and heard rumors at the ball about the possible engagement between the Riviera and Petty household. What if he had gotten her pregnant and was now trying to ignore his responsibilities? Iyanda found it hard to swallow the thought.

Aria dangled a key in front of Iyanda. "I knew you were here. Next time, I'll open this door and drag you through the streets to the proper authorities."

Iyanda rushed to Emiliano's room and changed her clothes, choking on the hot tears threatening to overflow.

Aria was pregnant.

How could she have been so stupid?

She stormed to the door where Aria stood with a satisfied smirk on her face. Iyanda stopped before her, looking her square in the eye.

She wouldn't be stupid anymore.

Gripping the necklace Emiliano gave her, Iyanda snatched it off of her neck and tossed it at Aria. Aria's wide eyes and gaping mouth gave Iyanda a twinge of satisfaction.

Iyanda left the apartment, ignoring the mumbling swears of Aria.

* * * * *

Ideally, Iyanda wanted to crawl back onto her pallet and sleep the day away. She had missed the funeral celebration and burial for Nana B.

It didn't matter.

She hated graveyards. Not because she was scared of them but because they were a constant reminder death didn't discriminate.

She was glad she had missed the burial. It had given her time to sort out her thoughts while riding the bus back to Stingray Cove. She had watched mothers with their daughters, training them to be pleasing to the eye while silent. A pair of lovers cuddled under each other the entire bus ride, oblivious to the show they were giving other riders.

Walking from the bus stop, she arrived at the house she once called home. Her foot touched the front step, hardening her tongue to words.

Staring at her reflection in the bathroom mirror, she brushed back her frizzy coils. After washing and moisturizing her face, she finger combed water through the tresses. Her heart grew heavy as she braided her hair back into its halo prison.

She came out of the bathroom, stopping inches from her mother's piercing gaze.

Adeyemi still wore the scratches from her sister's attack. "Where did you go?"

"I haven't gone anywhere, mama," Iyanda signed, not wanting to speak. She just wanted to sleep.

"I'm talking about that day," Adeyemi said, a suspicious expression etched on her face.

Iyanda's brows flicked up. Brushing past her mother, she made her way to the kitchen.

Accustomed to seeing her uncle at the small dining table, Iyanda frowned, then remembered he was still locked up.

She went into the refrigerator, hoping to find something to eat and to avoid her mother's questioning. Two plantains and a bowl of soaked black-eyed peas was all she found. Iyanda silently groaned. Her mother's angry steps stopped on the other side of the fridge's door. If only she could stay there until Adeyemi left, but that would only bring a whole new argument.

Closing the door, an impatient Adeyemi stood inches from her, scowling.

"I needed some fresh air. It was too much for me," Iyanda signed.

"For three days?"

Iyanda averted her eyes. How could she talk about the peace she felt for those three days or how the scent of Emiliano still lingered in her memory? How she wrapped her hands in his locs, bringing him in deeper as he tasted her.

She didn't want to fight. Her grandmother would have wanted her to show respect.

Adeyemi's eyes softened. "I know it's hard with your grandmother gone. We all miss her. But now you have to prepare for your wedding to Mason."

"I'm not marrying Mason," Iyanda signed.

Adeyemi raised a single brow. "What do you mean?"

"I'm not marrying him."

"Not this conversation again." Adeyemi sighed. "You cannot call off the engagement. Do you know how hard it will be to find another man who will want you?"

The words struck Iyanda. She swallowed the lump forming. *"I don't care."*

"What do you mean you don't care? Iyanda, you need this match. Not many men will take you because you're mute and don't have a father."

"I wasn't born that way."

"Doesn't matter. You are that way now. Men want women who are beautiful and perfect."

"If that were true, Baba would have stayed."

Adeyemi's hand felt as if fire originated from her palm when she struck Iyanda's cheek. Iyanda bit her inner cheek, swallowing the iron taste of blood. Tears burned her eyes as she looked back at Adeyemi.

The once loving eyes were hard and empty.

"You will marry Mason," Adeyemi said, "or you are not welcomed back in my house."

Iyanda stormed past Adeyemi to her room. Quickly packing a few clothes, she left home.

* * * * *

Even with no money to spare for a room, going back home was out of the question. There was one place. Iyanda hoped she would take her in.

Taking a bus to the upper part of Stingray Cove where many tourists and middle-class natives resided, Iyanda lugged her tattered suitcase, walked for five blocks before turning onto a dirt road.

The afternoon sun slowly sapped any strength Iyanda had from earlier. She looked straight ahead, fearful of looking into the thick forests on either side of her. Growing up, she believed bush spirits would kidnap her and hold her prisoner forever. When she was in middle school, there were reports of young women being attacked on roads such as the one she was on. The attacker was rumored to have skin the color of a vanilla bean and sky blue eyes. He lured the women into the bushes with honeyed promises of finding them a good husband or making them more desirable to the one they already had. Iyanda wasn't sure if the godlike man was real but she never took paths next to thick foliage.

She prayed Gaiana was home.

The path led her to an unpaved, circle driveway. She breathed a sigh of relief at seeing the blue two-story cottage and the familiar yellow scooter parked in front. Walking to the small set of stairs, Iyanda cringed at the thought of having to climb them. Her sweat drenched skin cried to be relieved of the sticky brown blouse. Her wobbly legs threatened to give out on her if she attempted to take a step. Closing her eyes, she willed her body to trust her just a little bit longer and then they would have a place to rest.

The sound of water came from the carport built under the house from the back. Remembering the outside shower, she placed her suitcase down and walked toward the garage. She rubbed her sweaty palms against her yellow adire wrap skirt. With each step she took, her heart pounded against her chest.

Walking up to the shower, Iyanda said, "I need a place to stay."

Gaiana yelped, attacking the shower curtain.

"Calm down, Ana," Iyanda said.

Gaiana stopped her attack and peeked from behind the shower curtain. "Iyanda?" Her brows met. "You're talking."

Iyanda gave an unsure smile. "Don't tell iya."

Turning off the water, Gaiana wrapped herself in a towel then walked out of the small cubicle of a shower. Flinging her arms around Iyanda's neck, she gave her friend a tight hug.

"What took you so long?" Gaiana asked, sniffling.

Warm tears spilled down Iyanda's cheeks. Gaiana would never tell her secrets unless it was necessary. Hopefully, she would support Iyanda in her decision not to marry Mason.

"Can I stay with you?" Iyanda asked.

Gaiana pulled away and wiped at the tears on her cheeks. With a comforting smile, she said, "You know you are always welcome here, my sister."

She motioned with her head for Iyanda to follow her inside the house. Using the stairs, they walked into the screened deck to get to the front door.

Iyanda stepped over the high threshold into a quaint living room. The white wooden walls were decorated with them at the beach and street festivals, oceanic scenes, and a twenty-four inch television.

Iyanda frowned.

How many jobs was her friend working to be able to purchase such an item? If she needed extra money, why didn't Gaiana come to her for extra hours in the herbal shop?

"Make yourself at home. I'll be right back," Gaiana said before going into the back bedroom.

The small, white kitchen beckoned to Iyanda to quench her thirst and feed her hunger. Looking at the polished counters and gleaming sink, Iyanda thought twice. She resigned herself to having a seat on the candy-striped couch.

Before she could give her legs a much needed rest, Gaiana was back in the living room dressed in a pair of Adire print shorts and a black blouse with wedge heels to complete the look for work.

Gaiana glanced at the kitchen before looking back at Iyanda. "I told you, get anything you want."

Iyanda gave a slight shake of her head. "It's fine. I know you have to go to work. You shouldn't have to worry about your kitchen being a mess."

"Aren't you going to work?" Gaiana asked.

Averting her eyes, Iyanda focused on the white refrigerator. Her throat suddenly felt dry at the thought of having to answer her friend's question. Going into the kitchen, she rummaged through the pantry for the ingredients to make her favorite deep-fried snack, chin chin. On not finding what was needed, she settled for an assortment of nuts kept in a clear container. Pouring the mixture on the plate and filling a glass with fresh-squeezed pineapple juice, she took the items to the small round dining table.

Gaiana sat across from her.

Iyanda tried to avoid her stare as she chewed the nuts slowly. She hated when Gaiana did that. Nana B used to tease that Gaiana should have been a detective. The way the young woman could stare a person down would make one confess things they did as well as the things one hadn't done.

Iyanda side-eyed Gaiana.

She stared back. "Still here, Iyanda."

Iyanda covered her nut-filled mouth to prevent the food from flying out as she chortled. Managing to chew and swallow the snack without choking, she cleared her throat then made eye contact with Gaiana.

"I left home," she said.

Gaiana pressed her lips together. "That is obvious. Why?"

"I'm not going to marry Mason. Iya was not happy to hear that. She told me I had to, or I couldn't live under her roof."

"Why don't you want to marry him?"

"Because Nana B wouldn't want me to. Because I don't want to. I don't love him and I know he doesn't love me."

Gaiana smirked. "Is this about Emiliano?"

Iyanda quickly took a sip of pineapple juice, her eyes shifting away from Gaiana.

Gaiana's brow raised. "Did you go out with him again?"

Iyanda took a longer sip.

"Did you spend the night with him?"

Iyanda dropped the glass, her body going into coughing fits to prevent the cold liquid from going down her windpipe.

"You slept with him!" Gaiana squealed in excitement.

Iyanda motioned for Gaiana to calm down.

"How was it?" Gaiana asked.

Iyanda's cheeks reddened.

Gaiana's eyes widened. "That good? Wow. That Yoruba blood is really strong in that one, o?"

Iyanda playfully hit Gaiana's arm, making the other woman giggle. "It was amazing." Iyanda sighed. "Three whole days, and he treated me like a queen. He even gave me-."

She touched the spot where the necklace had been then remembered the why of its absence. She gave a small smile. "Then he did something stupid to mess it all up."

"What?" Gaiana asked.

"Aria showed up."

Gaiana frowned. "Why was that his fault? They're not together."

"They obviously are. She's pregnant."

"Are you sure? It might not be his. She did run off with some self-proclaimed prince, leaving Emiliano during their engagement party. I'm surprised she's bold enough to show her face but then again, I'm not. Aria Riviera never backs down from the public eye."

Iyanda used a finger to draw a circle among the remaining nuts on her plate. Gaiana did make a point. But it didn't excuse the times Aria showed up with Emiliano. For all she knew, it could have been an act he performed whenever she was around. He and Aria were probably laughing at her right this moment.

"I don't know," Iyanda muttered.

"What's there not to know? Has he given you any reason to doubt him? Sounds very romantic."

Iyanda stopped drawing a circle and eyed Gaiana. "Romantic? His crazy ex is not romantic."

"Ignore her. She realized what she had and now she wants it back." Gaiana touched Iyanda's hand. "He is offering you the world."

Iyanda sucked her teeth. "How is he any different from Mason?"

Gaiana gave an understanding smile. "Mason isn't offering you the world. He's trying to fit you into a world he has created for himself. Didn't you tell me that Emiliano purchased an entire garden for you? And he protected you from one of Mason's tantrums."

"I don't need anyone to buy me anything. And someone would have stopped him."

"Who? You yourself said no one even looked in your direction when Mason raised his hand." Gaiana sat back and folded her arms across her chest. "Did Mason bother to even send his condolences when your grandmother died?"

Iyanda didn't answer. If Mason had in any way contacted the family during that time, Adeyemi would have made a fuss over it. Emiliano, on the other hand, came to the house dressed in funeral attire, ready to mourn for a woman he barely knew just to be there for her.

"You told me to stay away from Emiliano," Iyanda said.

"I was wrong. I was worried about upsetting your family. Worried about you because I know how people in Emiliano's class mistreat people. I shouldn't have been so hasty. Don't miss out on a chance of happiness, no matter how temporary, because of how others are feeling."

"Nana B said the same thing," Iyanda said, swallowing the lump in her throat.

She stared at her hands. Emiliano not only went out of his way to hire an interpreter for their date, Yesenia also caught him learning sign language with said interpreter. Mason refused to communicate through a piece of paper.

She did miss Emiliano. She missed the sound of his calming, deep voice. The memory of him speaking in her ear, awakening her soul, once again stirred the butterflies within her. The scent of lemongrass as she mapped his body with her fingers and mouth. She squeezed her thighs tightly to control the tingling coming from her center.

Gaiana reached out and touched her hand, her eyes speaking of sincerity. It was time for her to go to work. "I'll let your mother know you're staying with me so she won't be worried."

Iyanda nodded. As much as she didn't agree with Adeyemi at the moment, she didn't want to cause her mother more pain or worry. Gaiana grabbed her messenger bag and helmet. She glanced back at Iyanda and smiled before walking out the door.

CHAPTER 25

Emiliano barged into his mother's bedroom. Quilla sat at her vanity mirror, wrapped in a green, silk kimono. He glared at her reflection. She half-heartedly smiled then went back to the task of pinning her hair up.

"Good afternoon to you too, son," Quilla said. "Have we forgotten how to knock?"

"Are you so vindictive that you have to make others suffer because you can't control me?" Emiliano asked.

Quilla looked to the ceiling for a second then looked back at his reflection. "Yes. Yes, I am."

"Iyanda never did anything to you," he said.

"She was getting in your way. She was clouding your judgement."

"Just like you clouded father's," he shot back.

"Without the moves I made, you wouldn't be standing here all high and mighty. You are no different than me."

"I am nothing like you."

"You are holding my money from me," Quilla said.

"Father left money to me and my sister."

"I worked hard for it."

"Just like you worked hard to get at other people's husbands."

Quilla's eyes narrowed. He was the one smirking now.

"Father was aware of what you were doing," Emiliano said. "You put yourself in this position. No one else did."

Lifting her chin, she turned back to the vanity mirror and once again fussed with her freshly washed hair.

Emiliano turned to leave the room.

"Don't think of going to help them," Quilla warned.

Emiliano scoffed. "I do whatever I damn well please."

"The man will not take any money from you."

Emiliano looked at his mother's reflection. Cold anger still in her eyes but small creases were forming in the corners of her mouth.

"Everyone has a price," Emiliano said.

"If that was the case, don't you think I would have paid the little girl to stay away. Blessing told me about her. She said the little Cove girl was too pure for things like that. So, I had to find another way to get rid of her."

Emiliano made a mental note to speak to Blessing about telling his mother everything.

"I would be willing to have Edward's friend open the store back up," Quilla said.

Emiliano's eyes narrowed. He knew his mother. There would be a string attached.

She placed the last pin in her sleek low bun before walking over to her walk-in-closet, leaving the door open for Emiliano to hear.

"Of course, you stay away from the poor girl," Quilla said.

"And?"

"Pay more attention to Aria. Something big. Not a dating relationship. More of an engagement."

"No way in hell," Emiliano said icily.

"I wonder how long it will be before your little friend's family will starve and won't have a place to stay."

Emiliano clenched his teeth. "Fine," he muttered.

"And also you will give me access to my money."

Quilla emerged from the closet wearing a floor length, red gown. The neck plunged into a vee, exposing a peek of the bottom of her breasts. A split began at her hip and moved until it opened at the bottom of the dress, exposing more leg than a mother should.

Emiliano assumed she was going on a date with Edward. At least for the poor bastard's sake, he hoped she was.

She smiled at him.

"The only way you will get your hands on that money is if you kill me, my sister, or my uncle," Emiliano said.

Quilla's smile waned. With a slight tilt of her head, she studied her son.

Was she weighing her options?

Straightening her head, she shrugged and glided across the room to her shoe closet. "Fine," she said. "I'll wait on my money. One thing about Colombians is we're patient."

She had been weighing her options.

Emiliano felt sick to his stomach. He knew his mother could and would do some underhanded things, but to even consider taking the life of her own children was low even for her.

He turned to leave the room. He silently cursed. He would find a way to help Iyanda, he just hoped it wouldn't be too late.

Sticking her head out of the closet, she said in a singsong tone, "Emiliano."

He paused at the door.

"I know what you think of me, and I wish it wasn't so," Quilla said. "Just remember your madre knows what is best for you. And if you try to screw me on our deal, I will make your little friend wish she had never met you."

Iyanda came from the spare bedroom clutching a small cloth bundle between her hands. Lily Poe and Gaiana were seated on the colorful couches snacking on the freshly baked chin chin and sipping from cool bottles of water.

Inside the bundle were the waist beads Nana B managed to finish days before she died. Iyanda gave it a gentle squeeze, bringing it close to her heart, hoping her grandmother's essence might escape. She walked over to Lily Poe. Giving a last long look at the bundle then handed it over to her.

Lily stared at it sitting in the middle of her palm. She gave Iyanda a small smile then handed her the payment for the beads. With care, she placed the bundle in her purse.

"I'm sorry," Lily Poe said.

Iyanda nodded.

Taking a seat on the couch, Iyanda was careful not to touch the soft fabric of Lily Poe's pink and blue dress. A fashionable woman with a humble woman's attitude, Lily wasn't one to berate anyone for minor offenses against her clothes. Unlike others in Pleasant Heights, she inherited her wealth from hard work and investing in technology. Many tried to look down on her but she reminded them the only reason she bothered them was because she was thick, sexy, and intelligent with a style they tried to imitate.

"How are you?" Lily Poe asked, placing her hand on Iyanda's.

"Fine," Iyanda signed. It wasn't that she didn't trust Lily Poe to keep her secret, but the woman loved to talk and tell stories, and Iyanda wasn't ready for her family to know she was talking again.

"I wish there was something I could do about the store."

Iyanda glanced down at her hands. She did too. She tried to go into her own store, but the landlord hired the local police to watch the building.

"I don't see why our government allows these outsiders or their minions to take over. Aren't they what our ancestors fought to keep out?" Gaiana asked.

Lily Poe shushed her, shaking her head.

For the last twenty years, the foreigner's presence on Igbala soil caused nothing but trouble for the locals. But even worse than them was the natives who chose to forget their roots and bleed their brothers and sisters dry.

Lily Poe smiled sadly at Iyanda. "I hate that you and Emiliano didn't work, I hoped you would. You should have been the one in the Oló Mi announcement not the foreign aje."

Iyanda frowned. 'My Sweetheart' was a government issued bulletin that notified the island of the engagements of the high class. What was Lily Poe talking about?

"You don't know what I'm talking about?" Lily Poe asked.

Iyanda shook her head.

Lily Poe glanced at Gaiana whose curiosity was piqued as well. She bit her bottom lip and brushed a lock of her full, shoulder-length hair behind her ear.

"Emiliano." Lily Poe swallowed. "Emiliano is engaged to Aria Riviera."

The world slowed. Iyanda wasn't sure if she heard correctly. She made the sign for engaged.

Lily Poe nodded.

Her heart became heavy. She jerked away from Gaiana's touch.

The air was becoming too thick to breathe. She rushed out to the screened-in deck. It burned her chest with each breath of fresh air she sucked in. Hot tears rolled down her cheeks. Her legs were wobbly like cooked noodles.

What had she done? She refused to listen to the Ancestors and now her family was broken.

Her body shook from her heart-rending silent sobs.

She had to forget Emiliano. Forget his smile. His touch. She had isolated herself from her mother over a marriage she determined wasn't going to happen.

Emiliano's face appeared in the floorboards. She squeezed her eyes tight. He wasn't allowed in her thoughts anymore.

She opened her eyes, scanning the boards for any sign of him. The image was gone.

She fell to her knees. With open palms she looked to the ceiling. She opened her mouth to call out. But to who? Who would listen to her now?

CHAPTER 26

Mason watched Iyanda sweep hair clippings into a dustpan then dump them into a nearby trash can. He stared her down as she walked by for the tenth time without eye contact. For three days he sat on the tacky colored beaded couch, reading outdated fashion magazines, listening to chatty women, hoping she would notice him. And for three days she ignored him.

Stubborn, like the old woman had been. A trait he hated about Igbalaian women. She sprayed the display case containing his mother's special shampoo then wiped the glass in a circular motion.

His mother had been gracious to allow Iyanda to work in one of her hair salons to make some extra money. But she didn't have to work. He could make it so she would never have to work again. But only if she was obedient.

Her family's business was closed and still, she held her head high.

He would train her soon enough.

"She walks around here as if she is a queen and not a poor cripple," one of the stylists commented to their client.

"I hear that all the women in the family are like that. It's rumored they are royalty or the descendants of General Boaventura."

"If they are, they are poor now and need to remember that. My boss's handsome son keeps coming in here every day, and she ignores him."

Mason sat straighter at hearing the hairdresser praising him.

"Is she blind too?" the customer asked in a shrill voice.

The women laughed at this.

Iyanda leaned the broom and dustpan against the wall then walked to the back of the store, avoiding eye contact with everyone. Mason followed close behind.

He found her tossing wet towels into the dryer. She still had her nicely shaped frame from high school. Her hips filled out a little since then but she maintained her tiny waist with the beads she wore. Her breasts were too saggy for his taste but once they were married, she would get a breast lift if she wanted to keep him.

After starting the dryer, she turned and looked at him. She raised a brow as if not surprised to see him again.

He fumed. He would definitely teach her to be on her toes.

"We're going to lunch?" he said.

She shook her head then moved her hands.

Mason rolled his eyes. When she was about sixteen, she stopped speaking, which was fine with him. He preferred a girl who couldn't speak. But it gave her no excuse to act as if he needed to learn her strange hand language.

He repeated his statement, this time louder.

She pulled out a pad of paper and pencil from her apron.

He tensed.

She scribbled something on the paper then passed it to him.

He stared at the markings. The room became warm.

He couldn't read what was written. The only ones who knew his secret were his mother and the head of the school. His teachers stopped calling on him to read when he reached sixth grade under threat of being fired. His mother paid handsomely to make sure her son passed with excellent grades without his weakness being revealed.

Wanting to play it cool, he passed the notebook back to her then gripped her wrists, forcing her to follow him. She pulled away and frowned at him. When she tried to give him the pad again, he pushed it away. She stared at the white paper. Scribbling something on it, she then showed it to him.

The words were gibberish to him. Heat rose to his face. He slapped the booklet out of her hand causing it to hit the wall before landing on the floor.

Iyanda smirked. She knew. She figured it out.

Mason shoved her causing her to stumble back against the dryer. Her wide eyes looked up at him. She was frightened.

Good.

Mason grabbed her arm, squeezing it hard, and clenched his other hand in a fist. He needed her to know he was not to be made a fool of. She made him look stupid more than once with her running around and more than likely screwing the Petty boy. She was the cause of him being locked up. She rejected his marriage proposal. And then embarrassed him in front of the Council by dancing with Petty.

He struck her to the ground with his fist. His knuckles thirsting for more, broke through her barricade she formed with her hands.

She didn't scream. He wanted her to scream.

Damnit, why won't she scream?

The rage burned within him. She needed to understand that her silence annoyed him. She was being punished. Was she too stupid to understand that?

"Stupid bitch!" he shouted in Yoruba. "You can make those hand gestures but I know you can talk. Speak!"

He assaulted her face more. It was becoming gummy beneath his knuckles. Releasing her arm, she instantly curled into a ball, protecting her head with her hands.

Mason didn't want her face anymore. He wanted to make her suffer.

"You always thought you were better than me. Better in school. But you are nothing. A poor whore whose own father didn't want her. And now you fuck the Petty boy."

He pulled her up by her collar. "Where is he?" He shook her. "Huh?! Where is your precious Emiliano? You think I want his trash?" He released her, her body collapsing to the floor.

Kneeling down, he flung her onto her back. The left side of her face was bloody and already showing signs of swelling. She tried to move away but was held down with one of his hands. With his other hand, he struggled to undo his pants.

"I will teach you your place." Spittle flew from his mouth. "Your whore of a cousin knows hers, time for you to recognize yours."

Undoing his pants, he reached down to grasp her leg but something sharp attacked his eye. He jumped back, screaming in agony. He couldn't see. Pain coursed through his entire being each time his hand reached for the injured area. It was becoming harder to see. Where did she go?

Iyanda ducked out the back door. She ran, not daring to look back. She knew once Ms. King saw her baby boy on the floor bleeding from his eye, there would be no mercy for her.

She could barely see out of her left eye but it would heal.

His wouldn't.

She was thankful for the sharp rattail comb nearby. It had probably been rolled up in one of the towels and fell to the floor, but now lodged in Mason King's eye.

Hailing a cab, Iyanda jumped in before it came to a complete stop. Her tongue refused to release the words needed to tell the driver her intended destination, swollen from either fear or the attack on her face. She searched her pockets. Her notepad wasn't there. She tried to communicate Gaiana's address.

The driver frowned.

She kept looking back, fearing Ms. King would be coming around the corner with the police in tow.

Iyanda slumped back into the leather chair and closed her eyes. She hated this. If she had just stayed with Emiliano, she would be safely in his arms right now. Her heart broke at the thought of him. She wanted to escape. Not just from Mason but from this world.

Nana B's gentle hand squeezed hers.

"Ma'am, where are you trying to go?" the driver asked. "Don't waste my time."

Iyanda's eyes popped open, her tongue no longer swollen. It tingled with the words. She looked beside her, but the seat was empty. Nana B's touch was gone. Did she imagine it?

"I will call the police," the man said.

Iyanda looked back at him.

"I need to go to 254 Ominira Village," she said, her mouth pooling with saliva and probably blood.

"What did you say?"

Spitting out the window, she repeated the address then sat straight in the chair as the driver turned and drove toward her destination.

* * * * *

Iyanda was thankful Gaiana was not home. More than likely, she was out looking for odd jobs as well.

Iyanda made her way to the bathroom in her bedroom. Turning on the light, she flinched at her reflection.

Wetting a cloth, she gingerly dabbed at her split lip.

Her stomach rolled. Mason once kissed these lips. The dabbing became wiping, which turned into scrubbing. The pain was too much but leaving ancient traces of him on her lips was unbearable.

He was going to rape her. He was always demanding and a bit forceful during their relationship but never had he violently forced her.

Blood smeared across her cheek.

She dropped the cloth.

Her face was hot. She leaned on the sink, closer to her reflection. It reminded her of stories of people being half monster and half human.

Now she understood.

Those people weren't the monsters, the ones around them were. They were ordinary people, trying to live, striving to be what they were created to be. Others, out of envy, wanted that part of them. Beat it out of them with words, with hands, take the very innocence and essence of who these people were and leave them half whole. They only became whole again once they found love or took their own life.

Neither was an option for her.

Biting down on her bottom lip, she rocked.

"You are not a monster."

Iyanda turned to the familiar voice. Nana B's face was expressionless.

"I know, Nana B," Iyanda said softly.

"Then stop thinking it," her grandmother demanded. "He took nothing from you."

A tear fell down Iyanda's cheek. She took a shaky breath. "He hurt me. They all hurt me."

"And why should that stop you?" Nana B's eyes narrowed.

"He tried to rape me, Iya Mama Mi!" she sobbed. Iyanda slid to the floor. Bringing her knees to her chest, she buried her head and wept.

Seconds passed before Iyanda looked up to see if Nana B was gone. She wasn't. Her eyes were the soft eyes Iyanda was familiar with.

"But he didn't, did he?" Nana B asked. "He bruised your face, but he did not take away your power. You fought back. You have always fought back. Like I did. Like your grandfather did. You come from a people who have always fought back, who held on to who they were. Even when there were times that seemed they were losing, they fought back."

Nana B touched her chest. "We have never given up. When others around us have, our family has always remained strong."

"How can I be strong?" Iyanda sniffled. "My mother has thrown me out."

"You left."

"They've closed the stores."

"They will open."

"Emiliano used me."

Nana B stared at Iyanda. "Is that what you really believe?"

Iyanda frowned at the simple question but then paused. "No." she said softly. "I guess I don't."

Nana B extended her hand to Iyanda.

Iyanda stood, staring into her eyes.

"I can no longer be here with you physically," Nana B said, "but I'm never far from you. Your family needs you. He needs you just like you need him. You allowed your handicap to live for you, enslave you to its will. Do not let it do that any longer. Take back your power. Stop giving it away."

Iyanda turned toward the mirror. Staring at her reflection, she looked past the split lip and swollen eye. She could hear the beating of Batá drums. But they weren't coming from outside. She closed her eyes. They were within. Her heart came in sync with the percussion. Her head roll from side to side. The beat became faster. Her shoulders bounced. Faster. She swayed. Faster. Her hips begged to join the dance.

Nana B's words coursed through her. Mason did not take away her power. Neither had her father. Her mother. Not even Emiliano. She had given it to them.

The drums called. Their sound was louder. The dust from under her Ancestors' feet choked her lungs. Their feet demanding the Earth to awaken and share her power against their enemies.

She inhaled.

The healing abilities of Osain had always been natural to her. The herbs and plants were part of her. Mason wanted to take that away and her mother was willing to let it happen. Her brother had encouraged her gift but he abandoned her, leaving her without a voice.

No more.

She opened her eyes. The drums had stopped. Nana B was gone. Her voice remained. Iyanda stared at her reflection.

First, she would heal herself, then get back to preparation to be an onisegun. She undid the halo braid breaking the promise her mother had made to Mason's family. When she saw them again, there would be no wedding.

Banging from the front room startled her. She rushed out to the living to see a figure pounding on the door. She answered it to find Emiliano on the other side, breathless.

His eyes widened then grew hot with rage. He reached for her face but she pulled away.

"Who did this to you?" he asked.

"It doesn't matter now. Why are you here?"

He stammered to find the words. "I-My sister. Yesenia needs you. She's sick. Very sick."

Iyanda's heart dropped. She could still see the young girl's face full of sunshine and hope smiling at her.

"She needs your help," he said.

She studied him. She would deal with him later. Rushing to her room, she grabbed her bag of herbs and other instruments she would need and followed him to his car.

CHAPTER 27

Iyanda shifted under the death glare from Quilla. She pressed closer to Emiliano, hoping his presence would prevent her from darting away. Her heart pained at the sound of Yesenia's shallow breathing. The young girl's usual rich, terra-cotta skin was now ashen, near depletion of life.

"Why is she here?" Quilla hovered protectively over the motionless Yesenia.

"She's here to help." Emiliano escorted Iyanda over to the bedside.

"Get her out of here," Quilla's words hissed through her teeth. "I don't need any African witch helping my daughter."

"Have those doctors you paid for accomplished anything?" Emiliano glared at Quilla. "No, they haven't. Iyanda is not a witch. She can help."

Emiliano looked down at Iyanda. His expression hard and sure of his words, his eyes pleaded for her to prove him right.

Iyanda stared down at Yesenia. Taking a breath, she stepped closer and felt the sweat drenched forehead of the sleeping face. She was cold. Iyanda's brow furrowed. She pulled back the sheets and covers.

"What is she doing? We have to keep Yesenia warm," Quilla said, held back by Edward.

Iyanda ignored Quilla. Continuing her examination of Yesenia's body carefully, she found what she was looking for. A large red, pus-filled welt on the back of the upper thigh.

She grabbed a piece of paper and pen, quickly scribbled her diagnosis, and handed it to Emiliano. During the car ride, Iyanda made him promise not to tell anyone she could speak until the time was right. Emiliano didn't understand why but he agreed to it.

"What did she say?" Quilla asked.

"It's apani ọmọ," Emiliano read. The paper slipped from his fingers, his mouth open. His eyes seemed to stare past her and his sister. "Child killer."

Quilla gasped. Aria backed far from the bed.

"How is that possible?" Quilla asked. "Apani ọmọ has not been on the island for at least thirteen years. The doctors didn't even find it on her."

"Did they search her body?" Emiliano asked.

"Of course not! No one would expect a girl like Yesenia to get such a lowly disease," Quilla answered.

"It's a poor person's sickness. How did it get here?" Aria asked.

Emiliano's eyes narrowed. "Are you serious? A poor person's sickness? Plenty of people in Pleasant Heights died from this thing. You would've known that if you had been here."

"My sister died from it," Aria snapped.

"Then what made you think it was okay to say anything so ignorant?" Emiliano spat.

"Can she help her?" Quilla asked.

Iyanda nodded.

"She can," Emiliano said, "but you have to stay out of her way. And we've got to tell the doctors."

"That has nothing to do with us. We don't need this getting out." Quilla lifted her chin.

Emiliano's lip curled in disgust. "Lives are at stake and you're worried about appearances? Please keep showing me who you are."

Quilla stormed out of the room with Edward close on her heels.

Aria took a step closer toward Iyanda and Emiliano, her cold eyes watching their every movement.

Iyanda side-eyed Aria then quickly focused back on Yesenia. Emiliano needed to leave the room.

Opening her medicine tote, she pulled out a mortar and pestle and a bag of stems with pungent white flowers still connected. These were the first herbs Dunni had taught the class about, warning them to always have a fresh supply in case the infectious disease ever returned to the island. Opening the pouch, she pinched a few of the flowers and stems, and placed them into the mortar.

"Iyanda," Emiliano said.

Iyanda used the pestle to mash and grind the herbs. She had to ignore him so she could calm her fluttering heart.

Leaning over, he brushed her knee with his fingertips.

She shivered. She turned her knees away from him, keeping her focus on the medicine she was preparing.

"She can't hear you," Aria said. She walked over to Emiliano, her heels stomping on the carpeted floor. She grabbed his arm and tugged. "We need to plan our wedding."

"It's getting late." Emiliano snatched away.

Iyanda shifted under his piercing gaze. She didn't dare look under threat of angering Aria more.

After a moment, he left the room with Aria close on his heels.

Iyanda breathed a sigh of relief.

* * * * *

"Please stop following me." Emiliano stormed into his father's study with Aria close behind.

"How dare you bring her here!" Aria slammed the door behind her. She folded her arms across her chest. Her eyes, usually so unemotional, showed a spark of hurt.

"I bring whomever I choose. And right now, I'm bringing her for my sister." He plopped down in the desk chair.

"No, you can't! I am your fiancée. I will be your wife soon and you have to show me the respect I deserve."

Emiliano scoffed. "Trust me, I will. My mother gets hers and you will get yours."

Aria looked at him softly, pouting her mocha glossed lips. "I want to be with you, Emiliano. I always have. I just want to make sure I'm not entering into a marriage like the one my mother had with my father."

He smirked, amused by her confession. "And yet you're the one that cheated on me."

Aria threw up her hands. "Are you serious! That was so long ago."

"It was nine months ago."

She came around the desk and knelt down before him. She looked up at him with pleading eyes. She always did this. And he always gave in.

Not this time.

"I was stupid. I was caressed by the words he said. I didn't realize what I had with you. I want to make this right." Her hand slid up his leg to his belt buckle, her expert fingers loosening it. "I want to spend the rest of my life with you."

She undid the button. "I will be a perfect wife." The zipper. "All I ask is that you never see the deaf girl again."

Emiliano gripped her wrist and leaned in close. Her bright eyes beckoning him to sit back and fall under her spell. She thought he was giving in.

"You made two mistakes. She's mute, not deaf." He flung her hand away from him. "And I will never stop seeing her. Even when she will no longer see me, I will never give you the love and affection you think you deserve. I will loathe you for the rest of our marriage. I will have you followed everywhere. Everything will be reported back to me. And the moment I catch a whisper of infidelity, I will divorce you and make it so that we've never been married."

Aria's eyes widened. "Why?"

"You and my mother have tied my hands. I'm being forced into an arrangement that I strongly disagree with. But I can make this easier for both of us where neither of us get hurt," Emiliano said.

She cast her gaze down. "Wha-What is that?"

"Call off the engagement."

A small smile formed in the corner of her mouth, a glint of envy in her eyes. "No."

She stood and sashayed toward the door.

"So you're willing to be miserable with me?" he asked.

She paused at the door then turned around. "If it will keep you out of her arms, I'm willing to go to hell tied to your hip. You can have me watched until I slip up and take a lover, but the moment I have even a small feeling that you might still be seeing her, I will not only divorce you, I will publicly humiliate your family and have her arrested."

Emiliano shifted in his chair. Infidelity was a crime on Igbala. If reported, it would be a life sentence for the offender, usually the woman.

To publicly humiliate his family wouldn't bother his family's business, considering they dealt with others on different continents, but it would be an issue for his little sister. All possible prospects of marriage would be gone because of the shame connected to her last name. He couldn't do that to both of the women he loved dearly.

Aria smirked then opened the office door and left.

Emiliano listened as her footsteps faded down the hall. He rubbed the back of his neck. His jaw clenched. "Damnit!" he muttered.

He could easily take Iyanda for his wife, but it could possibly leave her family without their business. He needed to tell her about his mother being the reason the stores were closed. What would it solve?

Maybe she wouldn't blame him. He could take care of her and her family and open up new businesses for them. But what if she hated him for being the cause of their misery?

He glanced at the desk phone. He needed to call the Chief Medical Officer. He sighed then dialed the number. After speaking to the Head Physician and being informed the necessary precautions would be taken, he hung up the phone and leaned back in the chair. He closed his eyes.

His throat tightened. Iyanda was in the next room and yet he couldn't touch her.

A light knock on the door brought him out of his thoughts. Gaiana stood at the threshold, her face long with distress.

"Gaiana?" Emiliano's brow raised.

"Tambara is ill."

CHAPTER 28

Iyanda placed the moistened herbs on Yesenia's tongue then helped the young girl to swallow. She waited. Seeing no immediate adverse effect, she began on the compress. She had to focus on the task at hand but her mind refused. Seeing Aria follow Emiliano out the door worsened the heaviness she had in her chest.

During the drive, he tried to explain that the three days they shared meant something to him. She wanted to believe his sweet words but the knowledge of his engagement and Aria's alleged pregnancy made everything he said sound like a well-rehearsed lie. Not wanting to hear anymore, she asked him to stop speaking to her for the rest of the ride.

She needed to forget him. Just heal his sister and leave the island. Maybe go to Nigeria and find her brother. There was nothing else keeping her on the island. Her grandmother was gone, and her mother was selling her off to the highest bidder. She needed someone whose love she knew was stable and constant.

The sound of rushing feet startled her. She stood as Emiliano and Gaiana entered the room. Iyanda studied their faces. Something was wrong.

"Tambara is ill," Gaiana said.

"What do you mean?" Iyanda asked.

"She has a fever yet she is cold. She's barely breathing. Her skin is paler than usual. She had complained of stomach pains a couple of days ago but I thought it was just her cycle. She fainted while helping your aunt at home. They took her to the hospital, but the doctors told your mother and Aunt Ola there was nothing wrong and sent them home. Your mother asked me to get you. When I got home, you weren't there. I took a chance you might be here." Gaiana glanced at Emiliano. "With him."

Another person. Was the epidemic starting again?

"What's wrong with Miss Yesenia?" Gaiana asked.

"Same thing that might be wrong with my cousin." Iyanda reached into her bag and gave the pouch of flowers and stems to Gaiana. "Tell my mother and aunt to take a teaspoon of this and mash it, stick it on Tambara's tongue, and make her swallow it. Then make a compress. Place it on the welt they'll find on her body. She must stay wrapped in blankets and isolated. Do not open the windows or leave the door open."

Gaiana clutched the herbs tight to her chest and turned to leave.

311

Iyanda touched her arm. "Please tell my mother I love her."

Gaiana nodded then turned and left.

Iyanda stared at the sleeping Yesenia. She sucked her teeth.

"What's the matter?" Emiliano asked.

"I need more of the herb," she said. "I gave the last of it to Gaiana."

"Where is it? I'll have someone bring it for you."

She looked at him. "There are only two places where I keep this. One of them, I don't have access to." She looked away and sighed in frustration. "The other place is in the garden."

"You can't go there," Emiliano said. "I just told the CMO. They're going to start placing an island wide quarantine."

"It's not going to take long to get there." Iyanda picked up her shoulder bag. Giving a final glance at Yesenia, she made her way toward the room door.

He grabbed her wrist. "In a car, it doesn't. You have no other way to get back. Even if you manage to find a bus or taxi that is willing to take you, the risk is too great."

"Then I'll walk."

"If you're caught. They will kill you."

Iyanda swallowed hard. With each quarantine, the government caused a state of fear among the people. To prevent a riot, the government decided to kill anyone trying to travel outside of their city and the doctors agreed not to treat them.

Iyanda could stay and just monitor Yesenia, but the teen's chance of survival would be too low for comfort. Very few managed to make it out of alive once they contracted apani ọmọ and those that did had very weakened immune systems without the proper treatment. No. Yesenia needed the medicine or she would die.

"Let me take you," Emiliano said.

"No." She pulled away and turned toward the door.

"Do it for my sister."

Iyanda topped in her tracks.

"If you're not going to do it for me," Emiliano said, "then do it for her."

A sinking feeling filled Iyanda's stomach. She didn't want to be alone with Emiliano, but Yesenia needed the herbs. She chewed her bottom lip. If she didn't go, the girl could die. But to be alone with him. His deep-set eyes studied her intensely. She missed the feel of his touch, the way his body enveloped hers, the way her lips tingled after he kissed her.

She shook her head, refusing to succumb to the desire growing between her legs.

"Fine," she said, voiding her voice of emotion. "But no talking."

* * * * *

They sped through Pleasant Heights, Emiliano's locs dancing wildly in the wind. Iyanda's nails clenched the seat as her other hand tried to hold down the headwrap she fashioned from her blouse. Before the car came to a complete stop in front of Cynthia Boaventura's house, Iyanda hopped out and rushed to the backyard gate.

She squinted against the dimly lit garden wishing she had a flashlight. Searching among the tall bushes, she groaned. This was going to take all night. "What's wrong?" Emiliano came and stood beside her.

"It's too dark. It's going to take forever."

He pulled out his cell phone and turned on the flashlight. She gave a small smile of appreciation. Nodding, he motioned for her to lead the way.

They inspected each raised garden bed, searching among the various long grasses and herbs. After half an hour, they finally found it.

Iyanda pulled the entire plant out of the ground, making sure to cut the flowers and leaves from the root. She mumbled a prayer of thanks before wrapping the precious herb into a dampened cloth and sticking it into her bag. She stood and hurried back to the car, Emiliano close on her heels.

"What were you saying?" Emiliano asked.

"I was thanking the Earth for her healing medicine."

As they reached the top of the small incline, they slowed on seeing Cynthia Boaventura standing at the car.

"Did you get what was needed?" Cynthia asked with concern. Even in her golden nightgown and wrap, she carried herself as royalty.

Iyanda greeted her. The woman smiled and placed her hand on Iyanda's head before Emiliano helped the latter back on to her feet.

"What is the matter?" Emiliano asked.

"The roads are blocked. It will be too dangerous to drive back," the older woman said.

Emiliano cursed.

Iyanda looked toward the road, her head spinning. How were they going to get back to the Petty household? Yesenia needed the medicine tonight. The girl's skin had also been strangely flushed and her pupils were enlarged when they left, unusual for the apani ọmọ.

Iyanda had seen these symptoms with one of Dunni's patients. She didn't want to believe anyone would poison the young girl, but to be sure, she had placed a few hairy, brown tubers within her bag.

"We'll have to take our chances." Emiliano rushed to the car with Iyanda hot on his heels.

"Wait," Cynthia said in English.

"My sister will die!"

"How will *your* death help her?"

Emiliano leaned against the car, his breathing unsteady. Iyanda placed her hand on his arm. He gave it a squeeze. Her heart broke for him. Iyanda worried about Yesenia, but she knew the emotional turmoil Emiliano was going through was no comparison.

"I do have a solution," Cynthia said.

Iyanda and Emiliano gave the older woman their full attention.

"How is your horseback riding?" she asked.

As if on cue, the moon emerged from its hiding spot behind the clouds at the sound of approaching hooves. The salt-and-pepper haired butler rode on a tall chestnut-colored horse while leading a black one.

"I haven't ridden a horse in years." Emiliano stroked the satiny muzzle.

Iyanda took a step back. She had seen tourists ride the beasts but never cared to be near them.

The older man climbed down and held the reins steady for Emiliano.

Putting his foot in the stirrup and holding the horn of the saddle, Emiliano lifted himself up onto the tall horse.

Iyanda looked from the older man to Emiliano. She shook her head and took another step back.

"Trust me," Emiliano said.

She stared into his gentle eyes. If it hadn't been for him, she wouldn't have made it to the garden before being stopped. But he was also the cause of her heart being splintered in two.

Iyanda looked at the black horse. Its large eyes stared at her, dissecting her being. She clutched her bag strap. Yesenia needed the medicine.

Taking a deep breath, she edged closer to the horse.

The older man interlocked his fingers then stooped down before Iyanda. Gripping the saddle horn and placing one foot in his hands, she lifted on to the large beast. Handing her the reins, the butler's cloudy gray eyes searched for the reassurance she was okay.

She gave a slight nod, allowing him to release total control of the animal to Iyanda.

"She is docile," Cynthia reassured, referring to the black horse. "She'll follow her brother wherever he goes. There is a path in the jungle the horses are familiar with. Try to stay on it and out of sight."

"What do we do when we come to the end?" Emiliano gave the reins a tug to control the restless animal. "It only stretches so far before the rest of Igbala becomes villages and cities."

Cynthia looked over the trusted worker. "Call Tiago and have him meet them at the fork." She looked back at Emiliano and Iyanda. "He will guide you the rest of the way. Listen to him. He knows how to survive against the authorities."

"You mean, break the law," Emiliano said.

Cynthia smirked. "It's genetic. Leave. It's getting late and you need to get back before daylight."

Emiliano turned his horse toward the jungle.

Iyanda took a last look at Cynthia and the older man. She knew if they were caught and killed, the elderly woman and those who had helped them could be executed or imprisoned for life. Their families would lose everything. It felt wrong to put their lives at risk.

"I'm a Boaventura. Death fears us," Cynthia said, as if reading her mind.

The woman's eyes were unreadable and stern, like Nana B's, but Iyanda swore she saw a ghost of a smile in the corner of her mouth.

Nodding at the elders, Iyanda hesitantly turned her horse to follow Emiliano.

The jungle was pitch black. How were they supposed to see the path? Iyanda's hands gripped the reins tight. This was not a good idea.

Emiliano's horse took the first step into the jungle. Small ground lights illuminated the path. They smiled at each other, both relaxing at the prospect of the mission being completed.

CHAPTER 29

An hour passed and Iyanda still wouldn't talk to him. Emiliano had tried to speak to her earlier but Iyanda had rendered him into petulant silence.

She shifted in the saddle again before saying, "We have to stop."

Turning the horse, he made his way back to her. "We can't stop. We have to meet Tiago. We have to be back before daylight."

"I know. But I'm sore and tired." Iyanda moved from side to side, back and forth on the horse.

"What are you doing?" Emiliano asked.

"Trying to get off."

Before he could move quick enough to help her down, she lost her balance and fell on her rear end. Stifling a laugh, Emiliano quickly dismounted his horse and rushed over to her. Taking her arm, he helped her to her feet.

"Thank you." Iyanda rubbed her bruised posterior.

"I guess we can lead the horses," Emiliano suggested.

Taking hold of both reins, Emiliano led the horses on the path as Iyanda walked gingerly beside him.

Seeing her limp, he asked, "Do you need help?"

Shaking her head, she kept hobbling.

Emiliano slowed his pace amused by her stubbornness. It was cute on her. If her pain got worse, he knew he would have to carry her the rest of the way, even if she verbally objected to it.

Iyanda rubbed her arms as a slight breeze blew by.

"Cold?" Emiliano asked.

"No." Iyanda kept walking, bringing her shoulders in more.

Emiliano wrapped his free arm around her shoulder and pulled her closer to him, never disturbing his walking pace. Her fragrance, a mixture of palm oil, shea butter, and licorice, quickened his pulse.

The peaceful song of the crickets and jungle frogs relaxed her shoulders. He slowly caressed her arm, the burning memory of her soft, willing skin trembling beneath his fingers. If they weren't restricted on time, he would take her in the forest, inhaling and tasting again.

"When is the date for your marriage?" Iyanda's asked.

"Didn't plan on a date," Emiliano stated.

"So, you're just playing with the woman?" Her shoulders tensed again.

"I don't..." How could he tell her the engagement was not his idea but was his mother's way of punishing him for not bending to her rules? The knowledge of knowing she was the cause of the arrangement would bring guilt to her tender heart and possibly push her away from him forever. He couldn't have that.

"I doubt Aria is the type of woman to play with," he said. "I'm just leaving the arrangements to her and my mother."

"I'm really happy for you," she said.

Emiliano scoffed. "Don't be."

"Most people say thank you."

The flame rose higher. Not only was her voice pure and sweet but also made one feel as if they were being lulled to sleep by the soothing song it promised.

"You insult me with your happiness," Emiliano said.

"Why?"

"Because I'm not happy. She's not the one I want to be with."

Iyanda moved away, trying to walk ahead but he quickly caught up with her.

"I'm not doing this," Iyanda muttered.

He grabbed her forearm, forcing her to stop and face him. He looked longingly into her eyes. "I'm not leaving this jungle until you know. I would rather be with you over any woman any day. Since we met, I had to force myself to focus on other things, only to lose in the end."

"Pretty words to open my legs one more time," Iyanda said.

A naughty smile curled Emiliano's lip. He wanted her more than once. "I don't want you to open your legs without really wanting to. I have never forced you and I never will. Just hear me."

"Hear what, more lies?"

"Iyanda."

She pulled her arm out of his grasp. The eyes that were once so passionate and eager were now so cold and distant to him. She was pulling back. He couldn't let her go back down that path.

Emiliano reached down, claiming her mouth, forcing her lips to part. Her hands went to his chest, trying to push him away. Wrapping his hand on her waist, he brought her closer. His lips played and sucked on hers, his tongue darting in and out of her mouth, promising more, if she would just yield.

She did. For a moment.

Iyanda pushed him away and glared up at him, her reddened face and swollen mouth the only signs of her previous excitement.

"I will not be anyone's second choice anymore!" Iyanda's chest heaved up and down. Her coloring came back but her eyes were still moist. "You are getting married to another. Even if she's not the one to make you happy, keep your promise."

She averted her eyes, tears glistening her cheeks. "I've seen too many women broken over being the mistress or not the cherished wife. My father left because he wouldn't care for my mother. He couldn't even love his own children. Be better than that."

The last words racked her delicate body into uncontrollable sobs.

"Iyanda," Emiliano said in a gentle tone, "I can't fix what your father has done, but I can promise to always cherish you and stay true to you."

Iyanda peered at him from the corner of her eyes. "No, you won't."

Wrapping her arms around her stomach she brushed past him, rushing along the path.

They walked for another thirty minutes, the only sound between them was a thin breeze whistling through the trees. Iyanda led the way as Emiliano guided the horses, the weight in his chest dragging his feet. Her tears clung to his soul, each word she spoke pierced through his heart. He wanted to take away her pain. But would she let him? Did she see him as she saw Mason or her father? Before he could ask her, they finally came to the designated fork in the road.

Emiliano paused. The crickets and frogs had stopped their songs. His father used to say the only beings smart enough to still listen for danger were animals.

"Iyanda," Emiliano whispered. "Stop."

Iyanda stopped. She glanced back.

"You hear that?" Emiliano whispered."

She slowly backed up to him. "What's wrong?" she whispered.

"I don't know," he whispered back.

Dragging her to the side of her horse, he hoisted her onto the saddle. Once she was steady, he handed her the reins.

"Listen to me," he said. "If I tell you to ride, you ride."

"What are you going to do? You can't defend yourself."

"I kicked Mason's ass, didn't I?"

It brought a small smile to Iyanda's lips. "Mason didn't have a gun."

"I can stall them. I need you to help my sister." Emiliano looked up at her with pleading eyes.

"If it's soldiers, you could die."

"I'm a willing sacrifice," he said, his stomach clenched in a cold knot.

"Emiliano, I-."

He put a finger to his mouth.

Turning, he crept to the meeting spot. "Tiago," he called out in a low voice.

He listened. Nothing. He called out again, this time a little louder.

Still nothing.

He glanced back at Iyanda. She was safe and still waiting.

He focused on the bushes and overgrowth of the jungle. It was pitch black within.

"Tiago."

An owl hoot startled Emiliano. Then there was rustling. He braced for a fight.

The rustling got closer.

He put his fists closer to his face. Hopefully the hidden figure didn't have a gun or teeth.

A short, pygmy of a man emerged from the bushes. He wore a black military style uniform and had tribal markings on his face. He looked Emiliano up and down then scoffed, an amused smile on his lips.

"What were you going to do with those, pretty boy?" The man indicated to Emiliano's raised fists, his voice gruff and deep.

Emiliano righted himself and slowly put his hands down to his side, unclenching them.

The short man raised a brow.

"You must be Tiago," Emiliano said. "We thought something had happened."

"It did. I went and took a piss. Next time don't be late," Tiago commanded. "Let's go."

Emiliano rushed back to Iyanda and the horses.

"Leave the horses," Tiago said.

They gave him an inquisitive look.

"They'll be too loud," he said.

Emiliano helped Iyanda down then tied the horses to a nearby tree. He gave them a final rub. It felt wrong to leave the beautiful animals alone in the jungle. He hoped someone would be along shortly to get them.

Taking hold of Iyanda's hand, they followed Tiago into the darkness of the jungle.

* * * * *

Iyanda and Emiliano followed Tiago on a path that took them to the border of Bunkum and Pleasant Heights. It was a small community consisting of laborers employed by many of the Pleasant Heights households and no place to hide.

Tiago led them down the moonlit paved dirt road, keeping close to the sparsely wooded area, distancing themselves from the people traveling further ahead.

"Guess everyone has a guide tonight," Emiliano said in a low voice.

"It's rumored Talaka Village doesn't have the sickness," Tiago responded. "Many are trying to get there."

"Isn't that endangering others?" Emiliano asked.

"Not everyone has the luxury of a fancy doctor or a beautiful healer like you do, pretty boy."

Within seconds of those last words, armed guards emerged from the woods ahead of the other group, aiming and firing without hesitation.

Tiago led Iyanda and Emiliano into the jungle, zigzagging among the trees. The armed men shouted for them to stop while firing at the three runners.

Iyanda looked back in the darkness and saw the outline of the soldiers. She stumbled only to have Emiliano quickly help her to her feet. The thought of her mother finding out her daughter broke the law ran through her mind. Adeyemi would be heartbroken. With Nana B gone, no word from her son in years, and her daughter dead and labeled as a criminal, her mother would have no reason to keep going. And what of Yesenia? Even if the girl survived the disease, she still had someone in that house trying to poison her. *I have to survive, there are too many that need me,* she thought.

Emiliano grabbed her hand, forcing her to catch up with him.

"In here!" Tiago commanded, clearing away vines.

Iyanda and Emiliano ducked inside an abandoned house with Tiago close behind. Lifting a trapdoor, he motioned for them to get inside. Climbing into the empty, dark root cellar. darkness, they pressed against the corners as Tiago closed the hatch behind him. He motioned for them to stay down in the shadows.

Iyanda's heart raced, threatening to explode in her chest. Her lungs begged for more than just the small gulps of air she breathed. She shut her eyes, trying to close out the last screams and cries of the executed people from her mind. The ugliness of Igbala. The part the tourists pay not to see. She bit down on her tongue when she heard the squeak of the house door. Emiliano gripped her hand.

Boots scraped the rough floor above them. She flinched, her body screaming for her to run and find a better hiding spot. Emiliano pushed her behind him. Her heart thudded in unison with the heavy feet.

The guards searched the small house then left, except one. He paused above their head.

"Let's go, Ropo," one of the men ordered.

The boots were silent.

A chill ran through her. She envisioned the man named Ropo studying the floor, feeling their presence beneath his feet.

Ropo's name was called again.

His boots shifted.

She hid her face in Emiliano's shoulder. The last words she said to her mother played over and over in her head. If the orishas would allow her to live, she would ask for her mother's forgiveness.

The man roared Ropo's name. The boots stomped out of the house.

The three escapees breathed a sigh of relief.

"We'll wait a minute to make sure they've left," Tiago whispered. He posted himself at the trapdoor entrance.

Emiliano turned to her, sandwiching her face between his hands. "Are you okay, ife mi?"

Her heart fluttered at the sound of the pet name. She slid away from his touch and walked past him. "I'm fine."

"What the hell is the problem?" Emiliano's narrow eyes focused on her. "Why do you keep pushing me away?"

"You're engaged," she said in a timid voice.

"So are you. Did it stop you from staying with me?"

Iyanda's cheeks reddened when Tiago side-eyed her. "They need you more than I do," she said.

"Who? My sister? What does she-."

"No!" She leaned in. "Your child," she said in a hushed voice. She shifted when he tilted his head and stared at her.

"What child?" he asked, his eyes glancing at her stomach.

She frowned. "Aria! Aria is pregnant with your child."

Emiliano blinked rapidly, mouthing the word pregnant over and over.

"She told me the day she came to the apartment," Iyanda explained.

"She came to the apartment? Is that why you left? When I didn't see a note or get a call, I thought you felt bad for being with me."

"Whether I felt bad or not doesn't matter," Iyanda said. "What matters is that you are to be a good dad to your child."

Emiliano crossed his arms across his chest. "Aria is not pregnant."

"She's not?" Iyanda asked, rapidly blinking.

"If she is, it isn't mine."

"But she said-." Heat rose to Iyanda's face. Had she been stupid enough to listen to Aria?

"I haven't been with her since she ran off with that guy."

"That means..." She stared at the ground, warm tears of shame clouding her vision.

"That you fell for the oldest move in the book," Tiago chimed in.

Iyanda scowled at the rounded man.

Emiliano grabbed her shoulders. "Is this what this whole thing is about? Iyanda, even if she was pregnant with my child, I would not stop fighting for us. You are who I want to be with."

A wave of wholeness washed over her. She wanted to bury herself in his arms and never leave, daring the world to separate them again.

She touched one of his hands and sadly looked at him. "And you are who I want to be with but we can't. I have a duty to my family."

"You're not mute anymore. Tell them what you want."

"My lack of words was not the only thing bringing shame to my family. My father left us without a name. He told many people I wasn't his."

Taking one of his hands, she placed a kiss upon his knuckles then did the same with the other before releasing them. She gave him a wistful look.

"Give her your best, like you did for me," she said, her voice breaking.

Emiliano's averted eyes pinched at her already grieving heart.

"Let's go, lovebirds," Tiago said, pushing the trapdoor up.

* * * * *

Iyanda quietly exhaled at the sight of the Petty mansion. There had been too many close calls during the night to last her a lifetime. Thankfully two households, one of them supplying salve for her eye and lips, gave them shelter and water until the patrol passed then they had to quickly leave.

"Thank you," Emiliano said to Tiago. He reached into his pocket and pulled out a small fold of large money denominations. Sliding a bill off the pile, he tried to hand it to the hooded-eyed short man.

Tiago backed away from the money. "I don't want your money, pretty boy."

Tiago grabbed Iyanda's hand. She bent down and looked him in the eye.

"It won't come back if you don't want it to," he said.

Iyanda frowned.

"She expects to see you complete what you started." With those final words, Tiago disappeared back into the dark woods behind the Petty household.

Iyanda gripped the strap of her bag, her grandmother coming to her mind. She had already decided no one else would take her words. She was going to heal Yesenia then leave. What could he possibly mean by 'complete what she started'?

Emiliano grabbed her hand and began leading her to the house. She pulled away. He looked at her and frowned.

Wringing the strap between her hands, she looked at her feet before looking up at him. "We have to play our parts," she said. "Keep your distance." She rushed past him toward the house, the hollow words bitter on her tongue. The night breeze burned her misty eyes, but she wouldn't look back. She couldn't, even if her heart wanted her to.

CHAPTER 30

Iyanda sighed. Her suspicion about the poisoning had been right. Yesenia now slept peacefully after receiving the tuber and herbs, free of fever. Who would want to harm the innocent girl?

Iyanda prayed it wasn't the mother. Quilla Petty seemed like the type to move obstacles out of her way by any means necessary. It wouldn't be the first case on the island. Unfortunately, it was quite common among the high class to weaken or kill a member of their family. Because money was involved, the proper authorities looked the other way.

She stared at her young apprentice. What kind of obstacle would Yesenia have been?

Iyanda's mind wandered to Emiliano. She shuddered at his possible reaction to the news. Hopefully he would listen to the voice of reason when she explained the poisoning to him.

An emptiness gnawed at her stomach. She needed to eat but she hungered for more than food. Iyanda still wanted Emiliano but now he belonged to another. Or he would soon. She had to resist the urge to take him back. Then again, he was never hers in the first place. He and Aria had been a couple before. And now they were engaged.

After checking Yesenia's breathing and condition once more, Iyanda made her way to the kitchen to get some air and maybe something to eat.

The marble counters were scrubbed to a blinding shine. On the counter, red ceramic canisters lined the tan and white backsplash. The stainless-steel refrigerator and stoves shone with a factory finish. Iyanda's bare feet padded across the polished floor to the pantry. She skimmed the pantry and pots on the stove. Finding only fruit and bottled water to her liking, she searched for a knife to slice the small snack.

She was ready to go home. She prayed she would be able to go home earlier than the estimated day Emiliano gave her of two days. She missed her family, especially her mother.

Adeyemi believed she was doing what was best for her daughter. She always had. She went out of her way to learn Yoruba Sign Language so she could communicate with Iyanda. Adeyemi even reluctantly supported her dream of becoming an onisegun, believing Iyanda would grow out of the fascination to focus on getting married.

Iyanda caught a glimpse of her reflection in the countertop. Did her mother not realize she was taking her voice by forcing her to marry a man who wanted to destroy it. Emiliano claimed he wanted to give it back to her.

Picking up a piece of pear slice, she took a bite. The juices were almost as sweet as his kisses.

Her body tingled at the memory of his fingertips exploring her body. Her eyes closed. Heat started from between her legs and surged through her body. Her breath caught. His warm, wet kisses had perfumed the length of her collarbone. She felt him. She saw him. Their lives unfolded before her. The visions were warnings if she allowed him to marry Aria. Tears streaked her cheeks. She watched herself large with Emiliano's child and they were a family helping others, following the oro idile, the family traditions.

The clearing of someone's throat, forced Iyanda's eyes open.

Aria. With arms crossed, Aria's eyes spoke of the malicious intent she had toward Iyanda. Thankfully the counter stood between them.

Iyanda focused on her fruit. Taking a small bite, she slowly chewed until the pieces dissolved.

"You think you're special because he shows you a little attention?" Aria asked, her words angry hot. "I don't care if you're deaf, I'll say whatever I want to you."

Another person oblivious to the difference between deaf and mute. Good. Either way Aria believed Iyanda to be ignorant to her words. She unscrewed the top on her water bottle and took a drink.

"I'll do everything in my power to keep you away from him," Aria said, "and when we get married, I'll have you arrested if he even dreams of you."

Aria moved to the corner of the counter. Iyanda raised a brow. Obviously Aria believed her to be blind as well.

Aria turned her nose up. "I can't believe Emiliano thought you could ever compete with me. You're average. Below average, really." Aria smirked.

Iyanda took a bigger bite of her pear. Her body tensed.

"He was always looking for something to get over me, something 'better'." Aria held out her fist. "Sad, really, he thought he would find that with you." Aria opened her hand, allowing a necklace to dangle.

Iyanda's eyes narrowed. It was the gift Emiliano had given her. She clenched her jaw. Who did this woman think she was to wave a token of love as a weapon?

Iyanda's hand inched closer to the paring knife when Aria took another step toward her.

The movement didn't escape Aria. She glowered at Iyanda, raising a hand, she said, "I'll teach you your place."

She swung only to have it stopped mid-air by Quilla. Aria tried to snatch her arm out of the older woman's grip. Quilla stared her down.

"As much as I would love to put this pauper in her place, she is here to help my daughter." Quilla's eyes narrowed. "Don't interfere."

Quilla flung Aria's arm back. The younger woman cradled her wrist to her chest. She looked from Iyanda to Quilla, a frown creasing her flawless forehead.

"Take some time in one of the guest rooms," Quilla told Aria.

Iyanda internally scoffed. She wasn't offered a bed to sleep in.

Aria gave Iyanda an icy glare then stormed off. Without a glance, Quilla left Iyanda in the kitchen alone.

Iyanda's hand shook. Would she have used the knife if Aria had struck her? That's all she would need, a murder charge to add to her family's shame.

Leaving the kitchen with the fruit and water, she searched the quiet house for another place to enjoy her snack. She came to an office. She took a step onto the soft reddish carpet, mesmerized by five bookcases carved within the wall. The books were all leather-bound, some more worn than others. Her fingers slid across the smooth wood of the shelves as she read the title of each book. Some were in English but the majority were written in Portuguese, Igbalaian Creole, and Yoruba.

Her head tilted as she came to a series of books titled 'The Forgotten Ones of Igbala'. Her pulse quickened when she read the author's name.

Naade Olatunji. Her brother.

Naade always wanted to be a writer, a representative for his people. A joy to his father. He even wrote under the name of their father.

He had that choice. The family name had been bestowed upon him while she was denied it. Their father believed she wasn't truly his, resenting her for the doubt caused by her mother. Iyanda never understood or knew why her father would have such doubts about her faithful mother and she never bothered to ask.

Naade reminded her she was an Olatunji as well and no one could take that from her. He promised to make it his life's mission to prove it.

Blinking back tears, Iyanda slid one of the books out and with the care of a mother picking up her baby, she hugged it to her chest. Walking over to a nearby couch, she slowly sat so as not to disturb its contents. She stared at the cover.

How long had the book been out? Where was he? Why didn't he call his family? Why didn't the family know?

Her breath hitched at the first page. Her eyes read and reread the dedication, the prickling tears threatening the corner of her eyes again.

For my Little Sister,

I now give you what you were denied.
You have been selected to be special.

Tears stained the white page. She clutched the book to her chest, rocking back and forth. He hadn't forgotten her. He had kept his promise. She silently cried, his name escaping her lips. All the years that had passed. Her beliefs had become doubts. She had begun to believe the truths of her mother, that her big brother had also abandoned her.

"Iyanda?"

She looked up at the sound of Emiliano's voice.

He rushed over to her. Sitting beside her, he took her in his arms and held her tight.

Burying her head into the warmth of his chest, she continued weeping until her eyes were dry of tears. He rocked her, never asking questions, allowing her heart to release whatever pain she held within.

When she was able to silence herself, Iyanda sat up and handed him the book. "What happened to this man?"

Emiliano read the name. "He died."

A sudden coldness filled her center. "What do you mean died?"

"Yeah," Emiliano said. "I don't remember the whole story, but I believe it was six years ago. He was killed by someone he knew. Sijuwade Olatunji, if I'm not mistaken, was the name of the killer."

Iyanda clutched her chest, their father had killed her brother.

How? Why?

"Why? Do you know him?" Emiliano asked.

Iyanda moved away from Emiliano. Sliding off the couch, she returned the book to the shelf. She stood with her back to him, staring at her brother's name. Naade had tried to give her back what was rightfully hers. Is that what got him killed?

Emiliano made his way over to her, the clean scent of soap and lemongrass relaxed her mind a bit.

"He was my brother," she said in a soft voice.

"I'm sorry, love," he said, his expression pained.

"My father was the killer."

Emiliano looked away, all expression gone from his face. Walking to the desk, he took a seat and moved the computer mouse. His jaw flexed as he stared at the computer screen.

She deserved his silence. What more could she expect from him? He comforted her but she had made it clear he couldn't be there for her because of Aria.

"The poison is leaving your sister's body," Iyanda informed him, hoping to get an emotion out of him, no matter how small.

Emiliano paused then went back to clicking the mouse. "What kind of poison?" He didn't seem surprised.

"I'm not sure yet." Iyanda wiped the remnants of tears from her face and sniffled. "It wasn't severe, thankfully, but whoever has been preparing her food or drink has been slowly trying to kill her."

His brow furrowed.

How she would have loved to kiss the frown lines away, to take away his frustrating thoughts.

His brow relaxed a bit. "Thank you. I'll make sure you're compensated for your time." He waved his hand to dismiss her.

A ton of bricks had been thrown at her heart. He dismissed her as if she was beneath him. She turned to leave the room but stopped. Spinning on her heels, she marched over to the desk. Slamming her hands down, he looked up at her with unreadable eyes.

"Who do you think you are to treat me as if I don't have feelings?" she demanded. "I expect such things like that from your mother and Aria and anyone else in Pleasant Heights. But not you."

"Isn't that what you wanted?"

"I asked you to respect Aria."

"And she asked me not to talk to you or treat you better than what you deserve."

Burning tears stung her eyes. "So, I deserve to be treated like trash? No. Worse than trash."

"I've heard Pleasant Heights is known for their recycling program," he said with a sarcastic bite.

"You are worse than them."

Emiliano slammed his hand down on the desk, making Iyanda jump a bit. His once gentle eyes were now hard and furious.

"I go out of my way to give you what you deserve and what you ask of me," he said, "I've damn near lost my family for you."

"I didn't ask you to." She lowered her gaze.

"You didn't have to!"

Iyanda turned her head, her neck growing warm.

"You didn't have to," he said in a calmer tone. "I never demanded anything of you. I wanted you for who you were, even when you were mute. But that wasn't enough. You would love me with your arms keeping me at a distance. I told you I want to be with you and I mean it. I want to be the one to marry you. No, we don't have to get married right away. I would even be willing to pay the price for you. But that wasn't enough for you."

"What about Aria at your apartment?"

"You know why she came to the apartment," Emiliano said.

"Is she what I have to look forward to? Every time we move together, she'll appear with some lie or will she one day tell me something that is the truth?"

He turned his head.

She nodded, a sad smile in the corner of her lips. "I have enough people in my life trying to force me down a path I haven't chosen. I thought you were different."

"If I'm no different, then why stay with me? Why leave your grandmother's funeral with me?

"Because, I feel safe with you."

Emiliano raised a brow. His charming smile made her legs weak. "Present tense. You feel safe with me?"

Iyanda looked away, her cheeks growing hot.

He stood and slowly made his way from around the desk.

She took a step back. "I-I meant I felt safe with you."

He came closer. Her heart raced. She shielded her breasts from his enticing devilish eyes. The scent of lemongrass tempted her.

With one hand he lifted her chin. She looked at his sinfully sculpted mouth. She pressed her lips together, trying to control them from parting.

Using his thumb, he traced a line from her chin to her cheekbone to her lips.

"Never stop feeling safe with me," he said in a husky voice.

Taking one of her hands, he placed it upon his cheek.

Her hand moved to his long locs. The soft, textured ropes contained a calming energy. Iyanda saw into his eyes the familiar gentle wanting for her. She gripped a fistful of hair in her hand and forced his head down, claiming his mouth.

The guilt of him belonging to someone else subsided with the demanding kiss. He gripped the back of her neck, and thrust his warm tongue into her mouth, punishing her soft lips. His other hand possessed her waist, forcing her close.

Grabbing his shirt, she broke the kiss. They stared, breathlessly at each other. She led him to the red couch. Pushing him down on it, she straddled him, and reclaimed his lips.

His hands sent shivers through her body as he explored and massaged her body, moving the straps of her camisole down her arms. His lips created a trail from her chin to her full, round breasts. The expert touch of his tongue danced and circled the aroused buds, stealing the breath from her. She moaned.

Her sensitive spot pulsated, becoming wetter as she rubbed against his bulging erection.

Grabbing her shoulders, he broke the kiss. "I don't have protection."

She frowned. Her hands caressed his well-developed chest. She chewed on her bottom lip. The first day they didn't use any and he made sure, for the next three days not to repeat the mistake. She wanted to just forget the protection.

"You knew this before we started," she teased.

"You really didn't give me a moment to say."

Iyanda raised a brow and smiled. "I didn't give you a moment?"

Emiliano chuckled.

They stared at each other, both hungering for the other. Emiliano stroked her legs and the pulsing between her thighs started back up.

"I only want what you want," he said. He gave her rounded buttocks a squeeze.

"You don't want this?"

"I definitely want this, you, but not if it causes you shame."

She smiled. "Why are you so good to me?"

"Because you're my woman. No matter what."

Iyanda bent down and gave him a tender kiss. Their lips lingered before she broke away.

She smiled at him. "Thank you. We'll wait until I can be your woman in every way."

Emiliano nodded. Then blew air through his nose. "So, what do we do now?"

"I have to get back to Yesenia." She straightened the straps of her cami back.

He grabbed her waist to prevent her from getting up. She looked at him in confusion.

"I do need a taste to remember you by," he said.

Iyanda frowned. "I already gave you a kiss."

Emiliano smiled wickedly. "Need a bit more."

Shifting, he placed her onto her back on the couch. Reaching under her skirt, he slipped her damp panties off and dropped them onto the floor. His hands parted her thighs. Starting at her knees, he kissed a trail to the nest of moist curls.

She moaned, her head falling back. "Emiliano, what are you doing?"

"Grabbing a snack." His head disappeared underneath her skirt.

CHAPTER 31

Emiliano leaned back in the desk chair, his lips curved up in a satisfied smile. Iyanda had left the room an hour ago, but the scent of licorice and her sweet taste still lingered. He never had any woman so willing to please as well as be pleasured. Most, including Aria, were either too eager to receive pleasure or like dead fish in the bed.

A shrill scream made him sit upright. He listened. Maybe it was his imagination.

Another scream.

His blood froze. This one was from the depth of the soul. It had to be Yesenia.

He bolted for the door only to run into a wild-eyed Aria. She hid behind him, clinging to his shirt. He looked in the direction of her fear.

Quilla stormed toward them with flaring nostrils and Edward trailing behind her. Her eyes widened when she saw Aria's hands clutching Emiliano.

"Take your hands off of my son." Within a few steps Quilla snatched Emiliano away from the frightened woman and placed him behind her.

Aria trembled like a frightened animal, ready to flee or fight, whichever came first. With eyeliner streaked cheeks, her eyes darted from Quilla to Emiliano.

"What is going on?" Emiliano's stomach steadied. Thankfully it wasn't about his sister.

"She has the illness and is trying to spread it to the rest of us," Quilla said in Spanish.

He frowned. He slowly approached Aria.

"Get away from her!" Quilla commanded.

Emiliano glanced back. "Like you really care whether I live or die."

He focused back on Aria. Not seeing any visible marks on her face or arms, he bent down and lifted her pant leg. He breathed in sharply. A large welt on her calf slowly oozed pus.

"How long have you had this?" Emiliano dropped her pant leg and stood up straight.

Aria winced. "A day or two. I'm not sure."

He then noticed the beads of sweat forming in the corners of her temples. She had been hiding her symptoms. How did she manage to walk around? The temporary sickness made it hard for many to move, much less walk.

"You're not sure?" Quilla screeched as Edward held her arm, preventing her from rushing at the young woman. "You could have given this to my daughter? My baby is dying because of you! And to think I was going to allow you into my family."

"She's not the only reason for Yesenia's sickness," Emiliano said.

Anger churned in his chest at the nonchalant expressions of Edward and Quilla. He felt they knew more than they were letting on.

"If it's not her then it's that little native girl you brought here," Quilla said, her voice thick with accusation.

Just like her to put the blame of her crimes on everyone but herself, Emiliano thought.

"Did you forget that your children were born and raised here?" Emiliano questioned.

"You two are different."

He turned on his mother. "We are no different than anyone else. We breathe and die just like them."

"No, mi amor," Quilla lifted her chin. "You breathe in class and die in style."

They stared each other down. He couldn't fathom this woman was the one to have birthed him. How could his father have managed to stay in a relationship with a person like Quilla Petty?

Jack Petty was always so mild and fun-loving with his children. Emiliano couldn't remember one time the man ever raised his voice to him or Yesenia, not even when he had to discipline them. Everyone who came in contact with the senior Petty remembered him for his warm smile, wise words, and open hand to anyone in need.

Quilla smirked as if having read his mind. He knew there were only two choices: either Aria left or Iyanda did.

Aria could easily go home without the danger of being shot but not Iyanda.

He shut his eyes at the thought.

"It's settled then," Edward said.

Aria whimpered then screamed out for Emiliano. He couldn't move. Opening his eyes, his mother's smile taunted him as Edward dragged a screaming Aria to the door.

"She trusted you," Emiliano said.

Quilla shrugged. "No fault of mine."

"I thought she was the one you needed me to marry," Emiliano said.

"I no longer require her services to get what I want." She slowly walked up to him, her heels clicking on the floor. "You could always marry your campesina. But I wonder if her mother would be happy to know that her son-in-law is the cause of their struggles."

Emiliano towered over the short woman.

She didn't flinch.

"One day," he said through clenched teeth, "I'll make you pay for making her suffer."

Quilla scoffed. "I'm your mother. What son has the heart to harm his mother?"

The front door slammed.

With the flick of her thick, long hair, Quilla turned and left Emiliano standing in the hall.

Aria's screaming pleas resonated through him. He clenched and unclenched his fists. He had no choice. To save Aria would put Iyanda's life as well as Yesenia's at risk.

"And to think you were different."

Cold crept his spine at the sound of Iyanda's voice. She stood at the bottom of the stairs. Her disappointing eyes stabbing him in the heart.

"How much did you hear?"

"Enough." Her tone was cold and accusing.

"Iyanda, I-."

"You had my family's business shut down?"

"Let me explain."

"Explain what? Explain that you are the cause of my family's suffering?"

He motioned with his hand for her to lower her voice.

"Loud voices aren't strange in this house," she said.

He took a step toward her. She took one back. He stopped, his heart twisting in his chest.

"Iyawo mi," he said in a gentle voice.

"I am not your wife! I could never marry a man that lies." Her chin trembled. "I was the fish you wanted to catch." She chuckled. "You knew everything about me. You went out of your way to make me believe you could feel my pain and struggle. But you can't. You never have and never will. You are no better than Mason."

The words were a gut punch to Emiliano.

"And I hate I was too stupid to not see it." Iyanda rushed back upstairs and slammed the bedroom door before he could move toward her.

He fell back onto the wall, his hand at his chest. It was becoming hard to breathe.

How did he allow his mother's reach to get this far? He closed his eyes.

He needed the wise words of his father. Emiliano felt as if Jack Petty never left him, always giving him the right words to say and right actions to carry out. Why was he silent now?

* * * * *

Iyanda slowly opened her eyes. The rising sun peeked through the closed blinds of Yesenia's room. She lowered her legs to the cool floor, her body stiff from the balled-up position she'd slept in.

All men were the same. They preferred a woman silent or broken. If she was neither of these things then he would physically beat the voice out of her or take away what she had worked so hard for.

She wrapped her arms around herself and trembled. Nana B believed Emiliano to be different. She did too. Iyanda blinked back tears. She had almost given her body to him once again. Her womanhood pulsated at the memory of Emiliano's tongue magic.

"Not the time," she mumbled.

His smile and soft, encouraging words stirred within her.

Why couldn't she let him go? She had to.

Thinking of her mother, a single tear rolled down her cheek. She quickly wiped it away. Adeyemi deserved a better daughter. She was trying to make sure Iyanda would be taken care of, afraid history could repeat itself.

But Iyanda couldn't marry Mason. He would be worse than her father. And when she told Adeyemi what really happened to Naade then maybe she would see that truth as well. Maybe then Iyanda could go home.

Iyanda lifted her head at the sound of movement in Yesenia's bed. She slowly rose. Yesenia was propped up on her elbows. The young girl's eyes took turns opening and closing before she gained control of them. When she saw Iyanda staring at her, she gave a half-hearted smile.

"I knew no doctor could make me better, " Yesenia said in a scratchy voice.

Iyanda smiled back. She stood, her legs still a bit stiff, and walked to the bed. Feeling Yesenia's forehead and checking the now dry, crusted welt.

"What I miss?" Yesenia asked.

Iyanda applied another compress to the teen's leg.

"I had the strangest dream. I thought you were talking," Yesenia said, causing Iyanda to pause. "It was so strange. I heard you talk about going to the garden. But you still can't talk, right?"

Iyanda nodded with a strange smile, then coaxed the young girl to lay back down. She quickly left the room. Going down the hall, she rapidly knocked on Quilla's bedroom door.

The older woman flung her door open, her cold steely eyes locking on the intruder. "You better have a good reason, girl, for interrupting my sleep."

Iyanda swallowed the words and motioned for Quilla to follow her.

A naked Edward came to the door. Iyanda shielded her eyes. *With all the money the older woman had, why couldn't she buy her boyfriend a robe?*

"Maybe it's about your daughter," Edward said.

Quilla's brows arched, her face softening to a worried mother. She instructed Edward to put some pants on as she rushed from the room, zooming past Iyanda.

They made it to the room in no time. Iyanda was shocked at the speed the small woman had. Quilla barged into the room and rushed to the bed. Yesenia tried to sit up but was instructed by her mother to lie back down.

Iyanda watched from the door as Quilla assisted Yesenia in sipping some water then caressing the young girl's hair, soft words flowing from her mouth.

She pressed her lips together. The poisoning couldn't have possibly come from the mother. Unless Quilla was just that skilled at playing on people's emotions. Iyanda eyed Edward. Could he be the reason for the poisoning?

After a moment, Edward slid past Iyanda into the bedroom. He slowly walked up to the bed and asked Yesenia how she was feeling. The young girl mumbled she was fine but seemed to be enjoying the attention she was getting from her mother.

Quilla stood and came to Iyanda, her eyes not so cold, but definitely full of dislike for the younger woman. "Thank you. You can receive your payment downstairs. Do not grace my door again until I call you and stay away from my son. He's too high for you to touch."

Iyanda feigned a smile. She nodded, grabbed her bag and rushed from the room before the tears started. She hurried downstairs and made her way to the front door. A servant met her and tried to hand her an envelope. Looking inside, she saw the stacks of green bills and quickly declined the money.

She glanced back at Emiliano. She looked back at the meek servant and shook her head. She walked past, the sound of familiar heavy footsteps trying to keep up with her. Making it to the door, Iyanda grabbed the door handle. Emiliano's hand quickly covered hers.

Her grip relaxed under his touch.

"Iyanda, take the money." His warm breath blew on her ear, sending shivers to her toes.

"I don't need anything from you or your family." She swallowed. She had to regain her senses.

"I need you."

Her heart grew full at the sound of his words. Their fingers laced together as his voice urged her to turn around and forget the world outside those walls. Her eyes closed as his warm kisses caressed her neck, loosening her grip on the doorknob. Exhaustion, mixed with the desire to give in, wanted her to see that she needed him too. What would keep her from him? Fear, the mistress of memory, pointed out he was the reason her family struggled to eat.

An icy hand gripped her heart, squeezing tight. "Don't," she stammered. "Don't say you need me. Did you decide you needed me as my family starved?"

"Iyanda."

"Don't!"

Snatching her hand away from his, she opened the door and rushed from the house.

"Iyanda!" Emiliano called, following her. "Stop damnit! We don't know if the quarantine has been lifted!"

He was right. More than likely the barricade hadn't been lifted, but maybe she could prove she was one of Dunni's students bringing more herbs for the elder to cure the afflicted. It was a risk, but one she was willing to take. She couldn't stop, not now, not while he was nearby. She slowed when she saw Aria's vehicle still in the driveway. Her hand flew to her mouth when she saw the other woman's still body and vacant eyes. Looking away, she quickened her steps.

Emiliano's steps paused before he cursed.

She continued walking, ignoring her name being called as she rounded the corner.

CHAPTER 32

Iyanda sat inside Gaiana's screened-in porch. She stared blankly at the large yard. The late afternoon sun invited the birds' last minute chattering. Small clouds of gnats hovered in the yard, dancing left and right until they dispersed in different directions to complete their missions of irritation.

"How much longer will you sit here?" Gaiana asked.

Iyanda rested her chin on the top of her knees. She wasn't ignoring Gaiana, she just didn't know how to answer truthfully. Her friend had returned home two hours ago, finding Iyanda on the swing chair in the same curled up position. Gaiana, sensing it had something to do with Emiliano, sat down and tried to communicate with Iyanda.

It had been in vain.

Gaiana decided food would loosen Iyanda. She prepared the silent woman's favorite snack, chin-chin, and placed it on the space next to Iyanda and took a seat on one of the nearby rocking chairs.

She waited.

Two hours passed and the fresh, delicious smell of the chin-chin had dissipated.

"What happened there? Iyanda?" Gaiana asked.

How could she explain to her friend the truth she found out about her brother? That even though she saved two lives, she couldn't save a third. That her heart was slowly turning to stone to prevent anymore loss or pain?

"Nana B wouldn't want you sitting here being sad, she would want you finishing your training."

"I don't have the money to do that," Iyanda said, not breaking her focus on the large yard.

There was a pause of silence. Iyanda knew Gaiana had more questions but she didn't ask them under the threat of offending her friend.

"I would think being able to talk again would be a joyous occasion." Gaiana tried to switch the conversation.

Iyanda buried her face in her knees, hiding the tears.

"What good is a voice when it seems I'm the only one listening to it?" Iyanda's sobs were muffled by her skirt.

Gaiana rushed to Iyanda, kneeling beside her. "Don't say that. Nana B is always listening. She is here with us," Gaiana said.

"I know."

Gaiana paused. "And I'm always your ears. Were you talking about Mason?"

Iyanda lifted her head, her lips pressed together, her eyes asking if Gaiana was serious?

Gaiana softly laughed. A small smile appeared on Iyanda's lips.

"Why don't you call him?" Gaiana asked.

Iyanda dried her wet face with her skirt. She sat up, shaking her head. "Calling him will do nothing. He has shown his true colors. He's just a richer Mason."

Gaiana frowned. "Maybe you are mistaken."

"I know what I heard. He is the cause of the stores being closed down and for my family to suffer like they are."

"He closed the stores?"

Iyanda opened her mouth. Then closed it. She sat back and tried to remember the conversation. She didn't remember hearing Quilla outright accusing Emiliano of closing the stores. He was just blamed for it.

"I don't remember that being said," she said slowly.

"Did he say it himself?"

"His mother blamed him for the stores closing down."

The corners of Gaiana's lips creased up. She stood and moved the plate of chin-chin to the wooden floor and took a seat next to Iyanda. She placed her hand on top of her friend's hand and gave it a gentle squeeze.

"It sounds to me that you assumed wrong," Gaiana said.

Iyanda looked at the floor. Her heart had told her the same thing.

"Nana B trusted Emiliano would take care of you and that he really loved you," Gaiana said. "And I don't know a person alive who would ever go against Nana B's trust, besides Tambara."

They both softly chuckled.

Gaiana gave her friend's knee a gentle shake. "You love him, Iyanda. And I believe he truly loves you. He has to be hurting right now, if not more than you are. This man has been given everything at birth and could have anything, but he's willing to sacrifice it all to have you or to make sure you aren't hurt. What man does that for a woman? Mason definitely wouldn't."

The thought of her deceased grandfather came to mind. Iyanda had heard stories of the determined, loving man. Everything he had done and sacrificed, he did for the love of Nana B.

Just like Emiliano.

But how could she go to him now? She had made it clear she wanted nothing to do with him and that he needed to stay away. He would think she was an indecisive woman. What man would want to build with a woman like that?

Heavy footsteps halted the next words coming from Iyanda. Gaiana and Iyanda looked at the screened door.

Adeyemi came up the last few steps with Mason King and his mother in tow.

Iyanda's heart skipped a beat at the sight of her mother. Adeyemi's long hair was uncovered, sporting the protective yarn wrapped around sections of hair and her face was clear of the familiar makeup. Iyanda felt a pang of guilt at her mother's appearance. The beautiful woman had aged since the last time they had seen each other.

And the constant brain-numbing complaints of Ms. King probably didn't help the situation.

Gaiana quickly went and opened the door for them. Ms. King looked down at Adeyemi before brushing past the woman, placing herself inside first. Gaiana gave a slight nod to Adeyemi and stood to the side.

Disapproval gleamed in Ms. King's beady eyes. Iyanda and Gaiana glanced at each other then they reluctantly fell to their knees in greeting. Ms. King sneered then nodded for them to get up. Mason wore a black patch over one eye, with the other he sent a death stare in Iyanda's direction.

Iyanda looked at her mother. Adeyemi's shoulders hunched and her eyes were red and long from exhaustion.

"Do you see how disrespectful your daughter is?" Ms. King said in a shrill voice to Adeyemi. "An elder enters and she and her friend hesitate to greet me. She doesn't even beg for mercy at what she has done. Poor excuse for a daughter-in-law."

"I have already apologized for my daughter's actions, Ms. King," Adeyemi stated. "I don't know what else you could require. It is my fault she is this way."

"It is no one's fault but her own son," Gaiana chimed in. She glared at the Kings.

Ms. King raised her hand. "You dare call me a liar? Who are you to me?"

"Someone who can afford to pay for manners," Gaiana said.

Ms. King and Mason scoffed.

"You were an employee for them," Ms. King said, her nose high in the air. "They could barely buy food, I can imagine what you were making."

"Maybe she could work sweeping your floors," Mason suggested.

The Kings laughed. Iyanda touched Gaiana's arm. Her frustrated friend stood back, glaring at the two offending people.

Ms. King's brow raised. "Little Miss Deaf Bastard controls her guard dog, I see. Maybe you should have controlled yourself before stabbing my son. Now your mother has to pay by seeing you behind bars."

Adeyemi fell to her knees, rubbing her palms together. "Please. Don't press charges. Iyanda was just acting out. She didn't mean to. Please, there has to be another way for us to make it up to you."

Ms. King smirked. She glanced at Mason, who gave an eager head nod. She looked down at Adeyemi.

"We won't press charges if your daughter agrees to marry my son."

"Of course." Adeyemi nodded her head. "In five days."

Ms. King shook her head. "No. Today."

"Today?" A panicked expression etched across Adeyemi's features. "But everything is not ready. She doesn't have her bridal clothes."

"From what I hear, your daughter is far from bridal innocence. Either today at six or I press charges."

Adeyemi hung her head.

Iyanda couldn't take it anymore. She stormed over to her mother. Taking the older woman's elbow she helped her mother stand. Adeyemi tried to break away to resume her position back on the ground.

"Stand up, iya," Iyanda said, helping her mother to her feet.

Adeyemi's mouth fell open. She stared at her daughter and reached for her cheek. "You spoke?" Adeyemi said in a low voice more to herself.

Iyanda nodded. "Yes, iya. Your daughter has found her voice."

A tear fell down Adeyemi's cheek. She smiled then threw her arms around her daughter's neck, embracing her in a strong hug. Iyanda laid her head on her mother's shoulder, drinking in the strength and joy of a woman who loved her more than anyone.

Ms. King scoffed. "So, she does speak. And here I'm thinking I'm getting a silent daughter. Not surprising, considering your mother has lied before." Ms. King raised her nose in the air.

Iyanda pulled away from Adeyemi, glaring at Ms. King and Mason, who had slid a bit behind his mother.

Pathetic. Always hiding behind his mother's influence.

"You may say what you want to say about me, but you will not insult my mother." Iyanda puffed her chest out. "She is the most honest person I know."

Ms. King scoffed.

Iyanda stepped closer, stopping inches from the towering woman. "I will not marry your son."

"We paid the price," Ms. King said.

"And we will give it back," Iyanda said.

Ms. King made a tsk sound. "How much more shame do you want to bring to your mother?"

"If it brings us shame, so be it. I would rather live with the shame than to live with your weak son."

Mason stepped forward with clenched fists. "I'll show you weak."

"Shall I take your other eye?" Iyanda's tone promised bodily harm.

His fists unclenched. He stood back behind his mother. Ms. King looked at her son in disgust. She looked back at Iyanda, brows raised in annoyance.

"I will press charges against you," Ms. King threatened.

Iyanda came closer to Ms. King, her chest an inch from the woman. "Then I will press charges against your son. I'm still healing from the beating he gave me and he tried to rape me. I might be in trouble for stabbing his eye but he will serve life for what he has done. Think of what it will do for your reputation."

Ms. King's face softened to a blank stare. Everyone that knew her was aware of how much emphasis she placed on her reputation. She tried to stare Iyanda down, calling her bluff, but the younger woman's eyes were set and intense.

"Fine," Ms. King said.

"But, mother-," Mason began to protest.

Ms. King held her hand up. "If the full bride price is not back in our possession by six, you will marry my son."

"I'd rather go to jail,"

Adeyemi touched Iyanda's hand. Iyanda glanced at her mother. She sighed then looked back up at Ms. King.

"I will marry him, *if* we don't return it."

Ms. King surveyed them then, grabbing Mason's arm roughly, she escorted him out of the house and back to the car.

The three women breathed a sigh of relief the moment the Kings drove away. Iyanda turned to her mother and gave her a small smile. They embraced, sobbing the burdens away and welcoming the reuniting joy.

Gaiana touched their shoulders. They stopped and looked at her.

"As much as I love seeing you two back together," Gaiana said, "we have two hours to get the full bride price back to the Kings or you'll be giving your daughter away."

Adeyemi and Iyanda wiped their eyes as they followed Gaiana out the door.

* * * * *

Emiliano sat in a chair, a few inches from Mason. Behind them sat the council members, their eyes boring holes into the back of the younger men's heads. Emiliano took easy breaths through his nose. He needed to calm his insides before the Head appeared.

He stared at the curtained high podium. Did his father ever have to sit in his chair, staring at the podium, awaiting, what felt like, his execution?

Jack Petty had told his young son about how after the revolution, the commanders established a High Council to govern the newly freed slaves until they could find a way back to the land of their Ancestors. Because of her fierceness during the uprising, Adetowumi Temitope Boaventura, was believed to be the daughter of Ogun. The other generals advised their leader to stay hidden behind the black veil during the meetings to protect her from the spiritual attacks of their enemies.

Emiliano peeked at Mason. He sat back with a smug look on his face wearing a black eyepatch. Emiliano's mind went back to Iyanda's swollen face and his blood began to boil. He had a mind to finish the job that Iyanda had started but before he could stand, the announcement was made of the Head's arrival.

Everyone in the room stood.

A figure sat behind the black curtain and everyone one else took a seat.

"We are here concerning the Chairman position," a deep, rich feminine voice said. "A position that is, like the others, earned by blood right. The chair in question belongs to the descendants of Lieutenant General Damola. But the Elders of this council have forgotten this. You bring me a boy who cannot keep his hands to himself and has forgotten the ways of our Ancestors."

Emiliano smirked.

"And yet, the son of Petty returns after being gone for more than a year and requests to take his father's chair because it is his birthright. Do you know the suffering of your people, Emiliano Petty, Son of Jack Ropo Ògúndáre Petty or have you hidden behind the cushion of your luxuries to notice? You have been seen with another's wife, an offense on our island."

"She is his fiancée," Emiliano said.

"No matter. He has paid the bride price."

Emiliano shot out of his chair. "You have said yourself, he does not keep his hands to himself! My crime is not that I have broken a home but saved a woman from certain death under his hand."

He glanced at the council members before focusing back on the black curtain. "Yes, I have stayed away for too long and I've hidden behind my family's wealth, but I have not hidden from the people. I was just spat on for something many believe my father had done. There are many who are corrupted in the Council and I'm not going to lie, if you grant me my father's chair, I intend to clean up the corruption and finish the work he started. If you love this country as much as you claim, then don't give the chair to a boy."

Emiliano glanced in Mason's direction before reclaiming his chair. The Council members talked among themselves. Unease rolled through him as the Head sat silent behind the curtain. What would his opponent do if he was able to claim the chair? He imagined the state of the people would be worse than it was now. Women, like Iyanda would be in trouble if men like Mason were given the power over their lives. The sound of a gong brought everyone's attention back to the veil.

"Your words carry the spirit of your father," the Head said. "I had already made my decision before stepping out here but listening to your words have solidified my decision. Reclaim your father's chair and allow the legacy of those before you to carry on."

Mason shot out of his chair, his face reddened and beaded with sweat. "What the hell? Who are you to defame my character?" He pointed an accusatory finger at Emiliano then the black curtain. "I am better than this jackass and I'm way better than you! Come out here and show your face, you fucking coward!" His nostrils flared.

Gasp and lower murmurs from the Council members spoke of their disapproval. Of whom Emiliano wasn't sure.

"Sit down, boy," Mobolaji commanded.

Mason whirled on the older man. "You sit down, you bloated bag of bones! Listening to you was a mistake. You promised me that seat."

Mobolaji and his followers reddened in the face as they now saw their prodigy for what he was, a spoiled brat.

"If your mother had taught you the way of your Ancestors, maybe then you would have more respect for them," the Head said. "I will not lower myself, and neither will any of the other Council members to appease your childish fancies. You are dismissed. Go before I change my mind and have you punished for your offenses to our Founders."

Mason stormed out, uttering a promise to get even.

"Son of Petty. Next time you stand before me, it will not be for youthful foolishness. Keep your Ancestral seat safe that it might be passed on to your child."

Didn't the Head mean to his son? The only chair that permitted a woman was the Head, but the others had to be male descendants since the original Generals who had fought alongside General Boaventura had been.

Seye clapped him on his back and shook his hand, followed by a line of the other council members shaking his hand as well.

Except Mobolaji.

He stood at the exit, staring at Emiliano before leaving the small room.

Emiliano would ignore it for now. In time he would handle Mobolaji, but now there were more pressing matters at hand.

CHAPTER 33

Iyanda slowly walked the street toward WAISTED and her shop. Three days had passed and the streets were quiet except for a few tourists trying to find a nice place to have breakfast. Unbeknownst to the traveler's, it would be awhile before any restaurants or shops opened. Many of the residents who didn't catch the disease would have to wait for the Chief Medical Officer to give the go ahead to resume business.

She liked the quiet. After the excitement of returning the bride price and moving back home, Iyanda needed the moment to think. She was thankful for Gaiana willing to give her the fifteen thousand dollars to pay the King's back. Of course, she made a mental note to ask her friend where she had obtained such a large sum of money.

She still couldn't bring herself to sleep in her grandmother's bed so she opted for the couch, her cousin taking the floor to keep her company. Tambara seemed relieved to have her back home and she was nicer now that Iyanda could speak again. Her Aunt Ola was still distant, but cordial.

Iyanda's pace slowed as she approached the stores. Her body relaxed at the grand pink letters on the window. The large padlocks on the doors didn't deter the small smile on her lips.

A prickling sensation ran through her body. Nana B was nearby.

"Iyanda?"

Iyanda turned to the sound of her voice. Dunni was walking up. She met the older woman halfway and assisted her to a bench directly across from the stores. Making sure Dunni was stable, she took a seat next to her.

Dunni exhaled.

They both stared at the dark store.

"I remember the first day," Dunni said, "your grandmother opened WAISTED. I was no older than eighteen. I was in training and wanted to see what the old woman was offering. I bought a strand of white waist beads that day. She looked me in the eye and said, 'A sculptor is summoned and the woodpecker shows up'."

Iyanda frowned.

"It's like she knew what I was going to be," Dunni continued. "She never wanted me to think too highly of myself because there is always someone better in waiting. She told me not to lose my self-worth trying to be everyone's version of humble."

Iyanda stared at the store.

"She lived by that proverb. I used to believe she could see into the future." Dunni laughed softly. "She even knew that her family would own the store next door. At that time, it was a tourist souvenir shop. The Black American hated your family, thinking they were spreading their 'voodoo' on his store and that was why he couldn't get any customers."

She leaned in close to Iyanda. "He already had bad business," she whispered.

Iyanda smiled.

"Come back to finish your training," Dunni requested.

Iyanda looked away and shook her head.

"Your grandmother already paid for you to finish before she died."

Iyanda's heart swelled.

"What reason do you have not to come?" Dunni asked.

"I don't want to shame you," Iyanda said, her voice choking on tears.

Dunni lifted her chin. "I had heard that you found your voice."

She smiled, making Iyanda smile.

"Our people need healers like you," Dunni said. "I heard what you did for the Petty girl and for your cousin. You were willing to risk your life to save another. No matter what others say or think, I could never be ashamed of you."

"I wasn't able to save one." Her mind went back to Aria. She wanted to believe that if she had known about the woman's condition that she would have put her feelings aside and tried to save her.

"Sometimes, we can't save the majority but those we do manage to save, we owe it to them to try to keep going."

Reaching inside of her messenger bag, Dunni fumbled around until her hands wrapped around what she was searching for. She pulled out a hand-sized bundle made from purple adire cloth. She reached for Iyanda's hands.

Iyanda cupped them, her heart pounding. She knew her grandmother's signature purple cloth anywhere. It was one of the few designs that they did not offer in the store. Dunni placed the bundle in her hands.

Undoing the ribbon, the cloth fell open like flower petals blooming. Within the precious material were four strands of waist beads. A vibrant red, dark green, polished black, and a white one containing a set of stingray charms.

Tears welled in Iyanda's eyes.

"She wanted to give them to you for your marriage day," Dunni said.

"But I'm not getting married to Mason."

Dunni smirked. "She never said anything about Mason."

Iyanda touched one of the charms, feeling her grandmother's presence.

"She always believed that you had a strong connection with the Ancestors," Dunni said, "and the spiritual powers of the deities. She knew the Earth would open up her knowledge to you and you would use it for others." Dunni covered Iyanda's free hand.

Iyanda looked into her trusted mentor's gentle, glassy eyes.

"Carry her memory," Dunni said.

Before Iyanda could respond, Gaiana came up to the store with Adeyemi, Ola and Tambara in tow. Gaiana went up to the door of WAISTED and fumbled with the locks before it opened.

"What are you doing?" Iyanda asked.

Gaiana rushed over, her eyes bright with excitement. "We got the store back."

"How?"

"Your mother received a call from the former landlord. He said the building was under new management and that they demanded WAISTED and IYANDA'S EWE be opened back up before they settled the deal."

"How is that possible?" Iyanda asked.

"Does it matter? Your mother went to pick up the new contract and the man handed her these before leaving."

Gaiana handed Iyanda a small pile of folded papers.

Dunni came and stood next to Iyanda as she opened it. Iyanda scanned the first page, her hand rose to her mouth. Dunni took the papers and read them. A large grin curled her lips from ear to ear. She squeezed Iyanda's hand then rushed over to Adeyemi and Ola, embracing them.

Tears rolled down Iyanda's cheeks. Her feet and body refused to move.

"Yanda?" Gaiana asked.

She looked at Gaiana. "We own the buildings. They're ours forever," Iyanda said.

"Yes, oga." Gaiana smiled.

Iyanda smiled. Gaiana reached up and wiped the tears from her friend's cheek then embraced her.

The hairs on her arms stood up. "Thank you, ọkàn mi," Iyanda whispered to her grandmother, "thank you." She clutched the waist beads in her hand.

Time to finish training.

* * * * *

The setting sun cast a shadow over Nana B's headstone. Iyanda inhaled the mixed fragrance of fresh-cut grass and newly turned earth as she stood before the grave. Giving the purple bundle a gentle squeeze, she undid the ribbon holding it together. Kneeling before the mound, she spread out the cloth on the dirt, revealing the waistbeads her grandmother had made her.

She swallowed the lump in her throat and bowed her head. "Forgive me, Nana B. I should have been there to celebrate your transition. I was being selfish. I was always selfish when it came to you. I knew I could get away with anything, as long as you were there. At least, that's what iya use to say."

She softly chuckled. "Maybe it was little bit true."

She lifted her gaze, smiling at the headstone. "I'm talking now, but of course you know that. You always knew everything."

Iyanda clenched her skirt. "I shouldn't have left that day. My heart told me you were leaving me. Wouldn't be the first time I didn't listen to my heart. I just didn't want to disobey you."

She dropped her chin, tears quietly rolling down her cheeks. "I feel so empty right now."

A light breeze whistled by, stirring the leaves of the mango tree Nana B was buried under. Iyanda sniffed. "You always did like mangoes, but you loved breadfruit more. You said it could feed a whole family, and that yours would never be hungry because of it."

She paused "Family," she said softly, the word mulling around in her head. "I shouldn't have run away. But maybe you wanted me to. Maybe you wanted me to pull away from tradition, that tradition anyway."

Lifting her chin, Iyanda undid her headwrap, allowing her coils to fall to her shoulders. "No more halo, ọkàn mi. We'll never see Mason or his mother again. But you already knew that too. I feel like you planned that as well.

But," she sighed, "I wish I was wearing it for him. I think you like Emiliano." Iyanda shrugged, a ghost of a smile crossing her lips. "I don't think you were ever against him, you just wanted to make sure he wouldn't hurt me. I think you saw how he made me feel before I admitted it to myself. You were always so supportive of me. Lily Poe told me what he did for you."

Iyanda's breath hitched, she tried to swallow the tears choking her throat. "I messed up, grandmother. I rejected him. I couldn't trust him. I was scared of being hurt. I wanted a relationship like you and grandfather had that I was too blind to see I had it with him. I-I let so many people come between us. It's probably too late now. He'll find some other rich girl to get married to and forget about me."

A warm flood of tears trailed down her face. She wept uncontrollably, muttering to her grandmother that she wished she was there to hear her. While the warm tears she shed were for Nana B, the sorrow Iyanda felt was for the absence of Emiliano. She missed him. The way his sunset eyes calmed her spirit while his very presence brightened her day.

She took a breath. "Maybe I am stubborn. This man trusted me with his heart and I refused to open mine fully. How could I be so foolish?"

"You weren't foolish."

Iyanda whirled her head around at the sound of the familiar voice. Adeyemi came over and knelt down beside her. Her mother took her hands.

"You weren't the foolish one, Yanda, I was. I wanted so much to prove that my daughter was normal and that we were women who followed tradition, that I didn't think about your happiness."

"Iya-."

Adeyemi held up her hand, stopping Iyanda's words. "I should have listened to Nana B that night. She told me Mason was no good and that I was placing you in the same cycle I had been in. I was so scared of you being alone. I wanted everyone to know you were a good girl, that you knew how to listen to your iya and would bring honor to your family. When the Petty b- I mean Emiliano came along, I felt that he would hurt you, blinded to the fact you were already hurting."

Using her headwrap, Iyanda dabbed at Adeyemi's tears, careful not to mess up the older woman's makeup. "Iya, don't cry. I know all this." She sniffled.

"Forgive your mama?"

Iyanda smiled. "Always." She embraced her mother, another piece of her heart feeling lighter, the other part still empty. She couldn't remember the last time they were able to share a hug or a gentle mother-daughter moment since her engagement.

Adeyemi released her and took a hold of Iyanda's shoulders, looking her directly in the eyes. "Iyanda, you listen to me, if you still want him, you go get him. It's not too late. I've seen the way he looks at you, he loves you. Everything he did, I'm sure there was a good reason. Don't be like me and your aunt, married to men who never were raised to be good men. Love him and let him love you."

Iyanda glanced at Nana B's grave. She imagined her grandparents together, giving their approval of Adeyemi's words. She would keep them locked away in her heart, but she didn't know when she would get a chance to put them into effect.

"I feel you in my heart, ọkàn mi, take care of grandfather."

CHAPTER 34

A week passed before Yesenia was strong enough to move around. Emiliano had watched as his mother coddled his little sister. He knew it was just for show. Whenever the young girl reached out to her, Quilla would flinch before succumbing to a forced motherly instinct.

Edward tried to play father figure to Yesenia. After the second day, he left the house and wouldn't come back until nightfall.

Quilla didn't have the decency to attend Aria's funeral. Emiliano stood in as the family's representative with the excuse that his mother was still tending to Yesenia. He suspected that Chris knew otherwise. As the casket had been lowered into the damp earth, Emiliano knew he needed to make a decision for not only the safety of himself but for all who he loved and cared for.

He sat in his father's chair at the long dining table. Low voices of the servants working relaxed him a little. It meant Quilla wasn't nearby. His hands folded before his face in a steeple.

"Baba, I hope what I'm about to do is what you would do. If not, please make it impossible for it to happen."

The voices in the hall went silent.

The clickety-clack of heels echoed louder the closer they came.

He took a deep breath then slowly exhaled.

Quilla walked into the dining room. She looked at Emiliano with a lofty stare then with a swoop of her hand, flipped her hair.

He surveyed his mother's outfit. He never could understand why the woman still dressed like she was in her twenties. The white, ruffled dress hung off her brown shoulders, her large bosom stretching out the delicate material. The hem stopped mid-thigh, revealing large, meaty thighs and skinny calves.

"Is there anything in your closet that isn't straight out of a prostitute's fashion magazine?" Emiliano asked, averting his eyes.

"This is an Aqua original. Too high-end for a whore."

Emiliano bit his tongue. Now was not the time to be a smart-ass.

"Why did you call me?" Quilla asked. "I have to get back to your sister."

"You will not be going back to her today. Or tomorrow."

"What are you talking about?" she asked.

Emiliano put his hands down and leaned back in the chair. "I'm giving you two million dollars to leave this house and this island without Yesenia."

Quilla's eyes glistened. Emiliano's lips twitched at the money-hungry look in her eyes.

Then she frowned. "Why would I leave my daughter here? She needs to be with her mother."

"Let me make this clear. My sister, daughter of Jack Petty, will not be influenced by a gold-digger of a mother whose only concern is her innocent child's trust."

Quilla's hand pressed against her chest, her mouth open in shock. "I'm a classy gold-digger." She smiled with a white toothy smile.

He shot her a venomous look. Typical. She doesn't deny that her focus is on Yesenia's trust.

"You tried to poison my sister. Give me one good reason why I shouldn't have you arrested."

The smile faded from her lips. Quilla's eyes widened. "I-I would never hurt my children."

His eyes narrowed. "But he would."

"He wasn't trying to hurt her," she said in a soft voice. "Just make her a little sick. He said it would make it easier to get access to her trust fund. It would force your hand if you became too stressed about her."

"It could have killed her!" he roared. It took everything in him not to grab his own mother's throat. "Your child's life is worth less to you than all the money in the world."

Emiliano's darkened eyes made Quilla shrink back.

"I love you and your sister," she stammered.

"Those words should never come from your mouth."

"I'm your mother."

"It's the only reason why you're still standing," his words laced with more than just bitterness.

Quilla was visibly nervous. She inched toward the dining room door. "I need to get back to Yesenia," she said.

Emiliano stood up, the bottom of the chair's legs scraping the marble floor. His hand slammed down on the table, the loud bang echoing in the room. "Stay the hell away from her!" Emiliano's chest heaved as he glowered at his mother. Closing his eyes, he took a breath before looking back at her.

"Take the money, mother," he said in a calmer voice. "Take it and forget about us. Go anywhere you want just don't come back to Igbala. If you or Edward do, I swear I will have you buried under the prison system. Do I make myself clear?"

Quilla's chin trembled, her eyes hot with rage. Reluctantly she nodded to the agreement.

Emiliano gave a nod to one of the servants. She came over with a black duffle bag. "Two million dollars, cash. That should be able to hold you and your current lover over until you get bored with each other.

Quilla's eyes widened. She licked her lips as if she was about to consume a sweet tooth satisfying dessert. She snatched the bag and rushed from the dining room without a glance back at her son.

Emiliano wasn't surprised that Quilla would take the money. He wasn't even surprised she didn't fight back about Yesenia or even him.

No. Those things were expected.

It confused him as to why, her departure left a gnawing emptiness. He knew she was always like this. Maybe he hoped she would change, love them more than she loved money.

His father's memory would no longer be tarnished by the woman's presence and he was the one to make it happen that way. He flopped down into the dining chair, his line of vision having no target.

Yesenia was safe from their mother's financial plots and he was free. Free to think and act without someone he cared for being harmed by the conniving woman. He would need to move into the house with Yesenia until she finished school. But first he needed to take care of something else.

* * * * *

Iyanda smiled as Lily Poe's voice carried through the store. She was reenacting a story about her current lover to the other women in WAISTED. Her voice was a familiarity that Iyanda had missed. With a last turn, Iyanda screwed in the energy efficient lightbulb, brightening the once dim workspace of Nana B. She surveyed the small room.

"This is just the beginning, Nana B," Iyanda said.

After celebrating yesterday, her family decided that the store needed to be remodeled. They knew it would take a while before the store was allowed to open again. So with the monetary gift from their anonymous donor, they would be able to make a few changes to the beloved store. Today they decided to tear down the faded wallpaper and paint the walls like Nana B always wanted.

Lily Poe and Gaiana volunteered to help.

Iyanda slowly got down from the stool. She placed the lightbulb box on the nearby table. It still contained the calabash bowls loaded with beads waiting for their owner to return so they may aid her in her spiritual work. She lightly caressed one of the hollowed-out dishes, a weight sitting on her chest.

Reaching inside her work apron, she pulled out the bamboo knife and placed it on the table in front of the bowls. This would be her workspace now. Dunni had made it clear that her family could help with the making of the beads but it would fall on Iyanda to give them the full effect that her grandmother once gave them.

Iyanda gave the room one more look around. It needed more work, but there was plenty of time.

Moving the curtain of shells to the side, she entered the main part of the store.

As she told her story, Lily Poe would stop painting, twirling the brush in her hand to place emphasis on her words. Gaiana and Tambara stood, absorbed in the tale while Ola and Adeyemi continued painting in their designated areas, amused at the youth of the women.

Iyanda shook her head, breathing off an easy laugh.

Yes, everything would be back to normal soon. She made her way to her store. She needed to make the afternoon tea for Dunni's arrival and gather her things to go to the training house.

Turning on the small hot plate with the waiting teapot, she leaned against the counter as the water warmed. Everything was back to normal and yet, Iyanda felt empty. She knew it had to do with Emiliano.

She had finally decided to let him go but her heart was refusing the order. She didn't bother calling to check on Yesenia, knowing Quilla Petty would more than likely insult her and not give her an actual update on the young girl's condition.

The other day, Iyanda had received a response back from Aria's brother, thanking her for the flowers and condolences. She wished she could have done more.

Was Emiliano thinking of her? Probably not.

She wouldn't be surprised if he had got engaged again. She told herself she was fine with that. But was she? Iyanda wiped at the tear on her cheek.

The bell chime above the door signaled someone was there. It was too early for Dunni. In the years she knew the older woman, Dunni always showed up at the actual time that she said she would.

Iyanda rushed from the back room. "Welcome to Iyanda's Ewe! How can I-."

Her breath caught in her throat when her gaze landed on Emiliano. He stood wearing a pair of light beige sokotos, matching *Buba*, and fila. The green embroidery on the front of the *Buba* complimenting his brown dress shoes. Her heart skipped a beat.

"How can I help you, sir?" Iyanda asked, trying to sound nonchalant.

"I need to buy one item for my bride price." His demeanor was cool, almost formal with her.

"I wouldn't have anything in this store that you would need, sir. Our other store is closed right now. If you would like, you could come back in two days and we can provide you with the items you need."

Emiliano began walking through the small aisles. She kept her distance by staying on the opposite aisle of him.

"I was thinking of something," he said. "An herb that would make a woman forgive a man and make her love him once again."

"Sir, I have never heard of any herb like this. You mean to keep your new bride under a spell. I don't agree to such things so you might have to look somewhere else."

Iyanda turned in disgust. Whoever the poor woman was that Emiliano was getting ready to marry would be his prisoner. She made her way toward the back before Emiliano grabbed her wrist. She stopped and looked back at him.

She sized him up then pulled away. "Thank you for helping my family to get their stores back. But you need to hurry to your future bride."

"I didn't have anything to do with this."

Iyanda frowned. "What do you mean? It was bought by a wealthy benefactor."

"As much as I wanted to be that benefactor, I couldn't. Your landlord is a friend of my mother's boyfriend and she made sure I couldn't help you."

"Your mother is the cause of my family almost losing everything?" Something she had suspected as of late.

"Something that we can talk about later."

"How-you'll be getting married soon."

"Only if you say yes." Emiliano dropped to one knee. Pulling out a large diamond ring from his pocket, he presented it to her. "Iyanda Bankole, forgive me for not protecting you like you needed to be. But from here on in, your life, your honor, your family, will come under my protection. Marry me, Iyanda."

Tears welled in her eyes. She covered her mouth with the back of her hand. "But," she sniffled, "your mother won't allow it."

"My mother will never bother us again."

"How do I know I can be free with you?"

"I'm asking you to be free with me. I lost you once. I'm not going to do anything that would make me lose you again."

"The bride price?"

"Already paid in full plus more."

She frowned. "But how? You haven't spoken to my mother."

"I had it sent to your house and I'll speak to your mother once you say yes."

The corners of her mouth creased up. "And if I say no?"

Emiliano lightly laughed. "Then I'll be back tomorrow. And the next day." He stood slowly. "And the next day."

He took her hand and slowly slid the ring on her finger, his gaze never breaking from hers. "And the day after that. He pulled her close, his thumb caressing her chin.

"And the day after that," she whispered, trembling under his touch, warmth flooding her chest.

He bent down and tenderly kissed her, her salt-filled tears mingling with their moist tongues. He pulled away, his forehead touching hers.

"Yes?" he asked.

"Only if you kiss me again."

THE END

Made in the USA
Monee, IL
23 July 2020

36901152R00223